SEE

HOW

THEY

FALL

T0356311

SEE

HOW

THEY

FALL

RACHEL PARIS

SCARLET
NEW YORK

SEE HOW THEY FALL

Scarlet
An Imprint of Penzler Publishers
58 Warren Street
New York, N.Y. 10007

First Scarlet Press edition

Text design by Samantha Collins, Bookhouse
Typeset in 11.7/17 pt Sabon LT Pro by Bookhouse, Sydney

Library of Congress Control Number: 2024918144

ISBN: 978-1-61316-594-2
eBook ISBN: 978-1-61316-595-9

10 9 8 7 6 5 4 3 2 1

Printed in the United States of America
Distributed by W. W. Norton & Company

For my family

Behind every great fortune there is a great crime.

– HONORÉ DE BALZAC

AUTHOR'S NOTE

The Sydney location of the State Crime Command's Homicide Squad has been fictionalised.

ONE

SKYE TURNER

GOOD FRIDAY

I couldn't face another fight. Duncan had been irritable for weeks now – ever since his dad's funeral – so I was silent on the drive north from Sydney, picking ceramic clay out from under my fingernails while dusty paddocks and straggly trees flicked by. Despite the throbbing bass, somehow Tilly had fallen asleep in the back seat, one arm gripping her beloved Mouse, and the other cuddling our labrador, Bo.

Fog was still rising when we rolled through Yallambee's ornate iron gates. Those gates were the only hint of what lay beyond the forest of gum trees ahead. From the ridge line, manicured gardens sloped towards crystal water and white sand. Ten years ago, when Duncan and I first visited his family's private bay, I'd thought I was entering paradise.

The main residence wasn't visible until the road carved eastwards. Then the vast collision of concrete, steel and glass swooped into view. Duncan called it his dad's Taj

Mahal – a monument to the wife who died too young, leaving him with three school-aged sons. But really, Yallambee was a monument to Sir Campbell, by Sir Campbell. It was my father-in-law's announcement to the world that the poor Turner kid from Gawler had made it big, as well as an enclave where he could entertain powerful friends.

We usually only visited Yallambee in midsummer, when the light was golden and guests arrived by superyacht and helicopter to join Campbell's glittering beach parties, so the estate looked strange under a charred autumn sky. The watchhouse stood empty, and the entranceway was coated in a sludge of brown leaves, as though it were already in decline.

Duncan's older brother, Jamie, had suggested the family meet at Yallambee for the Easter break. It would be the first gathering of the Turner family since Campbell's funeral. No security, no chefs, no nannies, just family, Jamie had insisted – though his definition of family hadn't included Cody. That was partly why Duncan was on edge, and for good reason. This weekend would be his son Cody's first introduction to the rest of the Turners.

At the sound of the engine, our niece, Arabella, bounded out of the house, her pigtails flying. She darted across the cobbled courtyard and accosted me when I opened the car door.

'Aunty Skye, guess what?' She grinned, gap-toothed, and placed a ball of crumpled tissue into my palm. It weighed no more than a cotton ball.

Tilly, suddenly awake, lunged forward to see. 'Careful, Mumma,' she whispered over my shoulder.

I unwrapped the delicate paper to reveal her cousin's tiny front tooth. Tilly's own teeth were wiggly, and she was desperate for her first visit from the Tooth Fairy.

Jamie and Nina emerged arm in arm, like the lord and lady of the manor. As usual, Jamie was smart in a bespoke suede jacket and cashmere pullover, while my sister-in-law was dressed like the love child of a nun and a Stepford wife in an absurdly prim white silk pantsuit, her icy blonde hair pulled back in a chignon. She air-kissed me on both cheeks and complimented my dog hair-covered sweater. Jamie gave me a warm hug and shook Duncan's hand.

'We choppered up last night,' Jamie said. 'You're in the largest guest house. Now, can I help with your bags?'

Duncan was furious that Jamie had claimed the main house. As we unpacked, he grumbled that Jamie had always been an entitled prick.

Here we go, I thought.

•

At eleven o'clock, we stood around on a terraced lawn overlooking the beach while Nina served hot cross buns and English breakfast tea. Tilly and Arabella thieved down to the sand, and I watched them collect shells in an old metal bucket over the delicate chink of teacups and conversation. They laughed when a breeze whipped their hair into their faces and sent sprays of seaweed scuttling. Bo was having the time of his life, barking and running in giddy circles beside them. When Tilly looked back up at me, she waved and blew a kiss. I pretended to catch it and blew one back.

'Do I get a kiss too?'

A hand gripped my waist. It was Duncan's younger brother, Hugo, in his signature look – cashmere hoodie, box-fresh kicks, a chunky chain and gold aviators. He reeked of cologne and was already twitchy from coke. I faked a smile. As always,

Hugo grazed my breast when he leaned in for a kiss and aimed his lips at mine before I jerked away. A sleek young woman was lingering at his side. She had the homogenous beauty of an Instagram influencer, which made her seem vaguely familiar. What would Jamie think, I wondered, about Hugo bringing a plus one after his strict family-only edict?

'Are you going to introduce us?' I asked Hugo.

'Skye, meet Tamara,' he said, reaching across me to take the last hot cross bun.

Tamara extended her perfectly manicured hand. 'We met at Sir Campbell's wake?'

'Oh yes, of course,' I said. 'Sorry, it was a huge day.'

She flashed a sun-bright smile. 'I work in publicity at Turner Corp. I've been doing media training with Duncan recently.'

I laughed. 'God, that must be a challenge. Duncan's so weird about journalists.'

'I noticed.'

'That's why we keep Duncan hidden in finance,' said Hugo, as if he had any say in the matter. Jamie and Duncan only tolerated him in the family business to stop him wreaking havoc elsewhere.

Tamara kept glancing at Jamie over my shoulder. I understood why she was nervous. It was intimidating to be the newcomer at Turner family gatherings, and doubly so for her, given that Jamie was her new CEO. It was up to me to make her feel welcome because Nina would make no effort. She preferred to be admired from a distance.

'So, how long have you two been seeing each other?' I asked.

Tamara blushed. 'Hugo and I are just friends.'

The expression on Hugo's face confirmed that he had other ideas. 'I'm sick of always being the spare prick at these family things,' he said. 'Besides, Jamie okayed it.'

Before long, dark clouds began to roll in, so I summoned Tilly and Arabella back from the beach. Tilly had refused to wear her jumper, complaining that it was too scratchy, and I didn't want her to catch a cold and miss the upcoming book character parade at school. After much deliberation, she was going as Pippi Longstocking. Somehow I'd have to wrangle her mass of curls into two stick-out braids like Pippi's. I set a reminder in my phone to buy some pipe-cleaners and hairspray when we got back to Sydney, then I collected up the empty teacups and saucers and wandered inside to the kitchen – a magnificent statement in the most exquisite fragile Calacatta marble. I had an anxiety attack whenever Tilly went near it with a glass of juice or a felt-tip pen. The chefs didn't have to worry because this kitchen was just for show; all the meals were prepared in the huge stainless-steel scullery down the hallway.

I was jarred by the sight of Nina rinsing dishes at the sink in yellow gloves. Usually, a staff member would be hovering to take care of such a mundane task.

'We missed you at the gala on Wednesday,' she said in her cut-glass English accent, 'but it was so kind of you and Duncan to make such a generous donation.'

'I hope you raised a lot of money; it's a great cause,' I said, not quite remembering which of the Turners' worthy charities the gala was supporting – child cancer, marine conservation, Indigenous arts or women's empowerment. I began loading the rinsed plates into the dishwasher.

'Remember, the Limoges porcelain has to be hand-washed,' said Nina.

Why would anyone order plates that couldn't go in the dishwasher? Then again, a decade on, there was still a lot I didn't understand about the Turners. I unloaded the plates and rested them on the counter. To fill the pinched silence, I tried again. 'Can I help with dinner tonight?' I already knew Nina would decline my offer before she shook her head. No matter how hard I tried to connect with her, she always met me with polite resistance.

'Thanks so much,' she said, 'but we're all sorted. Hugo and Tamara are doing starters and dessert, and Jamie and I have the mains covered. It's going to be super casual.' She drained the sink and snapped off the latex gloves, one finger at a time. 'Actually, perhaps you could mind Arabella for us this afternoon while we prep? Usually the boys would entertain her, but I promised to let them go on their screens because they won their tennis tournament last night.' For once, Nina's twins, Olly and Finn, were zombified on the sofa like normal thirteen-year-olds, their faces glowing blue from their mobile phones. It was a rare reprieve from practising algebraic equations, piano scales or some other self-improvement activity.

'Of course. We'd love to look after Bella.'

'Thank you.' Nina smiled and squeezed my hand, which surprised me. She wasn't the touchy-feely type.

The clap of a car engine in the driveway startled us both. It had to be Cody arriving. Everyone streamed around to the side terrace to watch him climb out of his rusted Ford Falcon.

'So, this must be our nephew,' said Jamie, taking in Cody's shaved head and tattooed forearms.

Duncan was already striding across the courtyard to welcome him.

'Fuck me,' said Hugo. 'The secret son. What's the name again? Casey? Colby?'

'It's Cody,' I said.

Hugo smirked. 'Cody. Classy. I wonder what Dad would have made of this fucking soap opera?'

'Give him a chance, guys,' I said. 'He's been sweet with Tilly. I'm sure Campbell would have approved.'

Hugo scoffed. The truth was that Campbell would have been appalled by Cody – both the fact of his illegitimate existence and his unrefined appearance, neither of which aligned with the Turners' carefully curated image. Then again, I didn't exactly fit the mould either, and Campbell had accepted me eventually.

When Tilly saw Cody, she yelped with delight. 'See, I told you I had a big brother,' she bragged to Arabella. Then she tugged my arm. 'Mumma, let's go down.'

Jamie smiled. 'Yes, Skye, why don't you introduce us?'

Up close, I was struck anew by how much Cody resembled Duncan and Tilly, with his bright amber eyes and sharp cheekbones. He was so beautiful, even with a bolt through his lip and a new eyebrow piercing. When I hugged him hello, he smelled of weed and coffee.

Jamie and Nina gave Cody a gracious welcome, while Hugo and Tamara hung back, watching on from the terrace.

'You can sleep in the room right next to me,' said Tilly.

Cody scooped Tilly into the air and dangled her upside down while she shrieked with joy. 'No one told me I'd have to sleep next to a monkey.'

My heart swelled to see them bonding after all the monthly disappointments that had left Tilly an only child.

•

At six o'clock, we returned to the main house for aperitifs. Through the floor-to-ceiling windows, the last of the daylight was burning itself out, and the horizon was a vigorous impasto of blood orange and cadmium red. Nina was prim in another white-silk-and-cashmere ensemble, and Tamara had changed into a scarlet bodycon dress that plunged at her pneumatic cleavage. I glanced down at my sweater and jeans and wished I'd packed something smarter.

I chatted to Duncan and Jamie for a while, but before long they were debating the impact that the Chinese economic downturn would have on large cap mining stocks, and Tamara and Hugo were scrolling on their phones. The kids had taken Cody on a house tour so, as a last resort, I perched beside Nina at the kitchen island. She was polishing the crystal glassware. So much for a 'super casual' dinner.

'Need a hand?'

'Thanks, but I'm almost done.' She wasn't. God, she was tedious. How did Jamie put up with her? He was a bloody saint. No wonder none of her nannies ever lasted long.

'What did you do to yourself?' I asked. There was an angry red blister on her palm.

'I caught it on my straightening iron.' She smiled. 'I should really leave it to the professionals.'

'I meant to ask: how's your mum's health?' I said. 'Is she improving?'

'Unfortunately not. I was hoping she'd be able to come out to visit this year, but her doctor won't clear her to fly.'

'Why don't you travel to her?' I asked.

'It's hard to find the time to get all the way back to England.'

I nodded, but it was a pathetic excuse. With unlimited money, nannies and a private jet at her disposal, she might have made more of an effort to visit her ailing mother. After all, she was an only child, and the poor old lady had been on her own since her husband had passed away three years prior. So many people took their parents for granted.

'Now, we're serving Thai dishes for the adults,' Nina said, 'but they're quite spicy, so I'm just doing burgers for the children to keep it easy. Is that okay for Tilly?'

I confirmed that yes, of course, a burger would be just fine. We exhausted all of the usual topics of conversation – the children, her charities, my upcoming exhibition, in that order. When she raised the dismal weather forecast, I decided I'd done enough and offered to fetch her a drink to escape.

The house tour had concluded, and Cody was now showing Tilly how to muddle mint leaves in the bottom of a tumbler. He worked as a bartender in the city and had brought supplies to mix cocktails. I ordered two mojitos, extra strong.

'Good job, that's it,' Cody said as he helped Tilly guide the pestle.

She glowed at the compliment.

As I presented Nina with her drink, a FaceTime call came through from Ana, my close friend and the owner of the gallery in Double Bay where I exhibited. Her topknot of flame-red hair and her black lipstick shuddered into view when I answered.

'You promised you'd send me a photo of the Kngwarreye,' she scolded in the husky drawl that betrayed years of Marlboros. 'How does it look? I'm *dying* to see it up close.'

'Sorry, I totally forgot. It's spectacular. Look.'

I swivelled my phone camera around so that Ana could take in the glorious canvas pulsing with life along the back wall of the lounge room, the intricate patterns of layered lines and dots glowing like tiny stars. Campbell had acquired it at auction from a private collection shortly before his death, setting a record price for a work by an Indigenous Australian artist.

'The lighting's wrong,' Ana declared through the speaker. 'We need to adjust the angles and perhaps add some recessed directionals. I'll send someone up next week to take a look. Right, I have to go – but don't forget about lunch on Tuesday. Let's meet at the gallery and we can walk from there.' As always, she hung up before I'd managed to get a word in.

I'd met Ana twelve years earlier, when I was waiting tables in Surry Hills. She was dining with a photographer who followed my work and raved about it in front of Ana. To my amazement, she called the next morning. Back then I'd only recently begun experimenting with clay. Ana came to my studio (if you can call a half-share of a leaking basement flat a studio) and was taken most of all by my ceramic sculptures – hand-coiled vessels that resembled crumpled, lopsided hives and bird's nests. I'd created them by instinct, but Australia's leading art critic would later describe them as 'ethereal meditations on the fragility of home and the need for belonging', like he'd peered into my soul. Within a fortnight of our first encounter, Ana had signed me to her prestigious gallery, Betjeman's, and my luck had finally changed.

A few months later, Ana and I had just finished up a meeting when Duncan arrived at the gallery to take me to lunch. Ana almost fell off her chair.

'Why didn't you tell me you were dating Duncan Turner?' she whisper-hissed, trailing me into the stockroom when I went to fetch my bag.

'Do you know him?'

'Skye, come on! Every red-blooded woman in Australia knows about Duncan Turner.'

I frowned. 'Really?'

'Are you serious? Have you been living under a rock?' She arched her thin brows. 'How in the hell did you meet him?'

'We got chatting at the Biennale. Went for a drink afterwards.' I glossed over the fact that my flatmate and I had blagged our way into a VIP event for the free champagne and found ourselves smack-bang in front of the event's sponsor. Just as he was about to turf us out, the hot guy behind us intervened and said we were his guests. The hot guy turned out to be Duncan. When his hand brushed mine, the electrical surge that passed through me could have blown the national grid. Later that night, we wound up together in a yakitori bar until closing time. He was so charming, so funny, so interested in what I had to say – nothing like the guys I knew, who still behaved like selfish teenagers. 'What's the big deal anyway?' I continued.

Ana shook her head in disbelief. 'It's like you just blew into Bondi on a scallop shell. Don't worry – I'll fill you in on all the gossip, and there's plenty of it. Sir Campbell Turner has been a client of mine for years. He's Duncan's father, you know.'

I'd learn later that Duncan's dad had a MoMA-quality art collection crammed with Basquiats, Modiglianis and Rothkos, most of which was sheltered in offshore vaults for tax purposes.

'Please don't tell me,' I said to Ana. 'I want to get to know him without any preconceptions.' All Duncan had said was that he worked for his dad, hated it, and didn't want to talk about it, which suited me fine.

Ana laughed at my naivety, not realising I was just trying to outrun the shadow of my own past.

On the dance floor at our wedding, she'd given me a big drunken hug, her red hair tumbling down her back and her lipstick smudged.

'Good luck, my darling Skye,' she said. 'You'll need it.'

•

By my third mojito, I was buzzing with a pleasant mixture of exhilaration and detachment. I drifted through to the lounge and sank into the armchair with the best view of the bay.

If I traced the ragged cuticle of coastline north to Queensland, I'd have wound up back in my home town, which was littered with broken bungalows and rusted-out cars, and where the scorching heat and cheap grog left everyone wilted and listless. Now, those memories felt like a reel of someone else's life.

'Mumma, what are you doing here all by yourself?' Tilly skipped into the lounge, her hamburger in one hand, trailed by Bo.

'Nothing much. Just thinking, baby.'

'I'm not a baby anymore.' She crawled onto my lap and tore off a hunk of her burger patty.

'You'd better not let Aunty Nina find you. She'll freak if she catches you walking around with your food.'

'I'm not walking around – I'm sitting,' Tilly pointed out. She tossed the meat to Bo, who was watching her intently, awaiting a morsel. 'I brought you a present.'

'Really? What?'

She tucked her hand into the pocket of her jersey and withdrew a heart-shaped grey stone. 'I found it on the beach. Do you like it, Mumma?'

'No. I don't like it. I *love* it.'

Tilly giggled at my corny joke. I kissed the top of her head and slid the stone into my jeans pocket. 'Now go and sit back down at the table with your cousins before we both get in big trouble.'

Tilly darted off to the kitchen. I drained my drink but wasn't quite ready to rejoin the others – there was only so much pretentious blathering from Hugo that I could handle on an empty stomach. I killed some time by studying the long gallery of black-and-white photographs in the hallway. Here was a young Campbell at Yallambee entertaining fellow billionaires. He must have been in his mid-forties then, and he was the image of Jamie, with his broad, handsome face, thick dark hair and those striking amber eyes that shone even in monochrome. And here was Campbell with a trinity of famous models on the deck of Campbell's superyacht, and in the next photograph smoking cigars with Hollywood royalty on the terrace of the Chateau Marmont.

My favourite photo was the one of Campbell at his sixty-fifth birthday party, sharing a joke with a former US president. He was tanned and confident, his eyes sparkling with mischief. That night had been my first visit to Yallambee, soon after Duncan and I had started dating. I ended up dancing on a table to Beyoncé's 'Crazy in Love', and then I shared a joint with one of the waiters before Duncan whisked me away to bed. It seemed like a thousand years ago now.

Campbell had been such a force, always surrounded by supermodels and celebrities, always the life of the party. His presence at Yallambee was still palpable, as if he might emerge from his private quarters to join us at any moment.

A noise startled me. The door to a guest bedroom along the hallway was ajar. When I approached, a rapid movement caught my eye. It was dark, but in the slice of light from the hallway, I glimpsed a silhouette. It took a few moments for my eyes to adjust, and I was shocked to see that it was Jamie, grinding hard against Nina from behind. She had her long skirt hiked up around her hips and her face pressed away from me into the wall. They were really going for it. She'd always given off such frigid vibes. Who knew that, behind the scenes, she and Jamie screwed like teenagers in heat? I felt a pang of envy.

I carried on to the powder room, but the door was locked. There was some rustling and the whoosh of running water, and then Tamara emerged, her make-up freshly reapplied. I couldn't imagine what she saw in Hugo, but at least she was another woman to hang out with. We chatted briefly, and I suggested a walk up to the ridge the next morning if the forecast storm held off.

When I finally returned to the lounge, there was no sign of Jamie and Nina. I was still rattled by what I'd witnessed between them.

'Mumma, I'm *starving*.' Tilly was tugging on my arm.

'Then you shouldn't have fed your burger to Bo, darling.'

'But it hurt my wiggly teeth!' She opened her mouth and poked out a neon-pink tongue.

'Oh my God. What on earth have you been drinking?'

She grinned and her cheeks dimpled. 'Cody made me a special fizzy drink.'

I sighed. 'You know you can't have too much sugar. It makes you crazy.' I was still traumatised by her hyperactive meltdown on a flight when she'd duped the steward into giving her a Fanta.

'Uncle Hugo let me have ice cream too.'

'Come on, honey.' I wrapped my arm around her shoulders. 'You need some proper food, or you won't grow.' In the scullery, I dished her up a bowl of the rice and veggies sitting on the counter, and then sent her off to watch a movie with Arabella in the media room.

•

We were all ravenous by the time Nina invited us to take our seats for dinner. Duncan and I helped her carry out heaving platters of spicy prawn and chicken curries and steaming white rice from the kitchen, while Jamie topped up the wineglasses. The long table was shimmering with crystal bowls of white tulips and flickering tea lights. Soft jazz was playing in the background. Typical Nina perfection. She made entertaining seem effortless in a way I never could.

Nina and Jamie were seated at opposite ends of the table. I'd been placed between Tamara and Hugo, who was being his usual boorish self, interrupting and talking over everyone. Once we'd all taken our places, Jamie tapped his knife against his wineglass and the table fell silent.

'Welcome, everyone,' he said. 'I'd like to make a toast to the late, great Sir Campbell Turner.' Jamie surveyed the table, making eye contact with each of us as he spoke, like Campbell used to do. 'Dad, you were an inspiration. We miss you every day. As your sons, we vow to continue your legacy, and to always put family first.' His eyes snagged on Duncan.

We all raised our glasses. In the Turner family, you didn't clink – that was considered basic, as I'd discovered early on, along with napkin rings, visible designer logos and flying commercial. Cody had a steep learning curve ahead of him if he wanted to become a regular fixture here.

'To Campbell,' we chorused.

It was a lovely, heartfelt toast, but across the table Duncan's jaw clenched. The fact that Jamie had slipped so comfortably into his father's role would be grating on him.

At the end of the first course, Duncan cleared his throat. 'I'd also like to make a toast tonight,' he began, and I found myself holding my breath. 'As Jamie said, family meant everything to Dad, and so I'd like to take this occasion to officially welcome my son Cody to his first Turner family dinner.' He patted Cody's arm. 'To new beginnings.'

Everyone joined the toast, bar Hugo, who took a deep swig of wine and leaned across the table towards Cody. His sneer announced something unpleasant would follow.

'Ah yes, Cody. My prodigal nephew.' Hugo wiped his mouth with the back of his hand then stared straight at Duncan. 'So, come on, tell us.'

'Tell you what?' Duncan asked.

'How long the two of you have been scheming about all this.' He feathered his hands at Duncan and Cody, as if he were a feudal lord addressing a couple of serfs.

Cody shrugged. 'Sorry?'

Hugo's face contorted into a grotesque smile – the same awful smile he gave to household staff before eviscerating them for poor service. 'Well, *Cody*,' he said, as if he'd just bitten into something sour. 'How convenient that you've crawled out from fuck-knows-where straight after Dad's funeral. I can only assume you're trying to claim some inheritance?'

A fog of silence rolled in. Cody shifted in his seat. A vein was twitching at Duncan's temple. I kicked him under the table – a warning not to react. The air was flammable, and he couldn't give Hugo an excuse to ignite it.

'I'm not after any inheritance,' Cody said.

'Then why are you here?'

'I just wanted to spend time with my father and to meet you all, since – well, we're all family.'

Hugo laughed. 'Family?'

Beside me, Tamara squirmed and studied the weave of her placemat. Duncan leaned forward, poised to intervene.

'Well then,' Hugo continued, 'I trust you'll have no objection to sharing the results of your DNA test with my lawyer?' He eased back in his chair, linking his arms behind his head.

'Ignore him, Cody,' said Duncan. 'He's just drunk, or high – likely both.'

'Yes,' said Jamie, shooting his youngest brother a warning look. 'That's enough, Hugo.'

'Hit a nerve, did I, Dunc? And I'm curious, because you've been so coy about the one detail we most want to know.' Hugo's eyes were glassy, and beads of sweat glistened on his upper lip. He was such a creep. 'I never did get to the bottom of it. Which whore is Cody's mother?'

The air crackled, and there was a second of silence before Duncan rounded the table and lunged at Hugo. I cried out when he seized Hugo's throat, upending a glass of burgundy which bled across the white linen cloth.

Nina sprang to her feet. 'Please, everyone, calm down! Don't spoil the evening.'

Duncan ignored her. Hugo sputtered; he was choking.

I screamed at Duncan and tried to pull him off Hugo, but he wasn't letting go. He was never physically aggressive like that, and for a horrible moment I had a flashback to my first foster father – the crunch of cartilage, the smack of fist on flesh, the metallic taste of blood.

By the time Jamie wrestled Duncan to the ground, a ghoulish purple tinge had crept across Hugo's face. There was a stunned silence as Jamie dragged Hugo out to the hallway.

Duncan brushed himself off and turned to Cody. 'You okay?' he asked.

Cody looked at his father, then slowly took in the rest of us. Tamara was crying into her napkin. Nina was staring straight ahead, continuing to eat her meal, as if pretending everything was fine would see order magically restored.

'This is fucked up.' Cody rose, almost toppling his chair.

'I'm so sorry,' I said to him. 'Hugo's an idiot.' I was desperate to salvage his impression of the family – or his impression of me and Duncan, at least – for Tilly's sake.

'I'll make sure he apologises to you,' Duncan added.

'I'm sorry,' said Cody, 'but I can't stay here after that.' He turned to Nina. 'Thanks for dinner. And Skye, give Tilly a hug from me.'

Skye, Tamara and I cleared away the half-eaten dinner in silence, while Duncan and his brothers brokered a fragile peace in low, muffled voices in the next room. I found Tilly curled up like a comma beside Arabella on the sofa in the media room. Duncan scooped her into his arms, and together we dashed back to the guest house through the hissing rain.

'Mumma, my tummy's sore,' Tilly said, all bleary-eyed, when I peeled off her wet clothes and slipped her *Moana* nightie over her head.

'Sweetie, it's probably that sugary drink.' I poured her a big glass of water. 'Have this, and then we'll brush your teeth and you'll feel much better.'

She drank obediently, then slumped against me while I buzzed the toothbrush around her mouth.

The rain was thundering onto the roof and rattling the bedroom windows when I put her to bed. She was asleep before I'd even snuffed out the lamp.

•

The next morning, I woke with a chalky mouth and my stomach heaving from the curry. God, what time was it? It was barely daylight outside, and rain was still lashing the house. Despite Duncan's loud snoring, I could hear Bo scratching to go outside. When I stumbled out to open the door, a colossal wave of nausea gripped me, and I barely made it down the steps before vomiting into a clump of banksia. Even Bo looked disgusted.

Sodden from the rain, I dried myself off with a sofa throw and staggered back to bed. Duncan was still out cold. For once, Tilly hadn't slipped in between us in the wee hours, so I could stretch out under the cool sheet. I'd had my share of hangovers, but none this savage. It must have been the mixture of cocktails and wine.

I lay there napping for another hour or so and woke to find Duncan pulling on a t-shirt and boxers. 'You okay?' he asked.

'No. I'm dying a slow, miserable death. Got any Nurofen?'

He smiled. 'I'll check the bathroom cupboard. I feel really rough too. Tilly still asleep?'

I nodded. 'Yes, that's the one small mercy.'

'I'll check on her.' He padded out of the room, and I suppressed another wave of nausea. I had to pull myself together.

'Jesus! Skye!' came Duncan's panicked call from down the hallway.

I tore into Tilly's bedroom to find her hunched over in her bed, crying softly, surrounded by stale vomit. Had she called for us and we'd slept through it? I should have checked on her sooner, knowing that she'd been feeling unwell when I tucked her in.

'Oh, baby.' I cradled her in my arms.

Together, Duncan and I peeled off her soiled nightie and bedding while tears slid down her cheeks. I was now covered in her puke as well – which was lumpy and bright pink. I silently cursed Cody for the disgusting drink he'd made her.

In the shower, I retched as I washed Tilly down with a flannel and shampooed her tangled hair before Duncan received her in a towel.

When I emerged from the ensuite, Duncan had set Tilly up in our bed, surrounded by a moat of bath sheets, with a kitchen bowl on her lap.

'Can you stay with me, Mumma?' she asked in a small voice.

'Of course.' I slid under the blanket next to her, rubbing her back. Bo sprang onto the end of the bed and nestled under her arm.

Duncan hovered over us. 'Shall I get some Panadol?' he asked.

I pressed my palm against Tilly's forehead and shook my head. 'She doesn't feel hot, and I'm worried it'll make her throw up again.'

I could feel Tilly's breathing shift as she drifted back to sleep.

Duncan phoned our city GP, who reassured him that Tilly had most likely picked up the contagious norovirus bug that was doing the rounds at primary school. She'd feel better in a couple of days. The important thing was to keep her well hydrated.

I went to fetch her more water. Before I stepped back into our bedroom, I sensed that something was wrong. I found her vomiting again, but this time crimson blood was gushing onto the towels, and she was emitting hoarse, guttural moans like no noise I'd heard before.

'Duncan!' I yelled, rushing to cradle her. 'Hurry!'

Duncan phoned emergency services, but all the rescue helicopters were grounded, as were the family's private choppers, because of the gale-force winds. The operator suggested driving to the nearest medical centre. I tossed some towels and Tilly's favourite *Bluey* PJs in a bag, along with Mouse, for the drive to Taree.

The rain was torrential, striking the windscreen in harsh needles, and I pleaded with Duncan to slow down when he sped around the blind corners.

Forty-three minutes later, we screamed up outside the Taree Family Health Centre, a tired building with peeling yellow paint and rain plunging into the gutter from a broken downpipe. The wind was so powerful that Duncan struggled to open the car door to scoop Tilly up. We burst through the entrance, drenched and wild-eyed, setting the bell jangling and startling the young pink-haired receptionist.

'Where's the doctor?' I asked, my breath ragged.

'She's on her lunchbreak until half-past. Take a seat and you can help yourself to water at the water cooler.'

'You're a fucking idiot,' Duncan yelled, and pushed through into the doctor's surgery, where a grey-haired lady was eating fruit salad out of a plastic container and reading a Terry Pratchett novel. When she saw Tilly's limp blood-streaked body in Duncan's arms, she jumped to attention, sending her long shell earrings swinging. She instructed Duncan to lay Tilly out on the examination bed. I gripped Tilly's hand, while Duncan stroked her matted hair. She was making a strange wheezing sound.

'It'll be okay, baby,' I whispered, willing myself not to cry in front of her.

The doctor checked Tilly's pulse and temperature, then ran her stethoscope over her chest and back. 'Your daughter's having trouble breathing, so I'm going to give her oxygen and call an ambulance to take her to Sydney,' she said.

A rush of alarm. 'What's wrong with her?'

'Possibly a viral infection,' the doctor said as she opened a cupboard and wheeled out a rickety oxygen tank that looked like a museum relic. I counted the white ceiling squares over and over again to calm myself, while Duncan paced up and down the room.

When the paramedics arrived, they whisked Tilly onto a stretcher, and I chased them through the oppressive rain to the ambulance. Tilly didn't flinch when they fixed the heavy oxygen mask over her mouth and connected an IV drip into the tiny crease of her arm. I took Mouse out of my bag and tucked him in beside Tilly's chest, kissing the top of her head and swallowing down tears. Then I sat in silence in the back of the ambulance, trying to spot Duncan's car through the rear window and stroking Tilly's hand with my thumb in time with the steady loop of the siren. The whole trip back to Sydney, I prayed to every god I could think of to keep her safe.

When we surged into the hospital bay, the ambulance's rear doors swung open and Tilly was slid onto a hospital gurney. The paramedics were exchanging incomprehensible medical jargon with the hospital staff, but it was clear from their faces that they were worried.

My phone vibrated in my pocket.

'Why haven't you been picking up?' Duncan snapped when I answered.

'Why aren't you here?'

'I've just handed Bo over to Ana. I'll be there shortly. Jamie called and said Nina's really ill as well. What do the doctors think is wrong?'

'We haven't seen a doctor yet,' I said. 'I'm not sure what's happening.'

'For Christ's sake, Skye, demand to be seen! It's our little girl!'

I grabbed an orderly's arm. 'When will they know what's wrong with her?'

'She's bypassing triage and going straight to emergency, ma'am. Follow that lady with the red lanyard.'

Bile scorched the back of my throat. I chased Tilly's gurney down mottled grey corridors washed with disinfectant and artificial light to a glass-fronted room within the children's ER. The woman with the red lanyard was barking orders. Nurses in blue scrubs clamped a mask over Tilly's face and hooked her up to the monitors. Then one of the machines started beeping. Where the hell was Duncan?

'She's losing consciousness.'

Panicked, urgent voices now. A bell was ringing. Blood rushed in my ears. An emergency call sounded over the loudspeakers.

'What's happening?' I screamed.

'Your daughter's in respiratory failure,' said a nurse. 'We need to intubate. Wait outside.'

An arm wrenched me away so the crash trolley could cut through. Hands were slicing through Tilly's pyjama top and clipping tubes and drips to her chest and tiny fingers.

A doctor inserted a thick plastic duct into her mouth. My throat was aching, raw. I was yelling, smashing at the glass, desperate to get to her. Red lights flashed and Tilly's body spasmed then stiffened. They were sticking pads on her chest and back. Someone shouted, 'Stand clear!' and the doctor delivered the shocks.

Clutched by seismic terror, I watched my baby's little body convulse.

TWO

MEI O'CONNOR

I needed to smash something, to hurl my plate onto the kitchen tiles or slam the front door so hard that it buckled off its hinges. But I couldn't, not with Mum lying in the next room, a pile of frail bones and sallow skin. Instead, I continued to doomscroll, zooming in on Vanessa's smug face while fury coursed through me.

I'd spent the afternoon on Mum's lumpy couch next to her pampered Burmese, Laifu, researching unpronounceable cancer medications to distract myself. But when I turned on my phone to address the scores of missed calls, Facebook reminded me that, exactly one year ago, Nick and I had moved into our new rental. We'd marked the occasion with pizza and wine, and I'd posted a selfie of us half-drunk and half-buried in packing boxes. He proposed the next day.

Life was perfect – right up until a fortnight ago, when Dr Lee told us Mum's cancer was terminal. Mum barely reacted, so at first I thought she hadn't understood. Only her hands, quivering in her lap, gave her away. Since she didn't approve of emotional displays, I held back my tears until she was tucked up in bed with a cup of tea. Then, back in the car, I'd broken, shuddering at the steering wheel, weeping so hard that a passer-by knocked on the window to check I was okay.

I couldn't return to the office in such a state, so I went home to repair my blotchy, mascara-streaked face before meeting with my boss, Wilson. In my rush, I didn't notice Nick's car in the driveway. But I certainly did notice him fucking his physiotherapist, Vanessa, on the sofa we'd just paid off on hire purchase.

Nick was eerily calm. He'd wanted to tell me about Vanessa for a while, he said, but he hadn't had a chance because I'd been so focused on work and Mum's treatment. In fact, he added, as Vanessa failed to cover her ample breasts with a puny throw pillow, it was a relief to have it all out in the open. I tore off my engagement ring and hurled it at him. It bounced off his chest and clinked onto the wooden floor, before spinning under the couch. Somehow I made it to the bathroom, fixed my face, packed a bag and went to work.

My bravado lasted until the end of the day, when I'd retreated here to Mum's brick-and-tile flat in an ungentrified pocket of Redfern, into the dank, poky room with the peeling floral wallpaper stuffed with ancient books and a fold-out bed. I couldn't bear to admit to Mum that it was over between me and Nick – one more reason to be disappointed in me – so I told her that I was moving in for her next round of chemotherapy. She acted annoyed ('You'll unsettle Laifu with all your stuff everywhere. You're so messy! This place isn't big enough for both of us, *lè lè!*') but I knew she was pleased by my display of filial piety.

For the past two weeks, I'd avoided social media, but this afternoon I'd finally caved. It was a delightful torture to keep checking Vanessa's feed while the storm raged outside. The two most recent posts had her snuggling a dachshund puppy and posing outside the Paddington terrace her father had bought for her birthday. I recognised the location, not far from the St Francis of Assisi Catholic church. I skimmed back further, through an illegal number of pouty selfies and shots of her performing advanced yoga poses at luxurious retreats. Vanessa lived in a parallel universe. I'd just reached a series of her flaunting her thigh gap in Bali when the doorbell chimed. We weren't expecting anyone. The bell was followed by insistent knocking.

'I'll get it,' I hollered to Mum, and opened the door to Yvette shaking out an umbrella. Somehow she'd made it to the door bone-dry, her make-up still flawless.

'You can't not return my calls,' she scolded, barging inside and almost scraping her head on the ceiling. She hugged me so tightly that I choked on her mane of jet-black hair. 'I've been really worried. How are you holding up?'

I bundled her through to my room, where Yvette arranged her long limbs on the listing bed while I caught her up on the details. 'I don't want Mum to know about the break-up yet.'

'You haven't told her?'

'No. She'll just worry. I'm trying to work out a plan.'

'Is Nick still at your place?'

'I presume so. I haven't heard from him.'

'Are you serious?' Yvette's face contorted in outrage. 'No apology?'

I shook my head. 'Nothing.'

'God, he's such a total fuckwit.' She shook her head in disgust. 'You know, I never liked him.'

That was a lie, but I was touched by her loyalty. Everyone adored Nick – he was cute, funny, easygoing. I was struggling to process how someone I'd thought I knew inside out could in fact be a total stranger. Had he always been like this, and had I been stupid and missed the signs? Or had he changed overnight into a calculating, insensitive arsehole? Or was this partly my fault, because – as he'd constantly griped – I'd prioritised my career over our relationship?

'So, what are you going to do?' Yvette asked. 'About your house? And the wedding?'

Unspooling seven years of togetherness was proving to be an expensive and painful process. 'I'm still figuring that out. None of the wedding deposits are refundable. At least my name's on the lease, so I gave notice last week. We have to move our stuff out by the end of the month.'

'I can't believe how together you are,' Yvette said. 'I'd be a total mess if I were you.'

It stung worse than a UTI to hear how shitty my life was, as seen through her eyes. Besides, I wasn't holding it together. My insides were molten and it wouldn't take much for me to explode.

'You should come out with me tonight,' Yvette continued. 'Blake's having a party.'

'I can't be bothered.'

'What else are you going to do? Stay here sulking? It's Saturday night.'

'It's hideous out there.' We were practically shouting at one another over the din of the rain on the roof.

I persuaded Yvette to go to the party without me, but when she left, the flat felt even more depressing. By ten o'clock, Mum had fallen asleep, and I was restless. My phone kept dinging with messages from concerned friends and calls from Yvette, now drunk, bossing me to head to Blake's. There was no way I was going to traipse all the way over to Bronte, but since the storm had died down by then, I grabbed my jacket and headed out for a bite to eat.

I drifted past the lurid dumpling joints, massage parlours and bric-a-brac stores, their neon signs blurred onto the wet asphalt. Papery leaves skittered past into the clogged drains. I followed a group of students into a graffitied alcove thudding with drum and bass. Inside, the bar had the sticky, fermented feel of a well-worn dive. I slipped onto a stool in the darkest corner. I'd lost my appetite, so I ordered a neat Scotch from the young bartender. It slid down too easily.

On my third drink, he turned up the lights. There was an early close before we ticked over to Easter Sunday.

'I have to ask you to finish up,' he said.

'Or you could join me for one more?' I asked, brazen from the whisky.

Afterwards, we drifted out into the street together. I loitered outside while he locked up, and then we Ubered to his flat in a grubby Art Deco block with Bob Marley posters taped to the walls. The room smelled of damp towels and incense, and the sex was raw and untethered. I wanted to drown myself in him, to be erased and reborn.

•

When I woke, the room was still dark, apart from the red flicker of a burger bar sign through the tangled venetians. The bartender was still asleep. I pulled on my scattered clothes and slipped out to the street. Under the wafer moon, the trees gave off a peaty rain-soaked glow, and everything seemed strangely still after the violence of the weekend's storm. When I reached the Catholic church, I realised Vanessa's house must be nearby. I'd just make a slight detour.

I found her row of Victorian terraces easily enough, their identical facades edged in iron lace and all with carefully tended flowerbeds out front. Vanessa's was the third one along with the red door. I pushed through the gate and crept up a couple of steps to take a better look. I don't know why I did it. I was compelled – a moth to the flame. It was the same self-flagellating impulse that had made me snoop around her Instagram.

At that moment, the front door opened and Nick emerged in his boxers, bleary-eyed, with the tiny dachshund in his arms.

'Mei?' he said, when he saw me on the steps.

My shame was total. I could only hope that he'd believe I was a figment of his guilty conscience – but that would have required the fucker to have a conscience in the first place.

'What are you doing?' he asked, his expression cold. 'Are you stalking me?'

My anger was momentarily jettisoned by shock, and my mouth locked shut. This was worse than seeing Nick and Vanessa together buck-naked at our flat. I'd convinced myself that he was satisfying a physical urge; that nothing serious would come of it. But if he was staying over at Vanessa's house, and helping to house-train her puppy, then it was much more. They were already playing happy families.

Instead of telling him to go to hell, I turned and sprinted out of the gate. And I kept running until I flagged down a passing taxi to drive me back to Mum's. When I arrived back at her flat, I crept into the bathroom, peeled off my stale clothes and scrubbed myself almost raw under the scalding water.

I was planning to languish in bed all day when my phone rang, Wilson's name flashing up on the screen.

'Morning, O'Connor,' he said. 'Meet me at the coroner's office in thirty minutes.'

•

By 8.30 am, the Chief Coroner, Barbara Cairns, and my boss, Detective Chief Superintendent Wilson, were already waiting for me, along with my colleague Macca – known more formally as Detective Sergeant Stuart McKenzie. The empty swivel chair plummeted when I sat down. My head was pounding, not helped by the room's nauseating custard walls.

'I received a phone call from St Vincent's Hospital yesterday afternoon,' Barbara began. 'A female patient presented to the ED with severe gastroenteritis and respiratory complications. She had become unwell following a family gathering at a private estate on the Mid North Coast, about forty minutes out of Taree. The patient died at 5.33 pm from pulmonary failure and hypovolemic shock.'

I waited for the punchline. So far, there was nothing about this death to justify Barbara summoning three detectives from the Homicide Squad so early on a public holiday.

'Given the death was unexplained,' Barbara continued, 'the hospital reported it, and we ran urgent toxicology tests overnight. The pathologist notified me of the preliminary results early this morning.' She ran her eyes over us to ensure we were paying attention. 'The results were most unexpected.'

'Meaning?' I said.

'They indicate evidence of arsenicosis – that is, acute arsenic poisoning.'

Arsenic poisoning. It sounded so old-fashioned, like something out of an Agatha Christie novel.

'Then, an hour ago, the lab called with a further update. A six-year-old girl was admitted yesterday to the ED at Sydney Children's in Randwick. She'd presented with the same symptoms, and it turned out she'd come from the same family gathering. Her lab tests also returned a positive result for arsenicosis. The child's currently on life support, and her prognosis isn't good.'

Macca shuffled forward on his seat. 'Didn't you say the family gathering was up near Taree?' he said. 'Maybe they were exposed to arsenic in one of the old goldmines up that way.'

Barbara nodded. A gold star for Macca. 'Yes, that is a possibility,' she said. 'I've asked DCS Wilson to supervise a scene examination at the family's estate. Forensics will test arsenic levels in the surrounding soil and drinking water. However' – Barbara paused – 'the pathologist found that the arsenic levels in both patients' urine was extremely high, consistent with deliberate lethal exposure.'

We were all silent as her words sank in.

'Of course,' the coroner finished, 'we will run further tests and order a full autopsy.'

'Is the family cooperating?' I asked.

'That's where it gets more complicated,' said Wilson, facing me for the first time. He looked as bad as I felt, with huge violet pouches under his eyes and a heavy dusting of dandruff on his lapel. His left eye was twitching – a tic that surfaced whenever he was stressed. 'We're dealing with the Turners – as in, the family of the late Sir Campbell Turner.' He waited for recognition to register. Everyone knew of Sir Campbell. He was an Aussie legend who'd bootstrapped himself out of poverty, made a fortune as a trader in New York and expanded it into a global luxury goods empire. He'd also donated astonishing amounts to worthy causes, including a huge endowment to the New South Wales Police Officers' Memorial Fund. We'd all been treated to sausage rolls and scones at the town hall to mark the occasion.

Wilson was in line for a promotion to Assistant Commissioner, so he'd be under close scrutiny for his handling of this case, and the Turners were famously litigious. No wonder Wilson was feeling pressured.

'The deceased,' Wilson went on, 'is Nina Turner, the wife of the eldest Turner son, Jamie.'

Over the years, I'd seen plenty of paparazzi photos of Nina and Jamie Turner. They were an Australian 'it' couple. Jamie was straight out of a Ralph Lauren spread, with curly brown hair, fine bone structure and an effortless old money aesthetic. One breathless commentator had described him as George Clooney meets Theo James when he succeeded his father as the chairman and CEO of Turner Corp. And Nina was a perfect English rose who channelled old Hollywood glamour. On Thursday, the *Sydney Morning Herald* had run a profile on her which I'd skimmed in Dr Lee's waiting room. She was an Oxford-educated lawyer who now oversaw the Turner family's philanthropic foundation.

'And what do we know about the child?' I asked.

'Tilly Turner is the daughter of Duncan Turner – Sir Campbell's middle son – and his wife Skye,' Wilson said. 'Only six years old.' He scratched his head, dislodging a fresh drift of dandruff that made me retch.

Barbara cut in. 'The pathologist says both Nina and Tilly would have ingested the arsenic within twenty-four hours prior to the onset of first symptoms. According to the statement the first attending officer took from Jamie Turner at the hospital, Nina became unwell after a family dinner party at their private estate on Friday night. The dinner was attended by Jamie, his two brothers and their partners and children. She'd had no contact with anyone else since Thursday evening.'

'We understand it's the same for the girl,' Wilson said, 'but we need to verify that with her parents.'

Barbara nodded. 'We only have a small window in which to gather evidence before it deteriorates or is lost. We'll need to exclude accident and suicide, but so far the evidence indicates foul play. We must assume the poisoning was a deliberate act.'

Macca and I exchanged a glance. Holy shit. This was huge. The media would go berserk once they caught wind.

'Does the family know about the arsenic?' Macca asked.

'No, not yet,' Barbara said. 'Since this is now a criminal investigation, you'll need to inform next of kin. We'll also request urine samples from everyone else present to confirm the extent of the arsenic exposure.'

Wilson leaned back in his chair and addressed me and Macca. 'Guys, we can't fuck this one up.' He was still smarting about our very public embarrassment on the Livvy Tweedsmuir case. 'Here's the plan: I'll deal with Jamie Turner and the youngest brother, Hugo Turner, who's still up north at the family pile. You two get across to Randwick to interview

Skye and Duncan Turner at the hospital. Then I'll need you to head into the office to run background on all the witnesses.'

On our way to the lift, Macca shot me a pitying look. 'You okay, mate?'

'I'm fine,' I said. 'Why?'

'You sure?' He glanced at my bare ring finger. 'I had a beer with Nick last night. Why didn't you tell me?'

Nick and Macca had been friends long before we all worked together in Homicide. It was inevitable that Macca would find out about the break-up, but I wasn't ready for his inquisition.

'I'm fine,' I repeated and quickened my step.

Macca shrugged. 'If you say so. But you look like crap. Big night out, was it?'

'No, just a quiet one.' I pushed the lift button with a little too much force.

•

For once, I let Macca drive. I prayed that my two long gargles of Listerine and a spray of Mum's dusty bottle of Opium would mask the alcohol fumes leaking from my pores.

We headed out of the CBD, past sandstone cathedrals and bronze men on horseback, and glided south on the empty M1 before turning east. On the way, I googled our interview subjects and gave Macca the lowdown. Duncan Turner was in his early forties, similar in appearance to Jamie but taller and leaner, with a brooding quality that shouted disaffected middle child. Like his brothers, he worked for the family empire, and the photos online were either black-tie Getty images or styled corporate mugshots. The little girl's mother, Skye Turner, was a bohemian goddess. An artist who made weird ceramic vases, she dripped with sex and glowed like the sun shone out of her arse – a poster child for Eastern Suburbs private girls' schools. This messy situation had no business interrupting their charmed lives.

A call came through from the police lawyer, Althea Baros. I answered on speakerphone.

'Hi, Mei. Are you with Tilly Turner's parents?'

'Not yet. We're on our way to the hospital to interview them.'

'Okay, good. I've just had a call with the Department of Communities and Justice and an army of advisers. Based on the coroner's briefing and Wilson's report, the DCJ has exercised its emergency protection powers to assume temporary care of Tilly Turner.'

'But she's in hospital,' I said. 'How does that work?'

'She'll stay in the intensive care unit under police guard. The order will prevent any suspects from having access to her until they have been cleared by the investigation.'

'Does that include her parents?'

'Uh-huh. It's a drastic step, but the DCJ has a statutory duty to prioritise the child's safety. They believe it's the most prudent course of action.' Althea explained that the DCJ would have until Thursday to submit the formal care application to the Children's Court, at which time a hearing would be scheduled. 'We don't want the parents to cause a scene at the hospital, so somehow you'll need to get Skye and Duncan Turner down to a station or back to their house before you break the news.'

Great. Presumably that would go down like a cold cup of vomit. Nothing about this case was going to be easy.

•

The Children's Hospital was located within the Randwick hospital campus. Its rainbow colours and cheerful murals made the place seem even more dismal, like some kind of sinister funhouse. We made our way up from the underground car park through the Prince of Wales Hospital to the Children's Hospital reception. After we presented our IDs, the elevator whisked us to the paediatric intensive care unit, known as PICU.

The air was sharp with disinfectant, and the silence in the waiting room was punctuated with the hum and beep of machines and an occasional infant's cry. Opposite us, a young woman was sobbing quietly to someone on FaceTime. Above her, the wall was clad in thank you cards with pictures of smiling babies and children. The air in the room had a strangled, anxious quality – an acknowledgement that we were at the membrane between life and death; between dumb luck and loss.

Eventually, a doctor asked us to follow her. She led us to a small internal office where Duncan and Skye Turner were seated. When we entered, Duncan's eyes flicked up. He was drawn and unshaven, his arm cinched around his husk of a wife. The doctor excused herself and closed the door.

'Mr and Mrs Turner,' I said, 'I'm Detective Senior Sergeant Mei O'Connor.' I flashed my badge. 'This is my colleague, Detective Sergeant Stuart McKenzie. We're very sorry about your daughter.'

Skye nodded, but her eyes were glazed, as though she wasn't fully present. She was kneading a small grey stone between her thumb and forefinger like a rosary bead.

'What's going on?' Duncan asked. He released his arm from Skye's waist and straightened himself in his chair.

'We understand you've been informed of your sister-in-law's death,' Macca said.

'Yes,' Duncan replied. 'It's a huge shock.'

'Since Mrs Turner's death is unexplained,' I said, 'and you were both with her in the period before she fell ill, we need to ask you some questions. It's part of the coronial process.'

'Can't it wait?' Duncan said. 'Our daughter's in a critical condition.'

'Our investigation could help determine what happened to Tilly, too,' I said.

'Really?' asked Duncan. 'Last night they said Tilly had most likely contracted a virus.' He shot a furious glance towards the corridor where the doctor was waiting. 'I knew they were stalling.'

'Mr Turner,' Macca said, 'we can either interview you down at the police station or, for your privacy, we can conduct the interview at your home.'

Skye shook her head. 'I'm not leaving Tilly.'

Duncan turned to his wife. 'We need to go home at some point to get some spare clothes and check on Bo.'

'I'm not leaving her,' Skye repeated.

'Mrs Turner,' Macca said, 'I'm afraid you don't have a choice. We don't want to make things more difficult for you, but we do need you to come with us.'

Duncan turned to Skye. 'Ana will be here shortly. She can sit with Tilly for an hour until we get back. Tilly's heavily sedated. She won't know we're gone.' He looked at me. 'It won't take long, will it?'

I assured him we'd do our best to make it an efficient process. I couldn't meet Skye Turner's eye.

•

'Shit, that's a brand-new Aston Martin DBX,' Macca said when the Turners emerged from the parking building in a black SUV.

We tracked them north-east, towards the canopied slopes of Bellevue Hill. I lowered the window and let the cool air rush in. You could almost smell the money in this neighbourhood, with its leafy avenues and manicured lawns.

The higher we climbed, the more imperious and solemn the homes became, sequestered behind glossy hedges and inclined towards the harbour. Skinny blondes in activewear – the type that survived on bone broth and organic air – power-walked past us at the lights. Somehow the streets had already been cleared of storm debris, as if the chaos unleashed on the rest of the city had spared the upper echelons.

Number 91 Victoria Road was concealed behind solid steel entrance gates fitted with a high-tech camera system. A brass plaque announced 'Thornfield'. According to Google, the house had once been the Swiss consular residence. The gates swung open as the Turners' car approached, and we followed them along a winding driveway, fringed with clipped topiary balls and clusters of perfect white roses, passing a helipad, a tennis court and an elaborate gazebo. Eventually, we arrived at an enormous three-storey white house that resembled the tiered polystyrene wedding cake displayed in Lorraine's Bakery across from the office. Beyond it, a pristine sapphire pool was flanked by a stately ivy-bound stone pool house and a sprawling formal garden that opened onto a jaw-dropping harbour view. Macca and I exchanged a shocked glance. So this was how billionaires lived.

The Aston Martin slipped around the side of the house and was swallowed into a cavernous garage of gleaming bonnets.

Apparently, the Turners changed their cars like we changed our underwear.

'Fucking hell,' said Macca, whistling under his breath. 'That's a McLaren, a Pagani, a vintage Ferrari, a Bugatti Tourbillon and the latest model Range Rover Vogue. Easily a few million bucks of metal.'

'Reckon they've got a cryonic chamber and a doomsday bunker tucked away in there too?'

Macca chuckled and scraped our Toyota Camry to a halt beside the grand front steps.

When Duncan opened the front door to us, a labrador hurtled out, wagging its tail in misplaced excitement. Duncan led us down a long parquet hallway that smelled of citrus and wood polish, like the fancy hotel where Nick's brother worked as a concierge. We passed antique wooden sideboards, vases bulging with cut roses, bizarre sculptures and abstract jewel-toned paintings. Macca tugged my elbow and nodded towards a gruesome portrait of a woman beside me. I shrugged until I saw 'Picasso' scrawled along the bottom right of the canvas. Sweet Jesus. These people could snuff out poverty in the inner city by liquidating a single painting.

I glimpsed a ballroom-sized lounge furnished with a luminous black grand piano. Beside it, a child-sized violin teetered against a music stand. We continued down the hallway until we reached a vast library with a rolling ladder, its floor-to-ceiling shelves packed with books. In the middle of the room, a doll's buggy with a teddy strapped inside was parked askew. A little blue gingham purse with 'Tilly' embroidered across it dangled from the handle. Skye Turner perched on one huge sofa. Duncan settled beside his wife and invited us to sit down opposite.

I placed my contact card and a voice recorder on the coffee table, next to a half-built candy-striped Lego castle. The dog was gnawing on a loose turret by my foot.

'Are you happy for me to record the conversation?'

Duncan nodded.

'Mr and Mrs Turner,' I said, 'we have reason to believe that both Nina and your daughter consumed a toxic substance.'

Duncan jerked forward. 'What substance?' he asked.

'The preliminary toxicology finding is that both of them suffered acute arsenic poisoning. The high level of poison detected rules out accidental environmental contamination, so we believe the arsenic was intentionally administered. Consequently, this is now a criminal investigation.'

Skye collapsed forward with a pained cry. Duncan's expression shifted – to shock or anger, I couldn't say.

'That's why it's critical that you tell us everything you can remember about the forty-eight hours leading up to the onset of Tilly's symptoms,' Macca said. 'We need to know details of everyone she had contact with, and everything she ate and drank in that period.'

Duncan shook his head. 'Hold on. You're saying someone deliberately poisoned our daughter?'

'At this stage, based on the pathologist's report, it appears that way,' I said. 'He believes they must have ingested the arsenic sometime between Friday afternoon and Saturday morning, and obviously other family members may well have been affected, which is why—'

'You're wrong,' Duncan interrupted. 'This is bullshit. Tilly was with us the whole time. No one poisoned her, for God's sake. How do you know if the information you have is reliable? You said yourself that they're just preliminary results.'

Skye clasped her husband's hand. Tears were sliding down her cheeks and pooling in the well at the base of her throat.

'The lab's undertaking further testing,' Macca said, 'but the coroner is very clear that the initial tests indicate deliberate arsenic poisoning. We'll take statements from you separately, and then you'll need to head to the lab to submit a urine sample.'

Duncan's face soured. 'We'll be doing nothing until we've spoken to our lawyer.'

Skye stood to leave. 'Let's go back to the hospital,' she said to her husband.

'I'm afraid that's not going to be possible,' I said.

Skye's eyes snapped across to me. 'What?'

I struggled to hold my nerve in the face of her raw devastation. 'I know this will be difficult to hear, but because of the criminal investigation into the poisoning, the Department of Communities and Justice has assumed care of Tilly – just temporarily. Your lawyer can petition the Children's Court for access. In the meantime, Tilly will continue to receive the best medical care in hospital. Uniformed officers will also protect her, and you'll be kept informed about her condition.'

'No!' Skye screamed. 'You can't do this!'

'You'll be arrested if you try to re-enter the hospital,' Macca said.

Duncan's face twisted with disgust. 'How dare you? We'd never have left our daughter's side if we knew what you were planning. This is a fucking outrage!'

'Mr Turner,' I began, 'we didn't—'

But he cut me off. 'Get out of my house!' Duncan shouted. 'Now!'

Macca bristled beside me, but we couldn't force them to talk. They'd shred us for any procedural errors.

'Of course, Mr Turner.' I rose and retrieved my recorder from the table. 'We'll leave you to make arrangements with your lawyer – but as I'm sure you'll appreciate, time is of the essence. The sooner you cooperate, the sooner we can work out what has happened to your daughter. We'll see ourselves out.'

●

Back in the car, Macca turned on the ignition. 'Well, he's an arsehole.'

'It's understandable that he's upset.'

Macca gave me a searching look.

'What?' I asked him.

'Nothing.'

'Macca, what? Spit it out.'

He blushed. 'I thought this might be triggering for you.'

Triggering – a loathsome word he'd picked up from his perky life-coach wife.

'Why would you say that?' I demanded.

'The little girl's six years old. Wasn't your sister that age when she disappeared?'

We'd never discussed Grace before. I hadn't told any of my colleagues what had happened because they'd see it as a weakness in these sorts of cases. Bloody Nick must have told him.

I stared straight ahead. While we waited for the entrance gates to shudder open, I couldn't block a vision of Tilly Turner wheeling her teddy down the hallway in its pram, the little blue gingham purse slung over her shoulder. A lump rose in my throat.

•

Back at work, the lights sputtered on, bathing the office in a sickly glow. People often asked me what it was like inside the State Crime Command. They envisioned a high-tech war room with state-of-the-art screens and steel vaults. In reality, it was a charmless office on the top level of the Police Area Command in central Sydney: stale air laced with the sweet smell of commercial cleaner, sturdy grey photocopiers and tangled computer cords running under felt dividers.

Macca and I headed to our respective cubicles. Mine was internal, with no direct sunlight, but I liked it because it was quiet, was far away from the lift and had the fewest distractions. The only view was of an artificial potted fiddle-leaf fig, still strangled with Christmas tinsel and a few sad, sparse decorations.

When I stood up, I could see the top of Macca's head and the bald spot he tried to conceal with strategic brushing. Behind his computer, he'd pinned up Jayden's kindy artwork, which looked like a small animal had shat itself on a piece of blue cardboard. Beside it, his wife Saskia held a glossy sign that exclaimed 6 *months!* over a hot-pink baby bump.

My phone pinged with a text from Wilson. He wanted a briefing on our interview with Duncan and Skye Turner by noon. It was almost half-past ten. Our interview had been a total bust, and Wilson would be pissed if we didn't have anything useful.

'Let's make a list of possibles,' I said, 'and then divvy up the background checks so at least we have something for him when he calls.'

'On it.'

My phone rang. It was Mum, checking whether I'd refilled her fentanyl prescription because the Celebrex wasn't working. I'd meant to sort it out yesterday. I told her I'd swing by the pharmacy and drop it to her in twenty minutes.

'Hey, Macca, I have to nip out for a sec. Can you get started without me?'

'Sure thing, boss.' He gave me a dorky salute.

I was halfway home when Macca called. 'Hey, sorry to interrupt but I'm locked out of the database. Helpdesk's running an update, so I won't be able to start the background checks for a couple of hours.'

'Damnit.'

'Unless . . .' Macca said.

'Unless what?'

'I could try with your login? It's totally fine if you don't want to because of security and stuff. Just a thought.'

I checked the time. Realistically, I wouldn't be back until half-past eleven. It was better for Macca to get underway so we had something for Wilson by noon. I gave him my login.

'And what's your password?' he asked.

I paused. I'd only just reset it. 'Nickisacocksuckerx100.'

He stifled a laugh. 'No hard feelings then.'

•

When I arrived back at the office, Macca beckoned me over. 'I've put together a list of all the people that were at the Turner property. Based on the statements taken so far, neither Nina nor Tilly had contact with anyone else during the relevant period.'

He'd worked up a link chart on the whiteboard, with a photograph of Nina pinned at the top. She reminded me of the Sindy doll a distant Irish aunt had posted for my eighth birthday – corn-silk hair, pearl-white skin and wide-set blue eyes. That doll had looked just like my three fair-haired cousins in the photo inside the card, and nothing like me.

Beneath the words '*Nina Turner – deceased*,' Macca had listed the names of the other attendees:

Jamie Turner, husband of Nina

Oliver Turner, son of Nina and Jamie (minor)

Finn Turner, son of Nina and Jamie (minor)

Arabella Turner, daughter of Nina and Jamie (minor)

Skye Turner, wife of Duncan

Duncan Turner, husband of Skye

Tilly Turner, daughter of Skye and Duncan (minor) (suspected poisoning victim)

Cody White, son of Duncan Turner from a previous relationship

Hugo Turner, brother of Duncan and Jamie

Tamara Baruch, friend of Hugo Turner/Turner Corp employee

'We'll need to double-check the information is accurate, but it's a start,' he said.

'Anything come up on background?' I asked.

'Yep. Three of them have a history of criminal charges.'

'Okay, good. What are we looking at?'

'Let's begin with Duncan.' Macca put a red asterisk next to Duncan's name on the board and passed me his rap sheet. 'He got into a bit of trouble in his late teens. Told you he was an arsehole.'

I scanned the sheet: three counts of assault, including assault against a police officer, and two charges of driving while intoxicated. Even though he was found guilty, in each case he was discharged without conviction, which was highly unusual after so many offences. I made a note to ask Althea about it.

'Okay, who's next?' I asked.

'Hugo Turner, the youngest brother.' Macca passed across the second sheet and put a red mark next to Hugo's name. 'Got a diversion for possession of Class A drugs and driving offences, as well as a violent assault dating back to when he was a boarder at St Alban's. Looks like he and some mates beat up a younger student, and the poor kid ended up in a critical condition.'

'I can't see a custodial sentence.'

Macca shook his head. 'Nope. Just diversion and sixteen hours of community service. Not even home D.'

'Hmm.'

'And then there's Cody White.' Another red asterisk. 'Apparently, Cody is Duncan Turner's son, but that's not officially documented anywhere.'

I studied Cody's record. Mainly auto theft and burglary, driving without a licence, and possession of cannabis.

'Spent some time in juvie,' Macca continued, 'but, to be fair, he's had no run-ins with the law in the past eighteen months.'

'Anything else?'

'Just one anomaly – Skye Turner. She signed her marriage licence in the name Skye Mason, but I can't find any records for her under that name before 2012. I've lodged requests with all the relevant agencies.'

'That's odd. Maybe she had a starter marriage before she traded up to Duncan Turner.'

My phone started buzzing on the desk like a dying blowfly. It was Wilson. Wind rushed into the speaker, breaking up the line so I couldn't catch what he was saying.

'Sorry, sir, can you repeat that?' I asked.

The boss's gravelly voice crackled through the phone. 'We've hit a major roadblock in the Turner case.'

THREE

SKYE

The detective's words settled like a frost, numbing every part of me. Our baby girl, poisoned by someone at Yallambee. By someone in the family. Everything was shifting and cracking. Reality had dropped away.

I called for Duncan, but he didn't return to the library. Instead, after the front door clanged shut, his footsteps carried along the hallway and onwards up the staircase. I tracked him to his study. He was bent over his wide oak desk, scrolling on his computer.

'None of the lawyers are picking up,' he said, his gaze fixed on the monitor.

'Who cares? Let's get back to Tilly.'

'Weren't you listening? The cops will arrest us.'

'We have to at least try. Besides, we've got nothing to hide. If we just cooperate with the police, answer their questions, they'll let us see her.'

He glanced up, his face drained of colour. 'Don't be so naive. It doesn't work like that. We're not saying a damn thing to them without a lawyer present.'

'Why? Don't you want to know who did this to Tilly?'

When Duncan turned back to his screen, liquid rage shot through me.

'For fuck's sake. Someone in your family tried to kill her! She might not make it. Don't you care?' I was screaming now, grabbing fistfuls of his shirt. 'Answer me!'

'Skye, stop it!' Duncan rose and gripped my shoulders. Then he steered me into a chair and held me there until I broke down into gulping sobs. 'Don't you dare take this out on me.' His voice was low, his eyes glistening. 'Babe, listen to me. When we find out who hurt Tilly, believe me, I'll fucking end them. I will. I promise you. But for now, you've got to be strong.'

'Why can't we help with the investigation? I don't understand.'

'Skye, think for a minute. Who will they suspect first?'

I didn't follow. 'I don't know.'

'Do I have to spell it out for you? With your history, we have to be especially careful.'

His words winded me. My history? Those blurred months after Tilly was born, sealed and buried so long ago. Would they use that against me? The idea that anyone could think I'd hurt Tilly was abhorrent. But then Kate McCann, Madeleine's mother, darted into my mind. And Lindy Chamberlain, the mother of Azaria. Mothers who'd lost their children and been wrongly accused of the crime. I couldn't bear to think about it.

'Once this breaks in the media,' he continued, 'we're clickbait. We can't give the press any ammunition. They'd love nothing more than footage of you being marched away from our daughter's hospital in handcuffs. How do you think that will play to a jury? A good lawyer will make all of this go away.'

My head was throbbing. I couldn't bear to be separated from Tilly. I was going out of my mind.

Duncan leaned forward and kissed my forehead gently. 'Trust me,' he said. 'I'll handle it. Just sit tight.' Then he drew my mobile phone out of his back pocket. 'You left this in the car.' He hesitated before handing it over. 'Promise me you won't speak to anyone. I mean it. No one. Not until I have a plan.'

'What kind of plan?'

'A plan for dealing with the police and also with the media. A plan to protect you.

'I know it's a lot to ask, but we can't trust anyone. I've told the staff not to come in until further notice. And don't answer your phone, even if it's someone you know. They could be with a reporter.'

I nodded. He passed me the phone. There were already nineteen missed calls, probably from friends I'd phoned in the night who had woken to my hysterical messages about Tilly.

On the desk, Duncan's own phone began buzzing. *Jamie* flashed up on his screen. 'I'd better take this.'

'Of course.'

It was unfathomable that Nina was dead. Delicate, perfect Nina, turning grey and waxy in some strange, cold room.

'I'll check on you soon,' Duncan said, and he ushered me out of the study and closed the door.

I retreated to Tilly's room, trailed by Bo, and sank into her bed, pressing my face into the soft white sheets that were sprinkled with tiny silver stars. The pillow smelled of her apple shampoo. On her bedside table, a dog-eared volume of *The Magic Faraway Tree* that we'd been reading together was splayed face down, waiting for us to resume our nightly ritual. How could it be that my tangle-haired, rosy-cheeked, funny little girl with the dimples and the wiggly teeth was stuck in a hospital bed, in a web of tubes and wires, fighting for her life? Right now, we should have been watching Tilly and Arabella hunt for their Easter eggs in the gardens at Yallambee, not trapped in this nightmare.

The first thing I did was phone Ana. Thank goodness she was at the hospital. I'd beg her to stay at Tilly's bedside until the lawyer sorted things out.

'What's going on?' Ana said when she answered. 'Security just booted me out of PICU.'

'What? Did they say why?'

'Because I'm not Tilly's parent or legal guardian. The place is crawling with police.'

Panic strobed through me. Who would watch out for Tilly now? I told Ana about the allegations of poison, the police investigation, the care order.

'Oh my God. Skye. This is crazy. What can I do?'

'I don't know. I'll ring you back. I need to speak to someone on her ward.'

I waited on hold for what felt like forever. Finally, I was put through to the head PICU nurse, Sonia.

'I'm sorry, Mrs Turner, but my supervisor told me all reports on Tilly's condition have to go through her.'

'Please, Sonia. Just tell me how she is.'

'There's been no change. She's stable. We're keeping a close eye on her.'

Stable was positive, wasn't it? 'Is she conscious?'

'No. We need to keep her ventilated and in a medically induced coma while her damaged organs heal.'

'How long will that take?'

'There's no clear timeline, Mrs Turner. You'll be notified of any developments as soon as possible, I promise.'

She was preparing to wind up the conversation. I couldn't let her go. 'Can you video call me from her bedside? I need to see her. Please.'

She hesitated. I pushed again.

'Sonia, she's only six years old. I need to see my daughter.' I tried to fight the tears, but I couldn't hold them back.

A pause. 'Okay. I'll call you back shortly from my personal number.'

I held my breath until the phone rang a few minutes later. Sonia raised her phone camera so I could see slivers of Tilly – her dark curls, the camber of her closed eyelids, the black fringe of her lashes, her chest rising and falling with each metronome beat of the ventilator. I wanted so badly to reach through the screen.

'I have to go now,' Sonia said.

'Please, just a little bit longer.'

'I'm sorry, Mrs Turner, but I really do have to go. We're short-staffed and PICU's full.'

'Just let me speak to her. Put me on speakerphone, please, so she can at least hear my voice.'

'Mrs Turner, I'm sorry but I have rounds. I have to go, okay? We'll let you know if anything changes.'

In that moment, all of the exhaustion and frustration and rage and hopelessness crashed over me, and I broke. I screamed at Sonia that no, it wasn't okay for her to go. Nothing was okay. How could she do this to me? It was inhuman of her to cut me off from my critically ill child.

Sonia hung up, and though I tried to call back, neither she nor the PICU main line would answer my number.

After a while, I heard Duncan's quick footsteps on the stairs, and the front door slammed shut. From the second-floor window, I watched him stride down the driveway and then around the bend by the tennis court until he was obscured by clusters of yellow leaves. Where was he going? I called his mobile, but he didn't answer, so I hurried down the stairs and ran after him.

Bo scampered alongside me out the door, down the long driveway and through the still-open gates to the street. But there was no sign of Duncan. Just a boy on a green bike, and a black ute pulling out from the kerb. Had I only imagined I'd seen him? Was I losing my mind?

I drifted back to the house. Its shadow stretched like a stain across the lawn. It had been our surprise wedding gift from Campbell, and I'd been mortified by the extravagance. Until I moved into Duncan's apartment, I'd been sharing a crumbling cottage in Chippendale with five other artists.

'You'll have to fill it up with grandchildren for me,' Campbell had said with a wink when he'd handed me the key to Thornfield.

Before our wedding, Duncan and I'd had so many plans. We were going to move to Byron Bay. Duncan would restore classic yachts, and I'd have a studio by the ocean. We'd have four children and foster rescue dogs. Duncan swore he wanted a simple life, devoting himself to me and our family. It was his way of compensating for his own emotionally sterile childhood of nannies and boarding schools. But after the wedding, Duncan said that Campbell needed him to stay on with the business for a few more years. So I tagged along on the private jet when he travelled for work to New York, to Milan, to Paris, to St Petersburg. When we met up for dinner in the evenings, I'd tell Duncan all about what I'd seen while he'd been cooped up in boardrooms. He loved hearing about the discoveries I'd made and how they inspired my own work. He made me feel precious. He made me feel safe.

A year after our wedding, Thornfield remained unfurnished, beyond the small corner of it that we inhabited. Campbell sent in his interiors team. They loaded each room with designer furniture and important art – even a Picasso that Campbell had gifted us for our first anniversary. I could have insisted on furnishing the house myself, but Campbell liked taking care of us. It was important to him, and I'd learned early in life that it's best not to make a fuss with people who like to be in control; it's always safer to slide on through. So I spent more and more time working upstairs in the attic, or out in my garden studio. Duncan joined the Royal Sydney Golf Club. We stopped talking about Byron Bay.

My only requirement when we moved into Thornfield was that, unlike the rest of Duncan's family, we dispensed with a live-in household staff of butlers, chefs and housekeepers. It was absurd when there were only two of us rattling around in the place. Duncan wasn't easily persuaded, so we compromised on Betty, a Chinese lady who helped with the housework and laundry for a couple of hours each day, and an army of gardeners and pool valets who managed the exterior.

I'd taken for granted that babies would come, but by my thirtieth birthday there was still a stubborn single line on the pregnancy test. We saw a fertility doctor and a naturopath. I changed my diet and began acupuncture. Still nothing. Then the wearying rounds of fertility treatment began: pills, injections, blood tests, cramps, clots and ultrasounds. Doctors sucked eggs out of my ovaries with long, thin needles and syringed the viable embryos back into my womb.

Duncan and I lurched from the exhilaration of a flickering heartbeat on a sonographer's screen to the crushing disappointment of loss a few weeks later. I despised the word *miscarriage* – which my obstetrician casually explained was Latin for 'failure to carry'. Only a man could have coined such a heartless term for the moment your underwear fills with blood and livery tissue, and your heart fractures into tiny pieces.

And then, one day, an angel stuck. Every day that she grew inside me, she spoke in a secret language of curls and flutters. And finally, Tilly was born, soft-skulled, amber-eyed, with the tiniest half-moons on her fingertips and a cap of downy auburn hair. I'd expected the elation of that first day to wane, especially with the relentless sleep deprivation. Instead, it continued to swell in those first weeks until I was suspended in a euphoric bubble. The doctors later explained it was mania.

Then, one day, darkness fell. It was her crying. So much crying. I needed it to stop.

The antipsychotic medications blunted my memory of those months. All I had afterwards were fragments of the ward: a red plastic clock, its second hand twitching on the numeral two but never moving on. A plastered-over cavity in the wall that stared at me like an empty eye socket. A faded Monet print of a vase of sunflowers.

When I came home, something had shifted between Duncan and me. We sculpted our lives around Tilly – her routine and activities – so that we didn't need to address the change. Unlike my mother, I recovered. But, while he always denied it, in Duncan's eyes I would forever be a little bit broken.

•

It was nearly two hours before Duncan returned. I waited for him in silence, researching Tilly's prognosis on my laptop and despairing at the results. I needed to tether myself to hope, to the possibility that she was not in pain, to the belief that she would survive. My phone buzzed incessantly as word spread among my friends, but Duncan had asked me not to speak to them just yet. Besides, none of them could help. A thick glass dome had settled over me, separating me from the world.

'Where the hell have you been?' I demanded when Duncan entered the den where I was waiting with Bo. 'You can't just disappear like that.'

'Sorry. I had to clear my head after my call with Jamie.' He sank onto the couch beside me and pressed his palms together. 'He's really struggling.'

I softened then. I'd been so consumed with my own despair that I hadn't really considered Jamie or those three poor children who'd lost their mother.

'And I finally got hold of a good lawyer,' Duncan added. 'He's on his way.'

We were startled by the intercom system bleating in the hallway, which set Bo barking. Duncan rushed to check the cameras on the hallway monitor. 'Fucking vultures.'

I watched the screen over his shoulder. Two news trucks had assailed our berm and a crowd was pouring onto the footpath. A man was scaling the gates with what appeared to be a long-lens camera strapped to his back.

'Skye, go up to our bedroom – it'll be safer up there if any of these mongrels makes it to the house. I'll call for some security.'

I stood vigil at our bedroom window to see if anyone had made it onto the property. After a while, Duncan came upstairs to say that a security team from his work had arrived. He encouraged me to rest, but of course that was impossible, so I collapsed onto the bed and dared to check the news on my phone. The story was everywhere.

Breaking news – Police are investigating the alleged poisoning of a 41-year-old Sydney woman who died on arrival at St Vincent's Hospital yesterday afternoon. The deceased woman's niece, a six-year-old girl, remains in a critical condition in Sydney Children's Hospital. Both are believed to be relatives of the late billionaire businessman and philanthropist Sir Campbell Turner, who himself passed away in January. New South Wales Detective Chief Superintendent Mike Wilson would not verify the individuals' identities, but he did confirm that the incidents are being treated as suspicious. Investigations are ongoing.

I replayed the events at Yallambee over and over again. The detectives' theory just had to be wrong. It was inconceivable that anyone at Yallambee could have intentionally poisoned Tilly and Nina.

Sure, Duncan's family was complex. The brothers had had their disagreements, but that was the case in most families, and the three of them spent more time together than most because they all worked for Campbell's business. It had to have been a horrible accident. Perhaps a toxin had leached into the tank water supply or into some of our food. Or perhaps it wasn't poison at all but a lethal virus, like the doctors had suspected initially. I wasn't an expert, but surely the police had jumped to an extreme conclusion. Surely they needed to run more tests.

At the bone-crunch of car tyres on the driveway, I peered outside. A sleek silver Mercedes was nosing its way, shark-like, towards the front entrance. By the time I made it downstairs, Duncan was opening the door to a man with a broad tanned face, thatched with thick silver hair.

'Jack Harrod KC,' he said in a silky baritone, extending his hand to me. 'My sincere condolences to you, Skye.' His square teeth were the same crisp white as his shirt. 'That's an impressive security cordon you've got out the front there,' he continued, shaking Duncan's hand. 'Dare say you need it with those media barbarians at the gate.'

'Thanks for coming,' said Duncan.

'Of course. It's good to see you again, Duncan, although obviously not under these circumstances.'

Duncan led the way to the dining room, and the three of us sat at the table. Jack set a black leather folder and a fountain pen down in front of him.

'Let's start with this outrageous care order,' Duncan said.

Jack nodded. 'I've received a copy from the Department of Communities and Justice. I need some time to research the relevant case law, but the starting point is that under the Care Act, there is broad discretion to vest temporary care of a child in the state where there is concern for that child's safety.'

'But Tilly's in the PICU,' I said. 'She's already in the safest place possible, so surely there's no basis for the order?'

I waited for him to agree; to confirm that the authorities had overreached and that our access to Tilly would be reinstated. Instead, he cocked his head at me.

'The concern for your daughter's safety arises because you are both under suspicion for the alleged poisoning.'

'That's ridiculous,' Duncan spat. 'As if we, of all people, would ever harm Tilly. They can't do this.'

'They can, I'm afraid,' Jack said. 'But don't worry – it's only temporary, and I'm hopeful we can resolve the matter by Friday if we have a sensible judge.'

My head was spinning. It was Sunday now. Friday was almost a week away. 'No.' The word caught in my throat. 'Why are they doing this?'

Jack laid down his pen. 'Well, Skye,' he said, 'with your history, there is a reasonable basis for their concern.'

I stared at him. 'What do you mean?'

'Well, I understand there's a certain historical episode that will be of interest to the police, as well as a family history.'

'Sorry – why is that relevant?'

I looked to Duncan for support, but his eyes were fixed on the table. What had he told Jack about me?

'And I understand,' Jack continued, ignoring my question, 'that you were verbally abusive to an intensive care nurse on the phone this morning. That's not going to help you to regain access. For the time being, I'm afraid that all medical correspondence will need to go through Duncan.'

Jack opened his folder, and the only sound was the rasp of his fountain pen's steel nib against the paper inside.

'For now,' Jack continued, 'when it comes to the police investigation, I'd strongly advise you to exercise your statutory right to remain silent. Under the Law Enforcement Act, that won't prejudice the outcome if this ends up in court.'

An intense heat prickled at the back of my neck. 'Stop it.' I stood up, scraping the chair legs along the floor. 'You're acting like I'm some sort of monster.'

The lawyer glanced at Duncan and then laid down his pen. 'Skye, you're clearly very upset – understandably. But we don't know what evidence the police will find at the scene. We don't know what they're thinking. The important thing is that we're prepared for any outcome. That's my job.'

Duncan rounded the table and kneeled beside me, pulling me into his chest. I inhaled the familiar, musky scent of him. He urged me to go upstairs and lie down while he and the lawyer worked out a strategy. I couldn't possibly rest with my stomach and mind churning, but I was relieved to get away from them both.

I escaped to my attic studio, Bo at my side. It was the only part of the huge house that had ever really felt like mine. It was there that Tilly and I spent hours together shaping clay. She had such a natural instinct for it. Like me, she loved the rhythm of layering and moulding, and the alchemy of creating new forms out of blank matter. When I plunged my fingers into the cool earth, I felt her there beside me.

Hours slipped past as I pressed, folded and coiled. By the time Duncan joined me, I'd created a series of white shapes, as smooth and blank as dried bones.

'Has he gone?' I asked.

'Yes.'

'Good.'

I knew Duncan wanted to say something in the lawyer's defence, but he let it go. He stepped up behind me and put his arm around my waist, then drew me towards him, onto the couch. I let my head drop to his shoulder. After a while, I could feel him shuddering. He was crying too.

We sat there for a long time together in silence. Shadows lengthened on the studio walls, and the waning light ignited the pale blue kintsugi bowl on the windowsill. An artist had gifted it to me when Duncan and I had visited Kyoto after my fourth miscarriage. Kintsugi was the practice of repairing broken ceramics with a golden lacquer to bond the fragments back together. With the fault lines highlighted in gold, rather than camouflaged with clear adhesive, the repaired vessel was said to be more beautiful than the original.

The art form embraced imperfection and transience; the search for beauty in damage and loss. That philosophy had resonated with me and informed my work. But that was before we risked losing Tilly.

FOUR

MEI

EASTER SUNDAY

Wilson's voice rumbled through the speaker from Yallambee. 'Jamie and Hugo Turner have lawyered up. Refusing to speak. Of course, they're citing emotional distress, but it smacks of a cover-up. How did you get on with Tilly's parents?'

'No better,' I said.

Wilson sighed. 'Jesus. It's the bloody Woollahra mafia.'

I pictured him pacing the perimeter of whatever room he was in, shoulders hunched, sliding his battered gold wedding band up and down his finger.

'I did manage to take a statement from the young woman, Tamara Baruch,' Wilson continued. 'She's here at Yallambee as a guest of Hugo Turner. She's pretty shaken. Some possible leads. I'll email you the transcript when it's been typed up.'

'What about Cody White, sir – Duncan Turner's older son?' asked Macca. 'Has he been located?'

'Not as yet. He left the family estate on Friday night straight after dinner, which is suspicious. I need you to track him down this afternoon.'

'Roger that. We'll put out a statewide alert.'

'Did any of them agree to provide urine samples?' I asked.

'No,' Wilson said. 'And according to Althea, we can't force them to.'

'How about Tamara?' asked Macca. 'If she provided a statement, then why wouldn't she give you a specimen?'

'She might have, but she's being advised by Hugo Turner's lawyer now. Anyway, the pathologist tells me that urine tests for arsenic are only reliable for thirty-six hours after exposure. Realistically, we're out of time if Nina and Tilly were exposed at some stage on Friday, which is the pathologist's assumption.'

'What about the scene exam?' I asked. 'Has that turned up anything?'

The forensics team would be fanning out across the Turner property with sniffer dogs, painstakingly dissecting food scraps, swabbing surfaces, collecting liquid samples and trawling through rubbish sacks with the diligence of archaeologists.

Another deep sigh crackled through the speaker. 'Not yet. Arsenic residue is bloody tough to find. Apparently it looks like flour, and you only need a pinch to kill an adult. Less for a kid.' Wilson muttered something inaudible and then said, 'There's a call coming through from the coroner. I'll check in again this afternoon.'

•

At two o'clock, we ordered takeaway kebabs from the Turkish place on the corner. I perched next to Macca on a torn vinyl stool while airborne grease from the mutton gyro soaked into my clothes and hair.

Across the road, a white family of four was strolling along the footpath. The son, who looked about eight, was dressed identically to his father in a miniature navy blue suit, white shirt and striped tie. The wife was wearing a pastel pink coat and kitten heels and carrying a little girl whose hair had been looped into ringlets. Macca and I decided they must have come straight from Mass, being dressed like that on Easter Sunday in the city. I wondered for a minute what it would be like to be part of such a perfectly symmetrical family. To believe in resurrection after death. To believe that a book written by a handful of men three and a half thousand years ago had any relevance in today's fucked-up world.

'Ever go to church, O'Connor?' asked Macca.

'Yep, for a while. Dad used to drag us to St Patrick's when I was little, but Mum put a stop to it.'

'How come?'

'The other women weren't very nice. Back then a mixed-race couple was still pretty weird, especially in the Irish Catholic church.'

Mehmet handed us our takeaway bags, already oozing brown liquid, and we peeled them open on our way back to the office.

'Must've been tough for you too,' Macca said. 'And then you had to deal with all that stuff with your sister.' He laid his hand on my shoulder. 'You sure you're okay?'

'How could I not be okay with a bellyful of Mehmet's finest doner kebab?'

He paused. 'O'Connor, Nick's an old mate and all but – well, if you ever need to talk, I'm here for you. I know you're going through a rough time right now.' He gave me a meaningful look and blushed. He was so awkward. I couldn't bear it.

'Thanks, Macca. Good to know.'

•

Back in the office, Macca tried to pull up information on Cody White while I researched murder by arsenic. There was nothing enlightening on the police database, so I resorted to Google, which confirmed that arsenic trioxide had been the 'king of poisons' since Roman times and has been used to bump off a pope, several kings and various emperors.

I had to admit, it really was the perfect murder weapon: odourless, tasteless and fatal in tiny doses. In seventeenth-century France, impatient heirs used arsenic trioxide to snuff out their wealthy relatives so commonly that it was called *poudre de succession* – inheritance powder. Across the Channel, it was the leading cause of British homicide during the Industrial Revolution. After that, governments worldwide made the poison illegal, and its popularity as a murder weapon waned dramatically. In modern times, arsenic trioxide was so highly regulated in developed countries that it was tough to access, so whoever had poisoned Tilly and Nina Turner must have prepared well in advance.

If we could work out where the Yallambee arsenic had come from, perhaps we could narrow down our list of potential suspects. I called around the forensics team to get more information, but they were all on site at Yallambee or away for the Easter break and didn't answer.

The first one to call me back was the Ferret. She'd briefly flatted with Nick at university and felt a proprietorial claim to him that she reliably brought up each time we spoke.

'Mei, it's been ages. First off, I have to say I'm devastated to hear about you and Nick.' News travelled fast. She couldn't have sounded any less sincere. 'What happened?'

'He fucked his physio. As I said in my message, I need to talk to you about arsenic trioxide.'

'That must really hurt.' The Ferret's voice was dripping with schadenfreude. 'And I hate to say it, but Vanessa is so gorgeous. I hung out with her over the summer. You should see her in a bikini!'

I visualised punching the Ferret in the face. She was weak and scrawny – I'd easily take her in a fight.

'I'm trying to work out how a person could get hold of arsenic trioxide given how tightly regulated its supply is in Australia.'

'There are various ways.' She was huffy now because I hadn't succumbed to her mind game. 'Wilson already asked me to look into it. The powder form is a by-product of smelting ore. It's also used as an industrial chemical in manufacturing and as a treatment for a rare form of leukaemia.'

It wasn't exactly the shortlist I'd hoped for, but at least it was a start. Turner Corp's main investments were in luxury brands, but they might have some interests in mining and manufacturing that we could investigate.

'Thanks, that's helpful,' I said.

'And then there's Gumtree, Etsy, eBay. Loads of vintage products sold online contain lethal doses of arsenic – antique wallpapers, flypaper, some paints. You just need to work out how to extract the poison. And all of that information's online too.'

'So you're saying anyone with the internet and half a brain could get hold of enough arsenic trioxide to commit murder?'

'Correct.' Her tone was smug. 'Was there anything else?'

•

After ending the call, I checked my emails. Tamara Baruch's statement had just come through from Wilson. When Macca and I had searched her name online, the image gallery revealed a blandly beautiful young woman in her mid-twenties with a touch of the Kardashian – inflated lips, botoxed face, groomed to within an inch of her life – pouting at openings for glamorous boutiques and hip restaurants. According to her LinkedIn profile, Tamara had worked in events and as an influencer before joining Turner Corp's publicity team the previous year.

I opened the link and read through the statement. Tamara confirmed the names of the people who'd been present at Yallambee before Tilly and Nina developed symptoms, and they were all consistent with our link chart. Nothing new there. The interesting part came on page two:

> . . . Hugo mentioned that he and his brothers planned to discuss their father's will over the weekend. There was going to be, like, some sort of meeting on the Saturday afternoon. I don't know the details. I think it's a pretty complicated family situation. Duncan invited his son Cody along and I don't think Hugo or Jamie were happy about that. Then Hugo and Duncan had an argument about it at dinner on Friday night. Duncan went crazy and started choking Hugo. I probably shouldn't have said that . . .

I really don't want to get involved. I don't want to lose my job.

Now we were getting somewhere. If we could get hold of a copy of Campbell Turner's will then we might be able to establish motive. I called Althea. When my call went to her voicemail, I immediately called back. This time, she answered on the fifth ring.

'Hey, Mei,' she said. 'You guys do realise it's Easter Sunday, right?'

'Yeah, sorry. But—'

She groaned. 'I know. I've been on the phone literally all morning.' I heard kids stomping and screeching in the background. 'Sorry about the noise. We've got the cousins over for an egg hunt.' Then she roared, 'No, Vinnie! You've got enough. Put them back. Now!'

'Althea, after a person dies, how long does it take for their will to become a public record?'

'Not until probate is granted. That usually takes a couple of months, for a straightforward estate at least. But I'm guessing you're interested in Campbell Turner's will?'

'Yup.'

'Well, probate will take a while because his estate will be complex and spans multiple jurisdictions. Possibly a year – probably much longer.'

'Could we get hold of the will sooner with a warrant?'

'You'd need to establish reasonable cause et cetera. But I'm guessing the estate's lawyers would challenge it, so it would probably be a waste of time.'

'It's worth a try. Can you draft something up?'

'Today?'

'Yes.'

A deep sigh. 'Fine.'

•

I checked on Macca. He wasn't having much luck with his inquiries into Cody White either.

'He's not a registered voter, hasn't filed a tax return, doesn't have any credit cards and there's no vehicle registered to his name,' Macca explained. 'The last address on his police file is a place in South Brisbane from four years ago, and they've got no idea where he is now.'

'What about social media?'

'I've ordered a report, but my initial searches haven't turned up anything. He's a ghost.'

Another critical delay. Fuck.

Macca's phone was ringing with a FaceTime call and *Saskia* flashed up on the screen.

'Daddy, when are you coming home?' came Jayden's lispy little voice over the speakerphone. 'I *miiiiiiith* you!' He was holding his mother's phone on an angle so that we had a clear line of sight up his snotty nostrils.

Macca answered Jayden in a drippy singsong voice, and then Saskia joined in to complain he was missing family time and the opportunity 'to make Easter memories'. It wasn't as if Macca was down at the pub with his mates; he was trying to solve a homicide for Christ's sake. Then I overheard Saskia snipe, 'Yeah, well, you have family commitments. Mei doesn't. Let her handle it – she's the one they promoted after all.' Ouch.

Macca rang off and kept clacking away at his computer. I tried to ignore Saskia's barb, but I found myself insisting that

Macca take his laptop home so he could finish off his work after doing the Easter egg hunt. Damn my Catholic guilt.

After Macca left, a wave of fatigue hit me. I stood at the window and gazed out over the city: the grid of empty streets cutting through the sprawl of metal and glass, and the sheen of high-rise towers in the last light of the day. All hard surfaces, locked grilles and shuttered windows. I had a sudden need to curl up in my childhood bed and pull the soft cotton sheets up to my chin. Instead, I made myself an instant coffee that tasted like liquid dirt, typed up our report and emailed it to Wilson.

On my drive home, I thought of the churchgoing family from that afternoon. They would be sitting down to dinner, something wholesome like roast chicken with homemade gravy and steamed vegetables, the children rosy-cheeked and damp-haired straight from the bath. The parents would tuck their children into bed, read them a story, and then perhaps retire to the TV room to watch Netflix. They wouldn't stay up late, because they'd have plans to meet friends for brunch on Easter Monday. I had let myself believe that I'd have that life with Nick. Two children. We'd already picked out names (Connor for a boy and Evie for a girl). We'd go on camping holidays with other families. His parents would help with child care while we both worked hard to save for a house in a decent school zone. I'd been foolish enough to believe it had all been within my grasp.

•

Every evening, Mum watched the SBS Food channel on the couch with Laifu sprawled across her lap. But when I turned into the driveway, a faint knuckle of moon overhead and the other flats glowing like a string of lanterns, Mum's flat was completely dark. I raced up the steps, panic flaring in my chest, to find Laifu yowling at the screen door. I jammed the key into the lock and twisted it open.

'Mum?' I called, pushing my way inside.

The door banged shut behind me.

'Mum, are you okay?'

There was no answer. I ran to Mum's bedroom. She was hunched up on her side, her breathing shallow and her face flushed.

'My God, Mum! What's wrong?'

'Mei.' She extended a hot, bony hand towards me. 'I'm so cold.'

'Why didn't you call?'

'You were working, lè lè.'

'Mum, you know you have to call me.'

I took her temperature and called Dr Lee. He didn't pick up, and the recorded message directed me to ring the after-hours clinic. I begged the receptionist there to connect me with a registrar and she finally relented.

'It sounds like your mother might be neutropenic and developing an infection, which means her white blood cell count is dropping,' the registrar said.

'What should I do?'

'Give her two paracetamol right away to break the fever. If her temperature hasn't started to come down in thirty minutes, she'll need to be admitted to hospital for IV antibiotics.'

My throat tightened.

I lay on the bed beside Mum until her fever dropped, and then dragged my mattress into her bedroom. We both struggled to sleep. When I finally slid into a dream, I was in a pub, the air sour with spilled beer. Dad was holding my right hand and we were foot-dancing with my little white sneakers on top of his brown leather brogues, while Mum jiggled Grace on her hip. I had my left arm clamped around Dad's waist, and the crowd was clapping in time to the fiddles. When the tempo increased, we started spinning, faster and faster, until I began to lose my grip. I squeezed his hand harder and harder, but he was slipping away from me. No matter how hard I tried, I couldn't hold on.

FIVE

SKYE

EASTER MONDAY

I had no memory of falling asleep on Sunday night, and I woke in the early hours with animal panic spreading inside me. I couldn't face another day without Tilly. It was torture to be so far away while she lay alone in that hospital bed. The sanitised updates the doctors sent Duncan were no substitute. What if she didn't make it? That horrific thought looped around and around in my skull.

Careful not to disturb Duncan and Bo, I slipped out of bed and crept into the dark hallway. A lattice of moonlight was splayed across the landing. In the silence, the oppressive weight of the house bore down on me: each cornice, each moulding, each archway. I ran my fingers along the walls, drifting on instinct towards Duncan's study. The door was closed, so I turned the doorknob, but it didn't budge. I tried it again, more forcefully this time, but it remained stuck. There was an old keyhole under the doorhandle, but I didn't recall ever seeing a key. Surely he hadn't locked it?

'What are you doing?'

I was jolted by Duncan's voice behind me further down the hallway.

'Nothing,' I said. 'I mean, I don't know. I couldn't sleep.'

'Why were you sneaking into my study?'

I straightened. 'Why did you lock the door?'

He moved closer. 'Skye, I'm worried about you.'

'Answer my question. Why did you lock the door? Are you hiding something?'

When Duncan reached me, he gave the door a firm push, and it opened. It had just been jammed. He stood aside and gestured for me to enter. 'Go ahead,' he said.

'I'm sorry,' I said. 'I thought . . .' I trailed off.

He shook his head, then left me and returned to our bedroom.

•

I spent the rest of the night alone in my attic studio. For what seemed like hours, I stood by the window with my forehead pressed into the clammy glass, studying the contours of the dark garden. The sick, glutinous feeling inside me was starting to set. It was morphing into something dense and heavy that tugged at the base of my stomach, drawing me towards the earth.

Once, Tilly and I had shared a body. And even after her birth and weaning, our physical connection was still vital – in my bathing and drying of her, in the washing and combing of her hair, in the holding of her hand to cross the road, in the lifting of her onto the high swing at the park, in the application of lotions and bandaids to her skin, in the trimming of her fingernails, in the cuddles and kisses we shared. It was the cruellest punishment imaginable to be separated from her when she needed me most.

I finally succumbed to sleep on the tattered studio couch and woke on Monday morning to the mournful song of a grey butcherbird that had nested in the eaves. When I went downstairs, Duncan was making espresso. The sweet smell of the freshly ground beans made me nauseous.

'How are you?' he asked, his voice even.

'Fine.' I edged towards the kitchen island. A pile of Tilly's crayon sketches – a series of her and me planting sunflowers, our smiling egg-heads stacked on vibrant torsos – and a stack of unopened mail had toppled against the fruit bowl. The mandarins were starting to rot. 'How's Tilly?'

'No change.'

'Heard from the lawyer?'

'Not yet. I'm chasing.'

'How about Cody – any word from him?'

Duncan shook his head. 'No. I've left messages but his phone's still off. Probably out of credit.' He slid a mug of black coffee over the island bench towards me.

'Don't you think that's weird? That you haven't heard from him? He must know by now.'

'He's not exactly an avid news follower, and we don't speak that regularly.' His tone was defensive. 'He'll get in touch soon.' Duncan stepped backwards and took a sip of his coffee – he was working up to something. 'Skye, I've asked Doctor Friel to come.'

'Why?' I perched on a stool at the bench and winced at the shaft of grey light streaming in through the window.

Duncan drew the curtain halfway to block it. 'Because you need help.'

●

The doctor arrived with a black medical bag and a grave expression. He prescribed sleeping pills and asked how I was feeling. What did he expect me to say? There were no words for this. We sat in the library. Between us, on the coffee table, stood the Lego castle that Tilly and I had built last Thursday night. I traced my finger over the candy-pink bricks that we'd assembled together – the block-headed princess still waving from the top tower where Tilly had placed her – and I was seized by the certainty that none of this was real. It was all elaborate make-believe. A macabre prank. There was no arsenic, no murderous plan. Nina and Tilly were just fine.

I must have spoken aloud because Duncan and the doctor were exchanging words like *irrational* and *delusional*. The doctor scratched on his notepad and told Duncan the medication would be delivered to the house that afternoon. Duncan was to keep a close eye on me; Dr Friel could prescribe something stronger if necessary.

I broke outside to breathe. Before, our autumn garden had been magnificent – a rich canvas of auburns, plums and buttery yellows. Now, it was a dismal ecosystem of decay. I threaded my way around sulphurous mounds of bruised petals and rotting leaves laced with slugs and crushed snails and past the dark stars of dead roses. On a recent weekend, to the head gardener's horror, Tilly and I'd spent hours digging up topiary shrubs to sow jonquil bulbs, but the rain had flooded the soil. Now they would be rotting too.

I paused on the stone terrace overlooking the harbour. Rain had curdled the water, and the jagged peaks of the Opera House and sweep of the Harbour Bridge glinted through the fog like spectres. A city of millions unfurled before me, but I felt so isolated. So alone.

When I married Duncan, somehow I'd lost touch with my oldest friends. At first, I tried to maintain contact, but the gulf of privilege was an embarrassment. I couldn't invite them to our preposterous home when they were struggling to pay their bills, and they wouldn't accept my charity. I'd hemmed myself into a world where I didn't belong. The years of fertility treatment, and then Covid isolation, had only set me further apart.

On the surface, I had plenty of new friends – the glamorous wives of Duncan's schoolfriends, my crew of fellow school mums, my yoga friends and, of course, Ana and my other colleagues at the gallery. But none of them really *knew* me. I was a shapeshifter, shrinking or swelling to fill the void in any relationship. Once it had been a survival strategy. Now it was a habit.

When I returned to the house, Duncan's phone was charging beside mine on the kitchen counter. The sense he was hiding something had been nipping at me like a dog at my heels, so I found myself picking up his phone. But when I tried to unlock it, the home screen bounced, prompting me to re-enter the PIN. I did, but it bounced again. It was the first time he'd changed his PIN since I'd met him.

'What are you doing?' Duncan was behind me.

'You've changed your code.'

'Yeah, so what?'

'Why did you?'

'For security, with everything that's going on. Why were you checking my phone?'

'Because . . .' I didn't know what to say. I felt foolish and paranoid.

'Skye, why were you trying to get into my phone?' He was staring at me now, unsmiling.

I tried to think of a reasonable explanation. 'To see if you'd heard from the hospital.'

'I'll tell you as soon as I hear anything. I promise.'

Down the hallway, Bo was barking and scratching at the front door. Duncan crossed over to the window.

'Ah good, that's the security guy from work. I've asked him to install some more cameras around the house.'

'Why do we need more cameras?'

'For safety.'

'So you can spy on me?'

'Jesus, Skye! I'm trying—' He caught himself. 'Let's not fight each other. I'm trying to protect you – to keep you safe. Give me a break, okay?'

'Don't pretend you're worried that the reporters are going to break into the house.'

He hesitated. 'It's not just reporters. There are trolls online saying some things.'

'What sort of things?'

Duncan cleared his throat. 'I didn't want to have to tell you, but – well, I suppose you should know. Someone leaked your medical notes on Reddit.'

'What?' My stomach gave way. 'Who would do that?'

'A nurse, possibly, or someone in admin,' Duncan said. 'The press give them backhanders. It's the price of carrying the

Turner name.' He placed his hand on my shoulder. 'Don't worry about it. I'm going to deal with this. Just stay inside. Those bastards have drones filming overhead.'

From the upstairs window, I saw Duncan standing in the driveway chatting to a scrawny, bald guy beside a black ute. There was something about the scene that kindled a sense of déjà vu, but I couldn't place it.

I sank onto our bed and turned on my phone. The screen lit up and buzzed with a battery of messages from friends and acquaintances. They were devastated to hear about Tilly, desperate to see me. They'd tried to visit the house but they couldn't get past security. How were we holding up? What could they do to support us? I'd promised Duncan I wouldn't speak to them; besides, I couldn't face their tears and banal reassurances just yet. It would make it more unbearably real.

The only person I dared to phone was Ana, but the call went through to her voicemail. I hung up without leaving a message and checked my newsfeed.

Police have confirmed the dead woman is Nina Turner, and that six-year-old Tilly Turner remains in hospital in a critical condition.

Pictures of Nina taken at last week's gala, regal in a gold floor-length dress, and Tilly's school portrait were plastered everywhere. Her amber eyes, little freckled nose and dimples peered back at me from the screen. How had the media tracked down that photograph?

I swiped down, and a Channel 9 banner popped up – *Turner poisoning scandal: exclusive interview* – across a video still of a woman I recognised as Debbie Reimers, an officious mother I'd once chatted to briefly at school pick-up. She'd subsequently harassed me to use her interior design services, so I'd avoided her ever since. I pressed the play button and turned up the volume.

Debbie was speaking to the reporter in her open-plan kitchen. She was fully made up with her hair styled in soft waves. 'We're absolutely devastated. We're a very tight school community.' Debbie sniffed and pressed a tissue against her eyes without disturbing her mascara. 'There are obviously all sorts of horrible rumours swirling around. It's just so devastating for the Turner family.'

Off camera, the reporter asked her what Tilly was like.

'Vivacious, artistic, a little darling. My daughter Lula and Tilly are besties. Our family is very affected by this tragedy. We are praying for Tilly's full recovery.'

Lula and Tilly weren't close friends. Debbie Reimers barely knew us. That bitch.

My phone kept bleeping with a torrent of Instagram alerts, so I clicked over to my studio account. Strangers had been posting comments, and I reeled, sick to my stomach, when I read their messages:

tayla's_mum: *you crazy bitch @skyeturnerart*

sprout91: *we all know it was you*

wozza: *how could you do that to your own daughter?*

sweepyface: *watch your back slut scum*

I cast my phone onto the bed and tore downstairs to get Duncan.

He was outside, farewelling the security guy. When the black ute moved off down the driveway, a memory sputtered to the surface. A vehicle just like it had been outside our gate the previous morning when I'd followed Duncan out to the street. In fact, I was certain it was the same one, unmarked apart from a thin white stripe down the side.

'Hey, that security guy – were you with him yesterday morning?'

'Huh?' He was distracted, texting someone.

'The security guy – I'm asking if you were with him yesterday.'

He glanced up from his phone. 'What?'

'I followed you when you left the house. That ute was outside our gate and then it drove off. Were you in it?'

Duncan rubbed his face, exasperated. 'Seriously? Can you hear yourself? You're talking nonsense.'

'Just answer the question.'

'I told you: I went for a walk.' He spoke slowly, as if he were speaking to a child. 'You've got to stop this.' He crossed the hallway towards me and raised his hand. For a second, I thought he meant to strike me, but instead he drew me into his chest. 'You can't relapse. Not now.'

I let him carry me to the den and lay me down on the sofa. He sat with me for several minutes while my heart roared in my chest.

'Doctor Friel gave me a few tablets to tide us over until your medication arrives. I think you should take one.'

He disappeared to the kitchen and returned with a glass of water and a small peach-coloured disc, then waited for me to swallow it. When he thought I was asleep, he went upstairs to his study and shut the door.

I didn't want to be medicated, but I didn't have the energy to protest either. It was easier to let him think he was helping me. When he left the room, I spat the tablet out.

The security system for the property was concealed in an alcove off the entrance hall. I double-checked that Duncan wasn't around before finding the settings menu for the camera feed. I'd never paid any attention to the system before now, but surely it couldn't be too difficult to operate. First, I had to input a PIN. I tried our alarm code, and then Duncan's old phone password. Neither worked. When I punched in Tilly's birthdate, the green light flashed.

On the menu screen, I located the feed for the cameras mounted on the main gate and rewound the footage back to the prior morning. Then I forwarded through at double speed. Couples in activewear striding past the gate. Mothers pushing baby buggies. A car roaring past. A stream of cyclists. Then the detectives arriving at 9.19 am. I kept going, listening for Duncan's footsteps.

At 10.43 am, there it was: a huge black ute – just like the one the security guy had driven out of our driveway a short while ago – parked across the road from our house. The gates swung open at 10.46 am and Duncan ran out, crossed the road and climbed into the ute's passenger seat. A couple of minutes later, as the gates were closing, I saw myself run out onto the footpath and look up and down the road. A boy on a green bike cut past me, and the ute pulled out from the kerb. I took a photo of its licence plate with my phone as a reminder that I was not going insane.

Duncan was lying to me. Why? Sweat prickled at my nape and in the crooks of my knees.

In the library, the female detective's business card was on the coffee table. *Detective Senior Sergeant Mei O'Connor, Homicide Squad.* I closed the library door and tried to recall Detective O'Connor from the previous day's visit. Liquid black hair in a slick ponytail, tailored monochrome outfit and a feline quality that was both sleek and hostile.

I tapped her number into my phone but hesitated before I pressed the 'call' button. What exactly would I say when she answered? I had to be rational. What had Duncan really done that was so bad? He'd changed his phone password and lied about meeting with a security guard, but was that such a big deal?

Duncan was right. I was paranoid and irrational. He was entitled to privacy for his messages, and I shouldn't have been checking his phone in secret. And perhaps he'd chosen not to tell me about the security arrangements because he didn't want to freak me out about the gravity of the online threats. In fact, everything he'd done – the improved security, the visits from the lawyer and the doctor – were to protect me. Like he'd always protected me. And if I called Detective O'Connor, then I'd be waiving my right to silence, which the lawyer had expressly advised against. Even worse, I'd be betraying my husband, who'd always had my best interests at heart. I deleted the detective's number on my screen and put her card back on the table.

I was still feeling light-headed, so I took a shower. The hot water rushed over me and fogged up the glass. I spent a long time watching it spiral into the drain between my feet. When I emerged from the ensuite in my towel, my skin steaming, Duncan was waiting in the bedroom with a tray of soup and buttered toast. 'Feeling any better, babe?'

I nodded.

'Good.' He smiled. 'I knew the medication would take the edge off.' He gestured to the soup. 'I thought you might want some lunch.'

'I can't eat.'

'You have to try. You haven't had anything since Saturday morning.' He set the tray on the window seat, and came and sat beside me on the end of the bed. 'You need to stay strong.'

'I'm going to go mad if I can't see Tilly. If I have to stay imprisoned in this house.'

'You're not imprisoned. And in case you haven't noticed, we're in this together.'

'But you won't let me see or speak to anyone! And where are your brothers? Do they even care about Tilly?'

'Skye!' His eyes flashed with anger. 'I'm talking to them all the time. Nina is dead, for Christ's sake. The kids are beside themselves. And like us, Jamie's got the police and media crawling all over him. So does Hugo. They're both shattered. Everyone's just in survival mode.'

'What about the lawyer? You said he'd sort this out quickly.'

'Jack's working around the clock for us. I'm heading out to meet him at his chambers in the city shortly.'

'Why aren't you worried about security for yourself?'

'It'll be okay. It's Easter Monday. He said no one else will be in the office.'

'Can I come too?'

'I don't think that's a good idea. Look at you – you're overwrought. Besides, there's a pack of photographers outside the gate waiting to get an image of you. The last thing we need is for you to be splashed all over the papers looking like this. Stay here and I'll fill you in when I get back.' Duncan pulled me into a hug. 'You know I love you, right? I'll look after you, I promise.'

•

After he left, I realised that I couldn't find my phone anywhere. I was certain I'd left it on the vanity before my shower, but it wasn't there or anywhere else I searched. I had no way of contacting the hospital and no way of being contacted. We didn't even have a landline anymore. What if something happened to Tilly and they couldn't get hold of me? Or what if some crazy person got past the security cordon? The high fence and thick hedges meant the neighbours wouldn't hear me if they reached the house. And I couldn't leave the property without facing the media at the gate.

At least I could message or call Duncan or the police through my laptop, but when I found it, it was out of battery, and the charger wasn't in its usual place. I must have left it somewhere stupid. I hunted everywhere, but to no avail. Duncan had taken his laptop to his meeting with the lawyer, so I didn't even have that as a backup.

Then I remembered Tilly's GPS smartwatch, which was connected to both Duncan's phone and mine. If we had an intruder, at least I could use it to call Duncan or emergency services. She hadn't taken it to Yallambee, so it had to be somewhere in her bedroom. I rummaged through her schoolbag and dresser drawers, finally finding the lilac smartwatch tucked in among her socks and scrunchies. When I turned it on, it still had some battery charge.

The screen opened on the Family Circle app, which Duncan had installed on all our devices so we could keep tabs on one another's locations. But the GPS pins were wrong, showing both Duncan's and mine in the south of the city, near the port. I zoomed in closer and saw the location was a property on Hale Street, in an industrial part of Botany.

Confused, I refreshed the app, but the location didn't change. It didn't make any sense. Duncan was in the city with the lawyer. It wasn't a historic location pin because Duncan and I had never been to that location together. The only rational explanation was that Duncan was meeting the lawyer there, in Botany, near the port. But why? Besides, hadn't he specifically told me he was going into the city, to Jack's chambers? And why would he have taken my phone with him?

There was another button on the app that showed the weekly driver report for each of us. With trembling hands, I scrolled down. Duncan had made a trip yesterday morning, at 10.46 am, from our address to the same destination – a building on Hale Street in Botany.

What the hell was going on? Why was my husband lying to me?

•

While I waited for Duncan to return, I couldn't settle. An excruciating pressure swelled within me and it was only bearable with constant activity. I tried painting, then sculpting, but my hands were unsteady, and I didn't trust myself to fire the fragile greenware awaiting the kiln. Heavy gusts of rain were pounding the garden, trapping me inside the house. In the end, I resorted to reorganising pantry staples to distract from my claustrophobia. The silence was interrupted only by the *plip*, *plip*, *plip* of the kitchen tap.

Life with Tilly was loud: constant chatting, wild stories, tinkling laughter. Sometimes crying, too, for a grazed knee or a bad dream. Clattering utensils as we made school lunches and dinners together. Shouting up the stairs. Blaring music with dancing and singing. Tentative violin scales. Little footsteps padding up and down the hallway, steering her dolly's pram or chasing Bo. The boisterous soundtrack to family life – so routine, so unremarkable that it was white noise. Until it was gone. Now, the silence was crushing. I needed her home.

The tap was still dripping, each bead of water trembling for a second before plunging and shattering into the porcelain sink. I needed to drown it out, but how could I? Without my phone and laptop, I couldn't connect to the Sonos, and there was no television in the kitchen area. Then I remembered Duncan's old transistor radio – despite all the modern alternatives, it was still his preferred method of listening to the cricket when he was pottering in his workshop, stringing up fishing lines or preparing for a weekend away hunting.

The workshop was at the far end of the main floor, abutting the garage. I couldn't remember the last time I'd been down there; I was always steering Tilly away from the dangerous tools. When I opened the door, the blast of artificial light and the scent of leather and oil made me queasy. Duncan kept everything in meticulous condition – saws, drills, grinders and clamps were wall-mounted in custom tracks, and the steel workbench gleamed as new.

I ran my eyes around the room. No sign of the radio. I checked inside the lockers where he stowed his hunting and diving gear, and all his fishing tackle. The transistor was tucked inside the last one, right at the back, on a shelf. No, not a shelf – a slim black metal filing case. I grabbed the radio and was almost at the door when I stopped dead. Duncan was pedantic about keeping everything in its place, and we kept all of our files in his study.

I shimmied the filing case out of the locker and hauled it onto the workbench. It was made of heavy metal with two latches on the front, either side of a silver eyelet lock. It didn't look like a storage box for fishing tackle. This was for documents – indestructible and designed to be fireproof. I forced open the latches and crimped my fingers under the lid to pull it upwards, but it didn't budge. I was being ridiculous. Paranoid. There wouldn't be anything important inside. But then again, why had he hidden this filing case down here? And why was it locked? A new knot was hardening in the pit of my stomach.

I was searching for the key to open it when the drone of the garage door lifting filtered through the wall. Duncan was back. I couldn't risk him finding me here, in his workshop. He'd accuse me of snooping, of paranoia. I shoved the case into the locker and dashed back to the kitchen.

Moments later, when Duncan kissed me hello, I feared he'd hear my heart slamming in my chest. He placed a pizza box on the kitchen bench.

'How was the meeting?' I asked, and continued decanting panko crumbs into a container, hoping he wouldn't notice the smudge of my damp palm on the glass.

'Frustrating,' he said, opening the wine fridge. 'The DCJ's stalling. Jack's in contact with the detectives and the Crown lawyers. It sounds like they're scrambling. No real theory of what happened, and no solid evidence so far.'

He opened a bottle, emptied the pale liquid into two glasses, and slid one across to me.

'What are you even doing?' He ran his eyes across the containers of crackers, biscuits, cereals and pasta lined up on the kitchen island.

'Trying to keep busy.' I scanned his face for signs of guilt, but he gave nothing away. 'When does Jack think we can get back to the hospital?' I snapped on the container lid and swept the spilled crumbs into the sink with my hand.

'It should be this week. Everything's delayed because of Easter, but Jack's got it under control.' He was brushing me off as if I were an annoying child.

'Duncan, you've been gone for hours. What were you and the lawyer talking about for all that time if there's no news?'

It was a direct challenge, but he wasn't fazed.

'There's a lot of legal procedure. I can bore you with the details if you want me to, but I'm starving. Let's eat first.'

He opened the pizza box and took out a slice, as if it were the most natural thing in the world to be sitting at the kitchen island eating takeaway while our daughter was on life support a few kilometres away.

'So, what's his office like?'

Duncan looked up. 'You want to know what Jack's office is like?'

'Yeah.'

'Okay, well, that's . . . odd. It's the usual sort of legal premises. Corporate. Decent art. Quiet, obviously, because it's a public holiday. Why do you ask?' He said it casually, but the vein in his temple had begun to twitch. He was agitated – and lying. My gut twisted, watching him do it so easily. I had to confront him. I'd been practising what I'd say all afternoon. The words were forming on my tongue, and I fizzed with adrenaline as I opened my mouth to speak them. But something – some deep instinct – stopped me. If he was capable of lying to me so easily, what else might he be capable of? I shouldn't push him.

'I dunno. I'm sorry, babe.' Trying to keep my voice light, I said, 'I've got serious cabin fever. I can't think straight. If I can't see Tilly, then I really need to get out of this house. Perhaps I could go and stay with Ana for a couple of days, just for a change of scene?'

Duncan liked Ana and trusted her. She wouldn't blab to the media. She also lived in an exclusive apartment complex where my privacy would be assured.

I busied myself with the containers, placing them back onto their shelves, to avoid his eyes. 'And that way you could keep working with the lawyer and I'll just rest up, like Doctor Friel recommended.' I rotated the glass jars of staples so their labels were perfectly aligned.

Duncan shook his head. 'I don't think we should risk it. It's better that you stay here, where I can look after you.'

'But you weren't even home this afternoon.' I rinsed a cloth and squeezed it over the sink. 'And I was scared.'

He didn't say anything, so I continued. 'Imagine if one of those crazy online trolls had gotten into the house. They wouldn't think to look for me at Ana's.' I bit the inside of my cheek. I couldn't sound too desperate; I didn't want him to become suspicious.

After a long pause, Duncan sighed. 'Okay, why don't you call her and see.'

A flicker of relief. 'Great,' I said. 'Oh, by the way, I couldn't find my phone anywhere. I must have done something stupid with it. Have you seen it?'

He shook his head. 'No, sorry. Want me to have a hunt for it?'

'Thanks.'

Duncan returned with my phone a short while later. He'd found it under the sofa, he told me. I must have mislaid it again.

When I checked the Family Circle app on my phone later that evening, the travel history had been deleted.

SIX

MEI

EASTER MONDAY

I woke on Mum's bedroom floor sweating like a pig under my doona. She'd switched on the wall heater when she had chills in the night, and the room was steaming like a sauna. Mum was still asleep, her waxy skin stretched over jutting bones and her breathing laboured. At least her temperature had returned to normal after her most recent dose of paracetamol at 4 am.

When I checked my phone, I had a missed call from Wilson and a message confirming no material updates from Yallambee. Bugger. The only good news was that a colleague in the Western division had located a probation report for Cody White connecting him to a hostel in Fairfield. I texted Macca to say I'd pick him up in twenty minutes.

I forced the bedroom window open for some fresh air and heard Sandy, Mum's neighbour, pottering in the garden strip outside her ground floor flat. It was an unseasonably wet, cold autumn, and Sandy's hydrangeas and gardenias had shrivelled into brown clumps, which caused her no end of distress. She had an unfortunate habit of sprinkling eggshells on the soil to fertilise it, which attracted rats. Laifu liked to offer up their disembodied heads on the kitchen lino. But eggshells aside, Sandy was a good sort. She'd often pop in to watch telly with Mum and bake her lumpy cheese scones that Mum complained tasted like cardboard.

I pulled on a jumper and popped downstairs to say hello.

Sandy was kneeling on her foam pad, pulling out fistfuls of weeds.

'Hello, Mei,' she boomed, her round face breaking into a broad smile. 'Aren't you a good girl, moving in to look after Lian?'

I instantly felt shitty for pretending to be a saintly daughter, when the truth was I had nowhere else to go. 'You're up early,' I said.

'Hope I didn't wake you, but I need to tidy the garden before the next downpour.'

'How was Lithgow? Did your grandchildren eat all those Easter eggs?'

She hooted with laughter. 'They did indeed. Amazing how much chocolate the little ones can put away. How's your mum?'

'Not great, actually. She had a fever last night. I have to work today, so would you mind checking on her?'

'Of course I can, darl. Leave Lian with me. Now, if you're working on a public holiday it must be important. Not this Turner case, is it?'

'I couldn't possibly comment, Sandy.' I grinned.

'I knew it!' she said, triumphant. 'I told my friends, Mei will be running that investigation. She's a top detective. It's a bloody tragedy about that beautiful lady who died. Oh! And that little girl, fighting for her life. You know what people are saying, don't you?'

'What are they saying, Sandy?'

She lowered her voice conspiratorially. 'That it's the girl's mother. Skye Turner.'

'Who's saying that?'

'It's all over Facebook. And my friend Janice – you remember the plain girl with the diabetes in my book club? – well, she heard from her cousin's friend that Skye's mental. Institutionalised at one point. Jealous of the sister-in-law. Probably jealous of her own daughter. But you didn't hear it from me, Mei. I wouldn't want it to get back to Janice that I'm your source.'

'I won't breathe a word.'

'Okay, darl. I'll just sprinkle these eggshells and then I'll whip up a batch of scones for your mum.'

•

Macca and I found Fairfield Heights Hostel slumped behind a strip of noodle bars and vape shops. It was basically a series of rickety extensions knitted around a crumbling core. The top coat of paint had flaked off the timber frame, leaving a speckled carcass of greens and yellows, like an old bruise. Empty cans and bottles demarcated the boundary between the hostel and the footpath.

Despite the rain, the front door was open to the street, so Macca and I ventured inside and smacked straight into the grim stench of body odour and stale smoke. Flaps of wallpaper curled loose like dried skin, and television infomercials whined from darkened rooms. At the end of the hallway, we entered a kitchen with a shiny laminate bench and a list of 'House Rules' sellotaped to the wall.

Pay on time!

Mind your own business!

No stealing!

No fights!

No drugs!

'Can I help you?' A man with a saggy face and wild grey hair stumbled out of a back room. He was sucking on a cigarette, and a faded Metallica t-shirt strained across his bulging gut.

'Detective Senior Sergeant Mei O'Connor,' I said, 'and my colleague Detective Sergeant Stuart McKenzie. Who's in charge here?'

'I would be the proprietor of this fine establishment, ma'am.' When he doubled over in a pantomime bow, I caught a vinegary whiff of unwashed old man. 'Tony de Luca.'

I extended my hand, and Tony returned a predictably limp handshake.

'We need to speak to you about one of your former lodgers – Cody White.'

'Ah yes, Cody. Him I do recall. What's the young fella done? Must be bad for you two to turn up here.'

'Is there somewhere more private we can speak?' asked Macca.

'I suppose you'd better step into my office,' Tony said, and ushered us through to a storage room jammed with a tiny plastic table and chairs. 'Fag?' He rattled a packet of Winfields at us as he sat down, snagging his belly on the table.

I shook my head. 'Mr de Luca, when was the last time you saw Cody White?'

'I'd say about a year ago.'

'Have you kept in contact?' asked Macca.

'Sadly, I didn't make his Christmas card list.' He guffawed, then broke into a wheezy cough.

'How long did Cody stay here?' Macca asked.

Tony tapped the tip of his cigarette into a coffee mug and tugged open a drawer in a metal filing cabinet with his free hand, skimming through the brown manila folders. 'Ah, here he is.' He extracted a thin one labelled *White, Cody* and opened it to a single page with dates, payments and a few other notes scrawled in biro. A polaroid headshot of Cody was stapled to the top left-hand corner. He appeared older than in his police mugshot, his hair longer.

Tony studied the page. 'Just shy of six months – left last March,' he said between drags on his cigarette. 'Quiet. Good lad. Had been in a spot of bother with the coppers, he told me, but he didn't seem like a bad joker. He was trying to clean himself up. Got a job working for one of the local places; labouring, I think.'

'Do you remember the name of the business?' I asked.

'Nah, mate. Anyway, one day he just up and left. Didn't say goodbye, but he did pay his rent. Like I said, he was a good lad.'

'Did any friends or family members visit him here?' asked Macca.

'Let me check the visitors' book, sir.' Tony cackled and exhaled a cloud of smoke into my eyes. He was really getting on my nerves.

'What about the other lodgers?' I asked. 'Did he make any friends among them? Anyone he might have kept in touch with?'

Tony coughed again, a deep phlegmy hack that echoed through his chest. 'Not that I remember.' He snuffed out his cigarette stub and lit a new one.

'And you have no idea where he might be now?'

'No, I'm afraid not, madam.'

'We'll leave our contact details in case you remember anything else,' said Macca.

'And if you do,' I added, 'we might forget about the firearm incident.'

Tony blanched. I always did my homework.

I was opening the car door when Tony came running out. He was wheezing so hard he had to double over and plant his hands on his thighs to recover.

'I thought of something,' he gasped.

'Yes?' I asked.

'There was a girl working up at the pub that Cody knocked around with. They had a bit of a fling. Don't know her name, but maybe she can help you.'

'Can you describe her?'

'Skinny, black, lots of piercings.'

'And where's the pub?'

'The Tavern on Alan Street – me mate Bruce owns it. It'll be shut today because of the Easter holiday, and Bruce has gone bush for the long weekend, but I can give you his number if you like?'

We phoned Bruce from the car on our way back to the office. His phone was off, so I left a message.

•

We didn't make any more progress that afternoon and called it quits at five o'clock. Yvette was trying to round up a group of us to watch a movie but I decided to pass and went straight home to make an early dinner. Mum wanted *zhou*, so I stood at the old enamel stove stirring the pot of rice porridge. The rain had eased, and I watched the sun crawl across the flats opposite. It flared off the metal banisters, sparking rainbows, and made the red brickwork glow. For a moment, everything was beautiful – even the scruffy pot plants and the rusty bikes hitched to the railings. At the end of the street, two sisters were kicking a soccer ball. The younger one had just started school. A few days after I'd moved in with Mum, the little girl been posing rod-straight in their entranceway, swamped by her uniform, while her proud mum took photographs.

She was the same age as Grace had been, with the same long straight black ponytail and big spectacles that made her look bug-eyed. I couldn't remember Grace's face anymore. All I had was her last school photograph – the huge framed one on Mum's mantelpiece, which was the stock picture they used in all the newspaper articles. Even now, when I searched Grace's name, that was the first image to surface – her brown-checked St Dominic's school tunic, gap-toothed smile and pale lake-green eyes, magnified through the lenses of those huge pink spectacles. I was so jealous of those glasses that I'd pretended I couldn't read the blackboard in the hope of getting my own pair.

In the end, Grace's beautiful, flawed eyes were the most likely reason she didn't come home that Wednesday. She tripped over on the way to school, and I helped her sellotape the cracked lenses back together in Sister Edith's classroom. At the end of the day, Grace had walked home alone. Mum and Dad never understood why she hadn't waited for me. I could never bring myself to tell them the truth – that it was my fault.

It was only two blocks along Spencer Street, then through the park, to get home. In those days, kids walked by themselves all the time. Because of those broken glasses, she'd mistaken the wrong person for a teacher, or for one of my parents' friends, on the shaded pathway at the entrance to the park. That was what the detectives had thought, anyway. From the top of the stairs, I'd strained to hear every muted word, pulling and twisting the beige carpet fibres with my fingers until there was a little bald patch on the landing.

•

It was only when a tear splashed onto my hand that I realised I was crying. Grace's disappearance had forged a deep chasm between Mum and me. There must have been a time when Mum had held me, a time when she'd soothed me after I scraped my knee or woke from a bad dream. But I could never remember her touching me or telling me she loved me, not even when Dad died. Although she'd never said it aloud, she blamed me for Grace's disappearance. Was that why I was really here, a child clasping hope to my chest like a favourite toy, seeking her forgiveness?

I dried my face with a kitchen towel and set Mum up with a tray in front of the TV.

'Tina Wong called in today,' she said, craning past me to see the screen.

'How's Tina?'

'Same as always. She's stayed at the top of the bridge ladder since I stopped playing.'

I hid a smile. Mum and Tina had a long-standing rivalry that began when Tina's daughter Paula and I met in kindergarten.

'Paula's a gastroenterologist in Perth now,' Mum continued, stirring her spoon around her bowl to cool the contents. 'About to have her third child.'

'Great,' I said.

'You were always much cleverer than Paula,' Mum added. 'She just bought her mum a brand-new RAV4. Tina says she's raking it in.'

This was Mum code for the fact I should have gone to medical school instead of police college, and that Mum should have been a grandmother by now.

Mum raised the ladle to her lips and swallowed a small mouthful. 'It's too watery. Next time let it simmer for longer.'

•

After I'd cleaned up the kitchen, I ran a bath. I eased myself in and slipped under the water, letting my hair fan around my face like seaweed, and held my breath until I came up gasping.

My phone was ringing when I sat up – an unknown number flashing on the screen. I seized it with my dripping hand.

'Hello?' My voice bounced off the tiles, cheap and brassy.

'Detective O'Connor?' A faint voice at the end of the line – almost a whisper.

'Yes? Who is this?'

'It's Skye Turner.'

I froze so she wouldn't hear the slap of the bathwater. 'Where are you, Mrs Turner?'

'I'm at home. I'm ready to speak to you.'

'I'll come now.'

'No, it has to be tomorrow. My husband doesn't know I'm calling. I'll text you the time and the address in the morning.' She ended the call.

Halle-fucking-lujah. Our luck was turning.

I drifted under the water once more and listened to the amplified thump of my heart.

SEVEN

SKYE

TUESDAY

Early on Tuesday morning, Ana arrived at the door, lips quivering. She dissolved into tears when she saw me.

'My darling girl,' she said over and over, while she hugged me to her. 'Tilly's strong. She's going to be okay. She's a fighter, like you.'

Soon afterwards, I curled up on the back seat of Ana's car and Duncan covered me with a blanket to conceal me from the waiting press pack. The wool chafed the skin on my face and neck, and it was dark and hard to breathe under it. When I heard the muffled shouts of the media at the gates, every muscle in my body tensed and I kept rigid for the whole journey, trying to read the vibrations and turns of the road. I didn't move until Ana opened the rear door and helped me into the eerie yellow light of her basement car park.

On the way up to her apartment in the private lift, I couldn't avoid my reflection in the huge gilt-edged mirror.

My long hair was matted and wild, my eyes bloodshot. When we stepped over her threshold, I locked and bolted the door.

'Skye, darling, calm down. You're safe here.'

I nodded, but I couldn't shake the anxiety stewing in my gut. She led me through to her lounge but I was off balance – the room was too bright, too shiny, too hot. I was sucking in lungfuls of air. Ana gripped my shoulders and helped me slow my breathing.

When I could finally speak, I told her about Duncan's lies and his refusal to cooperate with the police investigation. Ana was never short of an opinion and was renowned for interrupting in conversation, but she stayed silent, her eyes widening, as I took her through the events of the past few days.

'You probably think I'm crazy too,' I said when I'd finished my download.

'Duncan did say you've been acting irrationally,' she admitted. 'He thinks you're headed for—' She paused, bit her thumbnail and didn't finish her sentence. Instead, she leaned across and embraced me. I allowed myself to let go, to let the heavy weight rush out of me. When I pulled back, she wiped my eyes with her scarf, and then clutched my hands in hers.

'Skye, I believe you. I'm on your side. Tell me what you want to do.'

●

The detectives arrived twenty-four minutes after I texted Ana's address to Mei O'Connor. I was waiting for them on Ana's velvet couch because my legs were shaking too violently to stand. Had I made a huge mistake contacting them behind Duncan's back? He was my husband, my protector, my greatest champion. A long time ago, I'd made an error of judgement, and I'd vowed never to betray him again. And yet, I had to do this for Tilly. I would just tell the detectives what I knew so they could find out who had hurt her. My only duty now was to her.

Detective O'Connor was brisk and efficient, and she got straight down to business. She switched on the voice recorder and asked me to tell her everything I could remember about the Easter weekend. She asked lots of questions – about Tilly, my marriage, Nina and Jamie's relationship, and everyone who'd been at Yallambee. The thickset male detective, McKenzie, didn't speak much, but he appeared to be taking detailed notes. And as I went through it all again, everything crashed into focus.

Cody. He'd made us all cocktails on Friday evening. He'd brought his supplies with him, and he'd made a special drink for Tilly. He'd also mixed mojitos for me and Nina. My awful hangover – perhaps it wasn't alcohol after all, but arsenic that Cody had slipped into my drink. He'd disappeared on Friday night, and we had no idea where he'd gone. Duncan hadn't heard from him. It was already Tuesday – he must have found out what had happened by now. I hated to admit it, but perhaps Hugo was right, and the only reason he'd contacted Duncan was because he wanted money, or revenge against the Turner family. Or both.

'We're still trying to locate Cody White. Do you know where he is?' asked Detective O'Connor, as if she'd read my mind.

'No, I'm sorry, I've got no idea. I hoped you would have found him by now. He left Yallambee on Friday after an argument with Duncan's brother at dinner. We assumed at the time he'd driven back to Sydney, but who knows where he went? His phone's been off ever since.'

'Can you give us his home address?' This time it was McKenzie who spoke.

I shook my head. 'No. Sorry. We've never been to his flat. Whenever we've seen him, he's either come to our house or we've met up at a cafe or the beach. He told us he was staying with friends in Newtown while he looked for a place to rent, but he was pretty vague about it.'

Detective O'Connor frowned and tapped some notes into her tablet. I'd disappointed her.

'What about the relationship between Cody and your husband?' she asked. 'Can you tell us about it?'

'Well, it's only very recently that they've been in contact,' I said. 'Duncan didn't even know Cody existed until a few months ago. It was after Campbell died – that's my father-in-law – that Cody got in touch. His mother told him about Duncan for the first time when she saw the coverage of Campbell's funeral on the TV news. At least, that's what he told us.' In retrospect, I wondered whether I could trust anything Cody had said.

'Was a paternity test done?' asked McKenzie.

'Yes, Duncan insisted on that before he agreed to meet Cody. The results are all on file with our family doctor. I can give you Doctor Friel's details, if you want? But it was just a formality. You only have to look at Cody to see the resemblance.'

Detective O'Connor cleared her throat. 'You mentioned an argument on Friday night which prompted Cody's early departure from Yallambee. Can you elaborate?'

'Hugo, Duncan's younger brother, was being obnoxious. That's not unusual. He implied that Cody had only contacted Duncan because he was after an inheritance from his grandfather. At the time it was awful to watch – really embarrassing – but on reflection, I wonder if he was right.'

'Right about Cody chasing an inheritance?'

'Yes. I mean, I haven't seen Campbell's will myself, but Duncan did say there were some peculiarities in it. That's the main reason we all went to Yallambee for Easter – Jamie had called a meeting with his brothers to try to resolve things amicably.'

'What sort of peculiarities?'

'It's to do with how Campbell's estate is split, but I don't know the details, sorry. I keep out of the financial stuff.'

Detective O'Connor raised an eyebrow, and I realised I sounded pathetic.

I cleared my throat. 'After the argument on Friday night, I did ask Duncan what was going on between him and his brothers, and he said it was complicated. It's been really tense since Campbell died, and Hugo and Jamie aren't happy about Cody being on the scene.'

'Why is that?'

'Maybe it affects their share of the estate? Another grandchild might change the proportions or something based on the will.'

Detective O'Connor frowned. 'So Cody turned up because he expected an inheritance?'

'Maybe.'

'But how would Cody have known what was in the will?' she asked.

That was a good question. Cody couldn't have known – unless Duncan had told him. But why would he have done that? He was almost obsessive about secrecy when it came to his family. Unless he and Cody were in on some plan together. But that was crazy. Duncan and Cody had only met a couple of months ago, and they were both still in the early stages of adjusting to their relationship. There was no way that Duncan would ever have conspired with Cody to harm his own family. To hurt Tilly.

'I don't know,' was all I could manage. 'He was probably just hoping to get some money. He couldn't have known anything about Campbell's will.'

'Mrs Turner, what do you know about your husband's relationship with Cody White's mother?'

I'd expected this question, of course. When Duncan had told me about Rebecca back in January, I was irrationally jealous. Until that conversation, he'd always maintained that the girlfriends before me had been cookie-cutters – the ambitious daughters of Campbell's rich friends. But when he told me about Rebecca, it was clear she'd been different. He'd met her at work, and after eight months together she'd disappeared. I asked him what he meant by *disappeared*, thinking he must be exaggerating, but Duncan said that was exactly what happened: she'd vanished into thin air.

He explained that he'd been overseas on business. Rebecca texted to say she had something important to tell him, but it had to be in person, so he'd agreed to go straight to her place from the airport. By the time he arrived the next day, Rebecca was gone. Her flatmate had come home from work to find Rebecca's room empty. She'd left no note, no forwarding address. Even her mother hadn't heard from her.

Panicked, Duncan reported Rebecca missing to the police. Campbell, too, was beside himself, given that Rebecca was not only Duncan's girlfriend but also one of his employees, so he'd hired a private investigator to look for her. But the investigator had been unable to track her down. Then, a few weeks later, Duncan had received a handwritten letter from Rebecca in the post. She said she'd felt trapped in their relationship, didn't love him, and he would never make her happy, so she was moving on. When Duncan had recounted the story, I'd seen the hurt on his face – still so much hurt, even after two decades.

What Duncan hadn't known back then was that Rebecca was pregnant. When Duncan had asked Cody about his childhood, his son was vague. He said they'd moved around a lot, and that Rebecca had refused to tell him about his father. At some point she'd changed her last name to White, and that was the surname she'd given to her son.

Learning about Rebecca and Cody that day was a huge shock. I asked Duncan why he'd never told me about Rebecca before. He said that it had been such a long time ago, he hadn't seen the point. His injured pride must have had something to do with it. He assured me that he had no interest in seeing Rebecca again, but he was curious to meet Cody, if it wouldn't upset me.

So, I played the supportive wife and welcomed Cody into our family. And when Duncan and Cody met, there was an instant, undeniable bond. Cody was the son that Duncan had always longed for, the son I hadn't been able to provide. And as soon as I laid eyes on Cody, it was clear he couldn't have been anyone else's. The Turner bloodline was undeniable in the tall, lean build, the smooth olive skin and those distinctive amber eyes that Tilly had also inherited. I was happy for Duncan but also unsettled. I couldn't help but wonder why Rebecca had chosen to reveal the truth now, after so many years.

Detective O'Connor was still waiting for me to reply. She didn't need all of this information. It would make me sound jealous and petty. I chose my words carefully.

'As far as I'm aware, Duncan and Cody's mother were colleagues at Turner Corp in the late nineties,' I said. 'They had a brief relationship, then she left Duncan suddenly, and without telling him that she was going to have his baby.'

'Where did she go?'

'Sorry, I don't know. Duncan said she just took off. Maybe she freaked out when she discovered she was pregnant. Couldn't handle the pressure of his family.'

Detective O'Connor paused her note-taking and looked up at me, unconvinced. 'What about recently – has Duncan been in contact with Rebecca White since he met Cody?' she asked.

'No. No, he hasn't. Although . . .'

'Although?' Detective O'Connor prompted.

'Nothing.' I'd assumed Duncan hadn't been in touch with Rebecca, but I didn't know that for sure. Was that why he'd changed his phone password? Maybe it was Rebecca he'd been meeting secretly in that building by the port. Perhaps they were working together to protect their son. My heart dropped like a stone. Given everything that had happened in the past days, anything was possible.

Detective O'Connor tried a different tack. 'Mrs Turner, why do you think your husband is refusing to cooperate with the police investigation?'

'I'm not sure. He says it's because he wants to protect me.'

'Protect you from what?'

'He thinks you'll assume that it was me who – ' It was unbearable to say it aloud.

Detective O'Connor frowned again and rested her tablet on her lap. 'That you poisoned Nina and Tilly?'

I nodded.

'Why would he think that?' I couldn't tell if she was genuinely curious, or if she just had a great poker face. Surely she'd have received my records by now.

I calculated how much I should tell her. I needed her to trust me, but I couldn't risk her delving too deep. I had too much to lose.

EIGHT

MEI

TUESDAY

As we inched through Double Bay's morning gridlock, Macca and I agreed that we'd completely underestimated Skye Turner. The woman we'd interviewed on Ana Betjeman's sofa, frayed from sleeplessness and worry, was no spoiled trophy wife. She'd laboured to fit into her privileged world – not that she'd admitted that to us. Her only concession was an occasional broad vowel or inflection that spiked through the posh accent she'd cultivated. If it hadn't been for the email that had finally hit my inbox overnight, I would never have guessed her past.

Until the early hours of the morning, I'd been piecing together the patchwork of records supplied by the government agencies into a coherent narrative. Skye had been born in Far North Queensland as Nikki Sinclair, with no father named on her birth certificate. Her solo mother had battled addiction and depression until she drowned in the bath after overdosing on heroin when Nikki was ten years old. After a series of foster homes, where there were reports of physical and sexual abuse, she'd absconded at sixteen. Two years later, in Brisbane, she'd changed her name by deed poll to Skye Mason. By 2011, tax records showed she'd worked in hospitality in Sydney until her marriage to Duncan Turner.

Skye was a chameleon and a survivor. I respected that. Everything she'd told us about Cody and the Turner family could have been an elaborate smokescreen to protect herself, or possibly someone else, but her anxiety about Tilly was authentic, and whatever her motivation, she'd given us our first breakthrough – a legitimate reason to investigate her husband.

Our first call was to Althea, instructing her to prepare a search warrant for Duncan Turner's home and office. We were interrupted by Wilson ringing through.

'Any news of Cody White?' he asked. 'He's been AWOL for days.'

'Not yet, sir,' I said, 'but we have a promising lead.'

Bruce, the pub owner, had phoned with contact details for his kitchen hand, Jasmin Abele, who fitted Tony de Luca's description of Cody's former girlfriend. Since Jasmin wasn't answering her phone, we were heading straight to her house in Fairfield.

'Let's hope the girl knows something,' Wilson said, 'for all our sakes.'

●

The Abele house was a tidy white-brick block on North Street with a chain-link fence and a frazzled burst of palms out front. Jasmin's mother scrutinised our ID cards before inviting us into a cluttered living room that smelled of ground cumin and coffee. Jasmin slunk out of a bedroom, still in her pyjamas, wearing earpods and a thick septum ring, tendrils of green ink spiralling up her forearms.

'Take those bloody things out, girl!' her mother said.

Jasmin scowled and pinched the white commas from her ears.

'Please, take a seat,' Mrs Abele said to us.

The teenager glared at her mother and dropped into a dining chair.

'Jasmin,' I said, 'we're trying to find your friend, Cody White.'

'Why?'

'He's not in trouble. We just need to speak to him. I can't tell you any more than that.'

Jasmin paused and rolled her earpods against the table with her palm. 'Well, I haven't seen him in a while,' she said. 'A couple of months, maybe.' She yawned and arched her back in a languid stretch.

Jasmin insisted she had no idea where Cody might be. After some prodding, she shared his mobile number. It matched the number Skye Turner had given us, which was already being traced. She pretended not to have any names or contact details for his friends. Jasmin knew how to play this game.

After some more back and forth, Mrs Abele grew impatient. 'Jasmin, come on! You must know someone or something that can help the detectives.'

'They could check with his mum,' she said reluctantly.

'Do you know how to reach her?' I asked. 'We had an address in Queensland, but she hasn't been there for several years.'

'Yeah. I went to her new place. Here in Sydney.'

My pulse quickened. 'When was that?'

'Dunno. A couple of months ago? Maybe February.'

'Do you remember the address?' *Come on, Jasmin.*

Macca shot forward, as if to will the information out of her.

She yawned again. 'Yeah. On Azalea Street in Blacktown. It had a bright blue fence.'

•

We headed north up Prospect Highway and eventually wound our way to Azalea Street. The houses were mainly red brick, slung behind patches of sodden lawn. Only one had a bright blue fence – a forlorn greyish weatherboard, with closed blinds, cabbage trees and a rotary clothesline out front.

We climbed the slippery steps to the front door, dodging the scabby shrubs in broken pots, and knocked.

No one answered.

Macca pressed his eyes to the patterned glass door pane but couldn't detect any movement, so we ventured around the back. I was peering in through the laundry window when we heard an engine.

A battered Datsun had swung into the driveway. A white woman in torn jeans, tall and slender with a dark messy bun, stepped out with a brown bag of groceries. She slammed the car door with her hip and was halfway to the front door when she spotted us.

'Rebecca White?' I asked.

She shrank back like a hunted animal. 'Who are you?'

'We're detectives with the Homicide Squad.'

From a distance she had a fragile, girlish beauty, but up close she was drawn, with deep hollows under her cheekbones.

'What's this about?'

'We're investigating a crime and your son is a witness. We need to speak to him.'

'I don't know where he is. I haven't been able to get hold of him for days.'

'You must have some idea, Ms White,' said Macca.

'I really don't.' She looked at me. 'Is this about the Turners?'

'That's right,' Macca said. 'Your son has important information.'

'He should never have gotten mixed up with those people.'

Those people.

'Ms White, can we ask you some questions about your relationship with Duncan Turner?'

There was a shift in her then, like a dark cloud passing through. 'I've got nothing to say.'

'Why don't we speak about this inside?' I asked.

'I told you – I've got nothing to say.'

'Ms White, we really—' Macca began, but I cut him off.

'We can leave it there for now,' I said.

Rebecca was jittery and would be easily spooked. We didn't have the right to detain her for questioning, so we had to build up trust. I fished a card out of my jacket pocket. 'Please call me as soon as you hear from Cody.'

When she reached out to take it, her sleeve slid up to reveal jagged white scars on her wrist, like tally marks. She nodded and let herself into the house.

As we returned to our car, I could feel her eyes on me through the blank window.

•

'That was weird,' Macca said when I pulled out from the kerb. 'How about those scars?'

'I know. And she seemed terrified. I wonder what went on between her and Duncan Turner.'

'A lot of things are starting to point his way.'

'But why would he poison his sister-in-law?' I said. 'Not to mention his own daughter. What's the motive?'

'He could have been targeting his brothers,' said Macca. 'Skye said there had been tension. Maybe it was an accident, and Tilly and Nina weren't the intended targets.'

'Maybe. But it would have taken a lot of preparation to administer the arsenic, and Duncan Turner doesn't strike me as careless. If he'd planned to poison someone else, he wouldn't have missed his target, and there's still no motive.'

'A family feud? With his brothers dead, perhaps Duncan would be entitled to a bigger inheritance? That could fit with what Tamara Baruch said in her statement about the will.'

'Possibly. But imagine if both Jamie and Hugo Turner had dropped dead after spending Easter with Duncan. Everyone would have suspected him right away. I doubt he's that stupid. And besides, when you're already that obscenely rich, would you really murder your siblings for a bit more?'

Macca sighed. 'No. So, why's he lying to his wife then?'

'Dunno,' I said. 'An affair probably.' My cheeks burned as I thought of all the times Nick must have lied to me about Vanessa. 'We need to look into Duncan, for sure, but so far the circumstantial evidence points to Cody. He's got a plausible motive – whether he was seeking money or some sort of revenge.'

'Cody could have been avenging his mother for whatever went on between her and Duncan,' Macca said. 'Poisoned the drinks he served on Friday night.' He was nodding in my peripheral vision, warming to his theory. 'Plus he's got a criminal record, and he's done a runner.'

'When we get back to the office, get Rebecca White's house under surveillance in case Cody turns up. I'll follow up on his phone trace and the warrant.'

'On it, boss,' said Macca.

•

We stepped out of the lift's piped muzak into the cacophony of the office. Wilson's officious PA, Shaniah, summoned us over. She'd refreshed her fake tan over the break and was a bright Trumpian orange that matched the zesty poster behind her desk featuring a cat in sunglasses exhorting us not to forget to be awesome.

'He wants to see you right away,' Shaniah said, pointing a bedazzled talon in the direction of Wilson's office, 'but he's in a feral mood, just sayin'.'

'Where the hell have you two been?' Wilson barked when we slid onto the chairs in front of his desk. 'I've got the Commissioner on me, as well as the leeching bloody media.' He slammed his palm on the stack of papers in front of him. He wasn't wearing his wedding band. Ruth must have kicked him out again. 'And now the lab tells me that it could take weeks – if not months – before they've finished analysing the specimens we found at Yallambee. And we're completely under-resourced.' His eyes were bulging as though someone was squeezing the air out of his lungs. 'And while I'm busting my ball sacks, you two are nowhere to be seen. I have to wonder whether I've got the right team around me. There's a queue of other DIs desperate to work on this case, so if you're not going to step up, then please, do me a favour and step aside.'

It was standard operating procedure for Wilson to lash out when he was under pressure, like an overtired toddler. The trick was to speak calmly and to maintain eye contact.

'Sir, I messaged you this morning. We've been following up some leads. We interviewed Skye Turner—'

'She say anything useful this time?' He pushed up his glasses and pinched the bridge of his nose so hard that the skin flared red.

Macca and I brought him up to speed on Skye's revelations about Cody and Duncan, and our subsequent visit to Rebecca White.

Wilson rocked back in his chair and folded his arms under his paunch, as if cradling an infant. 'Okay, this is good work, DSS O'Connor,' he said.

'Sir, it's been a team effort.'

'Well, don't throw yourselves a party just yet. Get on with it.' He flicked his wrist at us to signal we should leave.

•

Back at my desk, I checked on Cody White's phone trace. The last signal recorded was by a cellular tower nearly a hundred kilometres south of Yallambee on Friday night. That meant he'd either disposed of the phone at that point or had kept it switched off ever since. Either way, it didn't give us any indication of whether he'd headed back to Sydney or fled to another destination. He could have made it across state lines into South Australia or Victoria before the highway patrol officers had been alerted. We'd have to speak to Wilson about escalating the search.

An email from Althea pinged in my inbox, asking me to sign off the draft warrant so she could submit it to the judge for approval. With any luck, we could search Duncan Turner's home in Bellevue Hill and his office at Turner Corp by late afternoon.

I was waiting for the printer to spit it out when Sandy rang.

'Sorry to bother you, love, but I'm a bit worried about your mum. She's got a nasty fever. I think she might need to see the doctor.'

'What's her temperature?'

'It's over thirty-nine degrees, love. And she's having a hard time breathing.'

'Shit. Call an ambulance, Sandy. I'll meet you at the hospital ER.'

I grabbed my laptop, told Shaniah that I had an emergency, and made her swear to have Wilson call me immediately if anything came up.

•

When my car swung into the hospital car park, the familiar hive began to thrum in my chest. Inside, the soupy, chemical smell and fluorescent lights wrenched me back to those final days with Dad. At least back then, Mum had been there too. Now it was just me, navigating the stark corridors that flowed like tributaries to rooms swollen with the sick and the dying.

Mum had been transferred straight to oncology in the bowels of the old wing. I found her and Sandy jammed into a six-patient ward behind a crinkly plastic curtain. Mum was sealed under a green sheet, her face flushed and her lashless eyes half-closed, with tubes streaming from her atrophied body. A nurse was replacing a collapsing bag of fluid.

'What's happening?' I asked her.

'We've taken bloods and I've just started your mother on antibiotics,' she said. She picked up Mum's chart. 'How are you feeling, Mrs O'Connor?'

'I don't need this fuss,' Mum said. 'Mei, don't forget to feed Laifu.'

'Lian, don't worry,' Sandy said. 'I'll feed him when I get home.'

If only Mum cared about me as much as that bloody cat.

'The doctor will be with you as soon as she can,' said the nurse before she trundled off to the next patient.

The doctor showed up three hours later. She apologised for the delay – hospital staff were striking to protest budget cuts, so she was run off her feet – and said Mum would have to stay on the drip overnight. Her white cell count was dangerously low, but hopefully the antibiotics would bring the infection under control and prevent sepsis.

Since there would only be an overworked skeleton staff on the ward, I decided to stay the night with Mum, as penance for having abandoned her to go to work.

Sandy waited while I popped out to get some essentials – a miniature toothbrush and toothpaste, deodorant, bottled water and a packet of rice crackers. I dragged a chair from the corridor next to Mum's bed so I could work on my laptop while she rested. The stucco walls interfered with the wi-fi and cell signals, so I had to keep popping out to an alcove in the corridor by the nurses' station to check and send messages, but there had been no update from the office.

Another nurse popped by during the night to check Mum's vitals, change her drip and scrawl on her file. By midnight, her condition had stabilised and her fever was dropping.

I eventually dozed off to the nervous bleep of the monitors and the rolling din of the ward, and woke up stiff and achy, with a red line seared on my forearm from the metal chair.

In the morning, a new doctor announced that Mum could switch to oral antibiotics and would be able to go home at lunchtime. 'I see that Lian's on Doxorubicin,' he said to me while she slept. 'Have you looked at other options?'

'Like what?'

'LDK153. Ask Lian's oncologist about it. It's prolonged the length and quality of life for many women with advanced uterine cancer. I was involved in the trials.'

'Can you repeat the name for me, please?'

I tapped it into the Notes application on my phone so I could ask Dr Lee about it at our next appointment.

'Unfortunately it's not fully funded yet,' the doctor added.

'How much is the co-payment?' The lost wedding deposits had decimated my savings, but I could manage a few hundred dollars a month if I postponed my super contributions on compassionate grounds.

'Off the top of my head, around eighty thousand dollars.'

I laughed, and then realised he wasn't joking when I saw the confusion on his pale, earnest face.

'That's the average for a full course,' he said. 'The actual cost will depend on the treatment period.' He put his hand on my shoulder. 'I know it's pricey, but worth it if you can tighten your belt.' He smiled and moved on to the next patient.

Eighty thousand dollars. Where the hell was I supposed to find that sort of money? No amount of belt-tightening would make the slightest difference, and unfortunately I didn't have a spare Picasso to flog.

At half-past eight, I checked my phone again in the corridor. Frustratingly, there was still no news on the warrant from Althea. I'd asked her to let me know as soon as it came through.

Neither Wilson nor Macca answered their mobiles, so I tried the office number. 'Can you put me through to Wilson?' I asked Shaniah.

'He's not here.'

'Okay, well how about Macca?'

'He's gone too. They left in a hurry.'

'Where to?'

'They're executing a warrant on the Turner case.'

'No they're not. The warrant hasn't been approved yet.'

Shaniah huffed. 'Don't bite the messenger, Mei. I'm just telling you what Wilson told me.'

I rang off and called Althea. 'Why didn't you notify me when the Turner warrant came through?'

Althea hesitated. 'It's not what you think.'

'What? What does that mean?'

'If Wilson hasn't briefed you, I can't say anything.'

'I can't get hold of him. What the fuck is going on?'

Silence.

'Althea?'

'Look, Mei, after we spoke earlier, Wilson called. Macca got a tip-off about another suspect and they asked me to apply for an urgent covert warrant. You know I can't tell you anything else.' She paused. 'I shouldn't even have told you that. I've got to go. I'm under some serious time pressure.' She hung up.

An intense heat crept up my jaw and spread along my shoulders. How could Wilson have executed a warrant on my case without letting me know? It wasn't the first time Wilson had pulled a bullshit stunt like this, cutting me out in order to take the credit after I'd done all the legwork. How hard would it have been for him to drop me a message? He'd never do this to Macca or any of the guys, and there was no damn way I was putting up with it.

NINE

SKYE

When the detectives left Ana's apartment, I was swallowed by a deep, underwater exhaustion. I clung to her balcony while my body dissolved at the margins.

Ana kept coming out to check on me. She urged me into a chair and tucked a soft throw over my legs. A little later, she brought out a pot of fresh mint tea and wedged a pillow behind my shoulders. She instinctively knew how to comfort me without saying a word. Was this what it felt like to have a mother? The proper kind – not the dope-sick kind for whom I was an afterthought while she spent the child welfare payments on her next fix.

At five o'clock, Ana drew me a steaming lavender bath. When I slipped into the water, I had an abrupt vision of my mother as she was that last time. Slumped in the tub, her eyes rolling back, her lips blue. The discarded needle on the chipped avocado-green tiles. The horrible gurgling sound. There had been no sign of her latest boyfriend with the barbed belt and the sour breath who liked to punish me for any minor infraction, or sometimes for no infraction at all.

I knew to dial 000 for the ambulance, but instead of picking up the phone, I forced the tap around to full and went to school. When the receptionist came to my classroom to shepherd me into Mr Dennis's office, my wrists tingled in expectation of the cold metal handcuffs I'd seen on TV. But the policemen were gentle and kind. They explained that my mother had had an accident, while the receptionist sniffed into a Kleenex.

•

I woke in the spare bed to Ana tapping my shoulder. 'Sorry to disturb you, my darling. It's Duncan.'

The room was still dark. 'What time is it?'

'Nearly nine o'clock on Wednesday morning.' She swished back the curtain to admit a grey rectangle. It was raining again. 'You've slept for fifteen hours straight.'

I blinked hard and sat up, waiting for her to pass me the phone, but Ana placed her hand on mine. 'He's here.'

A surge of panic. 'What's happened?'

'I'm not sure. He says he needs to speak to you privately. Don't worry; I'll be in the next room.'

I stumbled out of bed and into the lounge. Duncan was watching the spidery clouds at the window, his back to me.

'How's Tilly?' I asked, dreading the answer.

The door clicked behind me, just as Duncan turned around. He was dishevelled and hollow-eyed – a grim version of his usual self. 'Tilly's stable. There's been no change.' He met my eyes and shook his head, his face solemn.

'Then what?'

He knew. He knew I'd spoken to the detectives. My heart broke free of my body and stammered in the space between us.

Duncan crossed the room and took my hands. 'The police have made an arrest.'

I felt a wash of relief, and then a lacerating blow – the certainty that Cody had tried to kill our daughter. 'Where is he?' I screamed. 'Where is he?'

'Skye, stop.' Duncan gripped my shoulders. 'It's Tamara. They've arrested Tamara.'

'What?' He tried to pull me into his chest, to comfort me, but I jerked free. 'Hugo's girlfriend?'

'I know. It's . . .' He faltered. 'It's so hard to comprehend. Sit down and I'll tell you everything I know.' He guided me to Ana's sofa. 'It turns out she's totally unstable. *Unhinged.* The police searched her apartment yesterday evening and found loads of evidence. She'd been planning this for a while, it seems.'

I picked through his words, trying to process what I was hearing. Just yesterday morning, the detectives had sat with me in this very room, and they'd barely mentioned Tamara at all. When they left, I was convinced they were hunting for Cody.

'But why?' I asked him. 'Why would she do such a thing?'

'Turns out she's been harassing Jamie for months. He didn't tell any of us about it because he didn't want to upset Nina or Hugo.' He clawed his hand through his hair. 'Jamie and Tamara were working closely on a project last year, and apparently she became obsessed with him – calling all the time and turning up at his office late at night. She even turned up at his house. The harassment stopped in January, but the police believe Tamara went to Yallambee with a plan to kill Nina. She's a total bunny-boiler.'

I scraped my mind for memories of Tamara. She'd seemed all right, aside from the fact she was friends with Hugo. Benign. Not *unstable*. Not *unhinged*. Not like someone who'd ever be capable of such horrendous acts. How could we all have misread her so badly?

'Why didn't Jamie say something?' I asked. 'If she was so unhinged, why didn't he warn Hugo? And why the hell did he let her come to Yallambee?'

'I don't know,' Duncan said. 'I have no fucking idea what Jamie was thinking. I suppose he thought he could handle it. You know how arrogant he is. He says he tried to warn Hugo off her, but Hugo didn't listen.'

'But why would Tamara hurt Tilly?'

'The police think that Tilly was just collateral damage.' Duncan's voice cracked. 'She must have accidentally ingested the poison meant for Nina.' Tears rolled down his face.

Collateral damage. A fresh burst of pain.

'The police are holding a press conference shortly,' Duncan continued. 'Jack will send us an email outlining the steps from here, but basically the formal legal process will kick in – court appearances and so on. He said we should both expect to be called as witnesses, so we'll need to give statements soon. And the media situation is spiralling out of control; Jamie's going to give a short statement on behalf of the family.'

'What about Tilly? If they've arrested Tamara, surely we can go straight to the hospital.'

'It's not that simple, babe. They still have to unwind the care order in court, and Tamara still has to be formally charged. I know it's frustrating, but Jack's on it. We have to wait until we've heard from him. Okay?'

No, not okay. Duncan had segued into business mode – talking about court orders and press conferences, filing his emotions into neat compartments, moving ahead – but none of it made sense. Cody was still missing, and none of this explained why Duncan had been lying to me. I didn't know what to say or how to feel. There was just a creeping numbness.

•

We sat with Ana in front of her television to watch the press conference. A *Sky News* banner ticked across the screen – *Breaking: Arrest in the Turner poisoning scandal*. The camera cut from the presenter's desk to a stage with the New South Wales Police insignia behind it, and we watched the backs of the reporters' heads bob along the screen as they took their seats in the darkened gallery. Several officers stood sentry either side of the podium. I recognised the burly male detective who had interviewed me yesterday morning – Detective McKenzie.

After a minute, a stocky middle-aged man with a thick blond moustache approached the microphone. A hush settled over the room. According to the caption, he was the NSW Police Commissioner. He unfolded a square of paper and addressed the waiting media in a solemn tone.

'*Good morning. I'm pleased to inform you that New South Wales police officers have arrested a twenty-seven-year-old Sydney woman in connection with the death of forty-one-year-old Nina Turner and the poisoning of six-year-old Tilly Turner.*'

A sharp pain fired in my chest when I heard Tilly's name in the mouth of this stranger.

The Commissioner continued: '*On behalf of the New South Wales Police Force, I wish to extend my heartfelt condolences to Jamie Turner and his children on the tragic loss of their wife and mother. I also wish to pass on our support and best wishes to Skye and Duncan Turner, whose daughter remains in a critical condition. Jamie Turner will shortly give a brief statement on behalf of the Turner family.*

'*Finally, I'd like to congratulate Detective Chief Superintendent Mike Wilson and Detective Sergeant Stuart McKenzie from the State Crime Command's Homicide Squad for their swift work on this investigation.*'

An explosion of flashing bulbs accompanied Jamie's walk to the podium. He looked presidential in his white shirt and dark suit, his face strained. I'd never forgive him for letting Tamara come anywhere near Tilly, but he was also suffering, trying to support his children in the aftermath of their horrific loss.

Jamie cleared his throat and waited for the commotion in the room to subside before speaking.

'*Our family wishes to thank the New South Wales Police for their tireless investigation into the death of my beloved wife, Nina – the mother of our three beautiful children – and the poisoning of my niece, Tilly, who is still fighting for her life. It's hard to comprehend why our loving family has been the target of this cruel and senseless crime. I would like to take this opportunity to thank the incredible staff at St Vincent's Hospital. As a family, we've been deeply touched by the outpouring of love and support from our community, and we ask that you respect our privacy at this very difficult time.*' Jamie's voice wavered on the final words.

When the press conference was over, Duncan stood up and reached for my hand. 'We should get going.' He turned to Ana. 'Thanks for being such a great friend to Skye.'

I hesitated. It hadn't occurred to me that I'd have to go home with him, but with Tamara in custody, the media would move on. There was no reason for me to remain at Ana's. Yesterday, I'd convinced myself that Cody was to blame and that Duncan had been involved in a cover-up; but now, looking at my grief-stricken husband, I realised that conjecture was completely absurd. Duncan loved Tilly more than anything in the world. He was devoted to her. How could I ever have doubted him?

TEN

MEI

WEDNESDAY

When Wilson and Macca materialised on my tiny rectangle of screen in the hospital corridor, I was gripped by a red-hot malignant rage. Motherfuckers. Neither of them had given me a heads-up they were executing a warrant, let alone making an arrest in my investigation. Let alone holding a press conference. I expected that sexist shit from Wilson, but not from Macca.

'Bugger. There goes five bucks.' A nurse was craning his neck over my shoulder. 'We've got a sweepstake going on the ward. I was sure it was that artist. Apparently she's nuts. You know – Tilly's mum.' He spoke with the enthusiasm of a punter at the races. 'On the radio, they said it was a twenty-seven-year-old woman, so it must be the nanny. Righto, this is for you . . .' He passed me a wad of hospital forms. 'Your mother is free to go home.'

•

I called Macca from the car on our way back to Mum's flat.

'I'm really sorry, O'Connor,' he said as soon as he picked up, before I had a chance to speak. 'Wilson told me he was keeping you informed, and it all happened so quickly.'

'You arrested Tamara Baruch?'

'Yes. I'll fill you in on everything, but I'll have to ring you back. The sonographer's just called us in for Saskia's thirty-week scan.'

'Fine. I'll take it up with Wilson. But you're not off the hook, mate.'

•

After Mum was settled in back at her flat, I carried on to work. When the lift jerked open, I thundered straight into Wilson's office, ignoring Shaniah's protestations. He was hunched over his computer, forking a reheated casserole into his mouth.

'What the fuck, Wilson?'

He glowered at me. 'Watch your language, DSS O'Connor.'

'You hijacked my investigation.'

Wilson heaved himself up, the dripping fork still in his hand. 'You disrespect me one more time and I'll suspend you. Sit down.'

I dropped into a chair without breaking eye contact. 'Sir,' I said in a saccharine voice, '*please* can you talk me through the evidence you've got on Tamara Baruch?'

Wilson sat and leaned back in his chair, gripping the armrests like a cranky mall Santa Claus. 'First of all, *I'm* in charge, so no one hijacked *your* investigation. Second of all, we got a tip-off when you were at the hospital with your mother, and we had to act immediately. You know the pressure we're under on this one.'

'What tip-off?'

'I can't reveal the source.'

'Why not?'

'I'm warning you: check yourself.'

I bit my lip. 'What evidence did you find?'

'A folder concealed in the suspect's bedroom with detailed information about arsenic trioxide – how to source it, how to administer it, and other murders involving the poison from around the world. It appears to be a copycat of a Japanese homicide from a few years back. We also seized her laptop. It's got a search history going back months that's consistent with the printed material in the folder.'

'How convenient.'

Wilson sighed. 'What's that supposed to mean?'

'You get a random tip and, like magic, there's a dossier of incriminating evidence in Tamara's apartment. Come on. When does that ever happen?'

'There's also the laptop. And phone and email records.'

'It's simple enough to fake an online search history,' I said. 'Have you asked forensics to confirm when and where the documents were printed? And what do the phone records show?'

I could tell Wilson was pissed with me from the aggressive way he'd begun to stir the remaining casserole around his Tupperware. 'For months, Tamara Baruch has been calling and messaging Jamie Turner. Jamie says that some of the material is graphic. He says he also has home security camera footage showing Tamara turning up at his residence at night. Macca's checking it now. The evidence paints a pretty damning picture of harassment.'

'Okay. So if Tamara Baruch was obsessed with Jamie Turner, why was she hanging out with his brother Hugo?'

'Our guess is she was using him to stay close to Jamie. Hugo gave a statement this morning. He said that Tamara was suffering from mental health issues, and that she was behaving erratically in the lead-up to the Easter weekend. He also confirmed that she prepared some of the food that Nina and Tilly were exposed to on Friday night. It all fits.'

'What does Tamara say to the allegations?'

'She's denying everything, of course. She's made up some fantastic tale, but Althea thinks that it should be a reasonably straightforward prosecution.'

'So, how did Tamara get access to the arsenic trioxide?'

'We don't have a definitive view on that yet, but she was actively investigating a number of avenues online.' He took another mouthful of casserole, and a glob of brown sauce snagged on his whiskers.

I had to change tack with Wilson if I had any chance of remaining involved. I took a deep breath. 'Sir, I'm sorry – I overreacted.'

He glanced up. 'I'm pleased you can recognise that.'

'How about I watch the footage of Tamara's interview? I might pick up on something – you know, from a female perspective.' I hated playing the gender card but needs must.

Wilson shrugged. 'Sure. Knock yourself out.'

•

I downloaded the file of Tamara's first interview to my laptop. The woman in the green prison tunic escorted into the interview room bore no resemblance to the Tamara Baruch I'd seen online. This one had long greasy hair scraped back into a ponytail, a blotchy face and dark smudges under her eyes. She looked like a teenager caught up in a meth bust.

Her lawyer – a chunky middle-aged woman with frizzy brown hair – slouched to the right of the screen. Wilson and Macca scraped their chairs up to the left of the red formica table, introduced themselves and began the interview.

Tamara denied the allegations that Wilson put to her. She denied knowing anything about the evidence found in her apartment. She was variously angry and emotional – the usual combination for a suspect.

'This is insane,' she kept saying. 'Someone put it there.'

'Who would do that?' asked Wilson.

'I have no idea. I told you. Wait until Jamie finds out you've arrested me. He'll be furious.'

'Ms Baruch, Jamie Turner has accused you of harassing and stalking him over many months.'

'What? Jamie would never do that.' She turned to her lawyer. 'I need my phone. I need to call him. He'll explain everything. He loves me.'

Wilson opened a file and slid a document across to her lawyer. 'These are phone records from Ms Baruch's mobile provider. The yellow-highlighted calls and texts are from her phone number to Jamie Turner's mobile. Ms Baruch, you phoned and sent Jamie Turner WhatsApp messages several times every day from last August until February. Many of those messages were explicit. Do you deny making those calls and sending those messages?'

She glanced at the sheets of paper. 'I wasn't harassing him. Some were work calls, and the rest were because he *wanted* me to send them.'

Macca and Wilson's heads cleaved together for a moment, then Macca spoke, in a softer tone. 'Ms Baruch, are you alleging that you had a romantic relationship with Jamie Turner?'

'Yes.'

'When did the relationship begin?'

'Last August.'

'And, Ms Baruch, do you believe you are still in a romantic relationship with Jamie Turner?'

'No. We ended things in early February, soon after his father died. It all got too complicated.'

Macca paused, working out his next question. 'Ms Baruch, according to the phone and email records we have here, during the six months you allege you were in a romantic relationship with Jamie Turner, he did not call, message or email you at all – save for a handful of work-related communications. How do you explain that?'

'God, don't you get it? He's married! He's also my boss. We had to be super careful. We couldn't risk his wife finding out.'

'But she could have seen the messages you sent him,' Wilson pointed out. 'How is that any different?'

She shrugged, exasperated. 'This was just how Jamie wanted it.'

'How do you explain the footage of you turning up at Jamie Turner's house late at night?' asked Wilson.

'Sometimes we'd meet in his pool house when his wife and kids were asleep or away.'

'Where else did your romantic encounters take place?' Macca spoke again, in a kindly tone. 'Perhaps there are records at hotels? Or we could check the security footage near your apartment?'

She shook her head. 'Just at his place, or at work. Mainly in his office at night.'

'Right. Is there anyone who can corroborate this relationship between you and Jamie Turner? You must have told someone about it – a family member? A friend or a colleague, perhaps?'

She shook her head. 'Jamie didn't want anyone to know. He was trying to figure out how to leave his wife. We had to be careful.'

Wilson shot Macca a sideways glance. 'Jamie said he was going to leave his wife for you?' he asked.

Tamara nodded. 'He still cares about me. We made love last weekend at Yallambee.'

The lawyer was whispering something to Tamara – probably something along the lines of *shut the fuck up* – but Tamara wasn't backing down. 'Just get Jamie on the phone. He'll explain everything.'

Jesus, the woman truly was batshit crazy.

Wilson leaned forward, planting his elbows on the table and steepling his fingers. 'Ms Baruch, Jamie Turner denies having any relationship with you whatsoever beyond an employment relationship.'

'You're lying. Let me talk to him.'

'In fact, Jamie Turner was so concerned about your behaviour that he laid two complaints with the Turner Corp human resources department – one last October and one in January. Here are copies.' Macca handed the lawyer a plastic sleeve containing the documents.

'That's bullshit!' Tamara's voice was high-pitched now, desperate.

'Ms Baruch,' Macca said, 'if you were in a relationship with Jamie Turner, then why were you at Yallambee with his brother Hugo?'

'Jamie encouraged me to come to Yallambee. He wanted to keep me close.'

Tamara was clearly delusional and her story could easily be disproved. Perhaps Wilson was right about her after all, assuming the evidence checked out. On the other hand, there was something too tidy – too convenient – about the whole thing. Who had tipped Wilson off about Tamara? There was no clue to the person's identity on file. Why would Tamara have left the damning evidence so easily discoverable in her apartment? And none of this explained why Cody White had gone into hiding, or the anomalies Skye Turner had observed in her husband's behaviour.

When Grace disappeared, the detectives were too quick to give up on her. If they'd tried harder, looked more closely, persisted longer, then they'd have found her. Now a woman was dead and a little girl was in a critical condition. I owed it to them both to keep going.

ELEVEN

SKYE

WEDNESDAY

When Duncan brought me home from Ana's apartment, we were engulfed by a tide of well-wishers. With the media trucks and security cordon gone, neighbours, friends and acquaintances swept in with offerings of Ottolenghi Chicken Marbella, vegetarian lasagne and unsolicited advice. The gate intercom buzzed constantly with flower deliveries. Their sickly sweet perfume infiltrated the whole house and made me retch. All I could think about was getting back to Tilly's bedside.

There had been no update from the lawyer. The DCJ was waiting for the last possible minute to lodge the court papers. Our supporters railed against the bureaucrats who were keeping us from Tilly. They all agreed we should sue the DCJ, sue the police, sue the hospital when this was over. I wondered, what did they mean by 'over'?

Some of our visitors stayed on to help. A few neighbours took charge of the hundreds of teddies that had been left at our gate, boxing them up for charity in the formal lounge. My yoga friends were burning white sage and palo santo in every room while Tilly's friends' mothers were in full mum mode, cataloguing the food deliveries for the fridge and freezer. Every time I entered the kitchen in one of my desperate orbits of the house, their gale of chatter would cease and they would rush towards me as a single many-headed monster to rub my back and assure me that everything would be all right.

In the old ballroom, Duncan's friends' wives were assembling the dunes of flowers and foliage into vases on the grand piano. They were scandalised when my old flatmates from Chippendale arrived in two battered station wagons and presented me with a bunch of homegrown dahlias, stewed rhubarb and solemn hugs.

I was touched by everyone's love and support, but I also felt irrationally anxious at seeing my past and present lives collide, as though it might trigger some further catastrophic rupture.

•

On Thursday morning I woke late, groggy and nauseous from the pills Duncan had given me to sleep. There was a calendar reminder on my phone screen for Tilly's book character parade. Her Pippi Longstocking costume was hanging ready in her wardrobe. We'd spent weeks planning her outfit: a dandelion yellow tunic with patched pockets that Tilly had helped me stitch on; her toy monkey, which we'd fastened to the shoulder of the tunic with safety pins; and socks in lollipop stripes we'd chanced upon at a charity shop. I could see her in front of me – twirling in her costume, excited to join the parade that Outlook confirmed would be starting at 8.30 am – and I was overcome with the most intense physical yearning to hold her. It was a violent ache, deep in my bones.

'Are you sure you'll be okay?' Duncan asked. 'I really don't want to leave you but there are some urgent issues I have to deal with.' He was heading in to the office. Someone else could have taken care of the work. He was just desperate for a distraction, for the charade of routine and normality. 'Why don't you invite some friends over?'

'Bridge and Vicky are coming after yoga,' I lied. All of my friends had offered to visit, but I'd brushed them off with excuses about the police investigation. If I couldn't be with Tilly, then I wanted to be alone. I would spend the day online, seeking out the miracle stories, the kids who'd returned to full health after prolonged intubation and sedation. But so far, everything I'd read was consistent on one point – every hour she remained in that medically induced coma, the worse the odds of her making a full recovery.

'Call me as soon as you hear from the lawyer,' I said. 'Surely we'll be able to see her today?'

'Here's hoping,' he said, fastening his cufflinks. 'Also, Betty's starting back. She'll be here at around eleven. And don't forget to take your medication.' He kissed my cheek.

About twenty minutes after he left, I checked the GPS app on my phone and felt a stab of relief when the green circle labelled with his initials pulsed at Chifley Tower in the city.

Bo was whimpering in the hallway, lying in wait outside Tilly's closed bedroom door. He'd been pining for her all week. He began swiping at the door with his paw, trying to force it open. A lump swelled in my throat. 'Come on, boy. Let's go for a run.'

At the word 'run', Bo's eyes flicked up and his tail started wagging. We'd both been cooped up inside for days and God knows we needed to get out of the house. I had to expel some of the crawling despair.

I didn't dare head for one of the parks on the northern slopes, where I'd encounter a bootcamp of school mums. Instead, I yanked my cap low over my eyes and took the alternative route south-east along Victoria Road. The rain had eased, and tentative white sunlight quivered in the puddles. I concentrated on the rhythmic slap of my feet on the footpath. Everything hurt. My abdomen was tight, my legs were stiff and my lungs lead-heavy, as though I was breathing through gauze. Bo strained on his lead, sensing that we were headed for Cooper Park. Usually, Tilly would be riding her bike alongside us, and I'd be watching ahead for cars in driveways, one arm poised to snatch her back from danger. That's the thing about being a mum: you're always on edge, alert to risk, primed to protect – and I'd failed her.

When Tilly was an infant, and I'd finally been allowed home, I'd bring her into our bed when she howled in the night and prop myself up on pillows while she suckled. Even when I was bone-weary, I never let myself fall asleep until she was back in her Moses basket. I was terrified of SIDS. But for the rest of the night, I'd jerk awake to search for her in the bedclothes, petrified that her tiny body was suffocating beneath our sheets and blankets. It was, until now, my most frightful nightmare.

I rounded the bend, passing the home of Tilly's schoolfriend Maysie. The parade would be finished by now, and the girls would be in literacy class with Miss Matthewson. Tilly and

Maysie had ballet after school on Thursdays. Would Maysie still go today? It was unfathomable that ordinary life could continue while we were trapped in this hell – cars kept whipping past, a postal worker was delivering the mail up ahead, a courier van had swung into the next driveway. The neighbourhood was alive with the buzz of leaf blowers and the grind of construction on a vacant block. The traumatic events of the past week had made a brief ripple before the world had closed over again. I sped up, my feet smacking the concrete harder and harder.

After a while, I sensed that I was being followed. I slowed my pace and glanced over my shoulder. About thirty metres down the road, just far enough that I couldn't make out the driver or the licence plate, a silver SUV slowed to a crawl. I checked myself – I was being silly – and resumed running, but just to be sure I peeled right down Riddell Street. When I looked back over my shoulder, the silver SUV had gone.

Bo and I turned onto Bellevue Road, passing the bakery and grocery store, and paused at the pedestrian crossing. I checked right before stepping out. The silver SUV reappeared and my heart swerved. It was probably nothing, I told myself. There were hundreds of vehicles just like it in this neighbourhood. I couldn't even be sure it was the same one I'd seen earlier. I thought about ducking into a shop, but I couldn't deal with bumping into anyone I knew and facing their maudlin expressions and glib sympathy, so Bo and I crossed the road and picked up speed.

The SUV edged forward.

I continued along the footpath to the top of the Cooper Park steps; there was no way the SUV could follow me there.

When I turned back, the vehicle had pulled over just down the road. I still couldn't make out the driver or the licence plate.

My lungs were scorched but I blazed down the concrete staircase into the damp belly of the reserve. When I hit the landing, the only other person I could see was an elderly runner who pounded past me and onto the soggy trail leading into the bush. Bo and I continued over the Moon Bridge, past the constellations of fraying wildflowers and into the Jurassic woodland. We followed the clay track where the buttress roots of ancient Moreton Bay figs spilled out like entrails and the earth smelled of wet moss and mould. Although my body was screaming, I kept on, in the doomed hope that I could outrun the panic thrashing in my chest.

Somehow Bo slipped out of his collar and darted through the ferns to the creek. He had just returned, covered in sticky black mud, his pink tongue lolling out the side of his mouth, when my phone rang. It was Duncan.

'What are you doing?' he asked.

'I've brought Bo out for a run. We're at the park.'

'What?' He was angry. 'What were you thinking?'

That was rich when he'd gone off to work.

'Right – so I can't leave the house, but you can?'

He lowered his voice. 'I'm in a secure office. I can't protect you when you're out by yourself in public. The media will still be tailing you. They'll be competing for the first photos.'

I hadn't thought about that. It explained the silver SUV.

As if reading my mind, he added, 'What will people think when they see pictures of you out for a nice little jog around the neighbourhood while your daughter is in hospital fighting for her life?'

He was right. A huge sob swelled inside me.

'I was ringing,' he continued, 'because I've just spoken to Jack. The DCJ still hasn't lodged the care application with the Children's Court. They have until close of business today to lodge, which means the hearing won't be until tomorrow at the earliest.'

Another gut punch. I'd been counting down the hours.

'But the police have arrested Tamara. Why can't the DCJ just drop the whole thing?'

'They still have to follow the statutory process. And even though Tamara's been arrested, she still hasn't been charged. Listen, I know you're upset, but Jack's doing everything he can, and we've got calls in to the Minister to apply pressure. When this is over, I'm taking those bastards down for what they've done to us.'

●

On the way home, I stuck to the back roads and kept an eye on the traffic. There was no sign of the silver vehicle. Maybe I was paranoid, but that was no wonder when Duncan was hiding things from me. I'd confront him when he got home. I had to know where he'd been on Sunday morning, why he'd taken my phone, and why he'd lied about meeting the lawyer. There was probably an innocent explanation, but he had to be honest with me if we were going to get through this.

Back at the house, I wrangled Bo into the vast laundry tub and hosed him down. Under the rush of water, clumps of black mud and leaves spiralled down the plughole while Bo squirmed against my leg. Before I'd finished towelling him down, he escaped and shook himself, spraying water all over the tiles, and then lolloped off into the hallway.

For a blessed few seconds, my mind drifted into autopilot as I mopped up the water and bundled the dirty towels into the washing machine. I pressed the button and turned to dry my hands, and there it was: Tilly's rumpled school blazer on the laundry benchtop. A single strand of her dark hair trailed down from the lapel. I picked it up and wound it around my index finger, then tucked it into my pocket, next to the grey heart-shaped stone that I'd carried with me ever since Yallambee.

Upstairs, the doorbell chimed. Betty was early; she must have forgotten her key. I braced for another tearful encounter. Betty would be devastated about Tilly.

But when I opened the door, it wasn't Betty standing there. It was Cody. He collapsed into me, and it took all of my strength to support him.

•

Cody and I sat together at the dining table, in the same seats we'd taken for Sunday dinner less than a fortnight ago. He'd played snap with Tilly while Duncan and I'd prepared the meal, and we'd all applauded heartily when Tilly performed a tortured recital of 'Twinkle, Twinkle, Little Star' on her violin. The memory was so vivid I could almost touch it.

Over pork belly and pinot noir, Cody had entertained us with anecdotes about working the city bars, serving conceited bankers and clueless tourists. He'd inherited Campbell's talent as a raconteur, if not his grandfather's finessed delivery. When Cody told us he'd enrolled in some programming classes at the Sydney Community College, Duncan had put his arm around Cody's shoulder like a proud father. In that moment, I'd felt uneasy. Cody and I were kindred spirits in many ways – both of us were outsiders who'd stumbled into the Turner family – but I saw then that he could also become a threat to our unit of three.

'So, where have you been?' I asked. 'We've been trying to get hold of you since Saturday. So have the police.' My voice was flat, unfamiliar.

'The Blue Mountains. My mate's got a cabin outside of Katoomba.'

'You really didn't know?'

Cody shook his head. 'There's no cell service up there – and anyway, my phone's out of credit. We had a heap of pills, and . . .' He trailed off. 'Shit. I can't believe it. Is she going to be okay?'

I shrugged. 'No one knows. We have to wait. Even if she survives, they can't rule out permanent damage to her lungs and heart, or neurological damage.' The words were bitter in my mouth. 'How did you find out?'

'This morning, on my way back to town. I saw a newspaper when I stopped for petrol.' He squeezed his eyes shut for a moment, as if to blank out the image. 'And she's in the hospital now?'

'Yep. And the DCJ won't let us see her, so she's there all alone.'

He began to cry again, and I felt a sting of shame. It had been too easy to convince myself that Cody was responsible for what had happened to Nina and Tilly, when really, here in the flesh, he was just a distraught child.

'So who did the police arrest? They said they have someone in custody.'

'Tamara,' I said.

His eyes widened in astonishment.

'Tamara?'

I nodded. 'The police think she poisoned some of the food we had at dinner on Friday night. Apparently, she's been stalking Jamie for months. They think she went there to kill Nina, and that Tilly's poisoning was accidental.'

'Are you serious?'

'None of us had a clue, and Jamie didn't tell anyone. If only we'd known she was so disturbed. I'd never have let Tilly anywhere near her.'

'Who said she was stalking Jamie?'

'The police.'

'But I saw Jamie and Tamara together at Yallambee,' said Cody. '*Together* together. They were fully hooking up.'

I frowned, disbelieving. 'What? Where?'

'In the storeroom. I was getting some more cocktail glasses and walked in on them. They were going for it.'

'No, that can't be right. You would have seen Tamara with Hugo, not Jamie.'

'Skye, it was Jamie. I'm one hundred per cent sure of it. I don't know if they saw me – I got out of there pretty quick.'

'There's no way.'

Cody's mind was obviously still bent with hallucinogens. Tamara wasn't Jamie's type at all, and besides Hugo and Nina had both been right there. And I'd seen Jamie having sex with Nina that night, around the same time.

'I know what I saw,' he insisted.

'If that's true, then why didn't you say something, for God's sake?'

He threw me an incredulous look. 'Honestly, why would I get involved? It's not like anyone wanted me there in the first place, apart from you and Duncan. And then at dinner

Jamie gave that phony speech about how important family is, and everyone was toasting him like he's such a great guy when he's just been boning his brother's girlfriend. And then Hugo laid into me, saying I'm just this gold-digger after their money. I know what I saw.'

'But that makes no sense. The police say Tamara was stalking Jamie for months. That she poisoned Nina and Tilly.'

'Skye, I don't know how this changes things, but I do know that Jamie was totally into Tamara on Friday night.' He stood up, his face earnest. 'You have to tell the police.'

I felt the walls and ceiling closing in, squeezing my brain and my lungs, tighter and tighter. I opened my phone, found Detective O'Connor's number, and passed it to Cody. 'Tell them yourself.'

Cody's version of events couldn't be right. It just couldn't. Because if Cody was telling the truth, then that meant Jamie was lying – and that changed everything.

TWELVE

MEI

At 11 am, on the fifth day of our investigation, Macca and I finally met Cody White. His features had matured and sharpened since his mugshot, and he had his father's striking amber eyes. Unlike Duncan, though, his head was shaved in a number one and tattoos unfurled from his hoodie up the side of his neck and onto his wrists. If I were ten years younger, I'd have been in serious trouble.

Cody surveyed the stark white gypsum walls before sliding into the vacant chair. He didn't seem nervous. I offered him a water. He declined. Macca glanced at me, impatient to begin the interview, but I signalled at him to wait. I didn't want to rush Cody. The kid had been through this process before and he knew his rights. At any time, he could choose to get up and leave. We sat in silence for what seemed like a long time. Then, all of a sudden, Cody White started to talk. His version of events rushed out of him like a pent-up tide.

On Friday night, he'd driven straight from Yallambee to his friend's cabin in the Blue Mountains. He denied speaking to any witnesses other than Skye since learning about the poisonings. Cody gave us the cabin's address and the details of the friends he'd been with since leaving Yallambee so we could confirm his presence there.

Then came the mic drop. Cody had seen Jamie Turner and Tamara Baruch having sex on Friday night. He was certain of what he'd seen. This supported Tamara's statement. If Tamara and Jamie had been intimate on Friday night at Yallambee, then she might have been telling the truth about their affair all along.

My gut told me that Cody was telling the truth and that there was more to this case than we realised. I thought back to our conversation with Rebecca White. She'd been twitchy as hell when we mentioned the Turners. 'One last question,' I said. 'What do you know about your mother's relationship with Duncan Turner?'

'What's my mother got to do with it?'

'Nothing directly. We're just trying to establish the family dynamics.'

He looked uncertain. 'Okay.'

'What did your mother tell you about Duncan when you were growing up?'

'Nothing. I didn't know anything about him. She refused to talk about my father.'

'So what changed?'

'We were watching the news and a story came on about Campbell Turner. About his funeral. Mum just went white, like she'd seen a ghost, and started crying. Eventually, I got it out of her. She told me she'd dated Campbell's son Duncan a long time ago.'

'And so you asked if Duncan was your father? And she confirmed it?'

He nodded. 'Yes. But after that she got all weird. She wouldn't tell me anything else.'

'So you tracked Duncan down yourself?'

'Yeah. I told Mum I'd been in touch with him. She tried to stop me, but – I dunno how to explain it. It was something I had to do.'

Why had Cody's mother been so resistant to him learning about his father? And why had she gone into hiding since their relationship ended? Rebecca White had dirt on Duncan Turner – I was certain of it.

●

After the interview, Macca and I took the lift back up to the seventh floor.

'If Cody's story checks out, Wilson's head's going to explode,' I said.

'I'm not buying it.'

'What?' I turned to Macca. 'Why would Cody have made it up?'

'He could be messing with us. Or maybe he and Tamara are colluding.'

'Possibly, but we've got to investigate his allegation. It affects Jamie Turner's credibility, and it gives both Jamie and Hugo Turner possible motives to harm Nina. Jamie might have wanted to dispose of his wife so he could be with Tamara, or Hugo could have poisoned Nina to punish his brother for sleeping with his prospective girlfriend.'

'I guess,' said Macca as the lift doors shuddered open. 'But how do you explain the evidence we found in Tamara's apartment?'

'Maybe it was planted.'

'Planted? You don't really believe that, do you?' He frowned. 'Sounds like you've been watching too many cop dramas. Personally, I don't think what he said changes anything. By the way, why did you ask Cody about his mother and Duncan?'

'Aren't you curious?' I said.

'A little. But how's it relevant to the investigation?'

'I'm still trying to figure that out.'

•

I asked Macca to verify Cody's story about his weekend at the mountain cabin and sent a transcript of our interview to Wilson, along with a meeting request. But after an hour Wilson still hadn't responded, and he wasn't in his office, so I went to check on his whereabouts with Shaniah.

When I approached her desk, she was yakking away into her phone headset, and held her index finger up to my face to indicate I should wait.

'Like I told you last time, I can't give you his direct number,' she was saying to whomever was on the other end of the line, 'but I will pass along another message.' She nodded, and said, 'Uh-huh. Okay. That's an American number, right?' Her tattooed eyebrows knitted together like a pair of plump slugs when she scribbled on her notepad. 'As you know, I can't reveal any more details.' Shaniah took unmatched delight in being the guardian of sensitive information. 'Uh-huh. Yes, I'm sure it's very important. I'll pass on the message, but I suggest you contact our Media Centre for more information.'

'Who was that?' I asked.

'Some pushy journalist wanting to meet with Wilson. He's been very persistent. Come all the way from New York to cover the Turner case. It's a big story over there. My cousins live in Alabama and they saw Wilson and Macca on the news. And isn't Jamie Turner a total DILF?'

'Where's Wilson?' I asked.

'He's with the lawyer. He said no interruptions. That includes you, by the way.'

I tracked Wilson down to a meeting room on the ninth floor, where he and Althea were working through court documents.

'Not now, O'Connor. We're in the middle of something. I'll catch up with you this afternoon.'

'Sir, I've sent you a statement from Cody White. He says he saw Jamie Turner and Tamara Baruch having sex at Yallambee on Friday night.'

I had expected Wilson to be surprised by this development, but his face was impassive, his mouth fixed in a straight line. He removed his spectacles and placed them carefully on the table in front of him. 'Althea, give us a minute?'

The lawyer left the room, closing the door behind her.

'Take a seat, O'Connor.'

I dropped into the chair opposite him.

'So, O'Connor, you'd overlook all the evidence that we have in relation to Tamara Baruch just because Cody White thinks he may have seen something? I've read the statement you sent through. Cody White is not a credible witness. He's got a record of drug offences.'

'I'm not overlooking anything, sir. I'm just saying that there could be more to all of this. The evidence you found in Tamara's apartment might not be reliable.'

He sighed. 'You have any proof of that?'

'Not yet, but I believe we'll flush something out when we search the Turner brothers' homes and offices.'

'That's not going to happen. We have our suspect in custody and we are charging her.'

'Sir, you can't charge Tamara yet. We haven't finished our investigation.'

He folded his arms and leaned back in his seat. 'So, what's your theory, O'Connor?'

'I don't have a solid one yet. But there are lots of possibilities.'

'Let me help you. Based on what you're saying, you seem to suspect that Jamie Turner, the respected chairman and CEO of Turner Corp, murdered his wife and also tried to murder his niece at a family get-together. Then he framed his mentally unstable employee for the crime. And all of this for no apparent motive and leaving no evidence. Does that sum it up?' Wilson was grinning, taunting me.

'Sir—'

He cut me off. 'Listen. Take this back to first principles. Tamara Baruch has clear motive, means and opportunity, as well as a large amount of compelling circumstantial evidence against her.'

'But Cody White's new statement is evidence that directly implicates Jamie Turner. He had a clear motive. And we don't have any other evidence because Jamie hasn't yet been properly investigated. Nor have his brothers. There's more to this. I know it.' Heat was rising in my face as I spoke.

'So, you want Tamara Baruch to walk free?'

'Not necess—'

'Because, as you well know, if we do not charge her within the next four hours, then we have to release her. And I am not going to let that happen. Not again.'

Wilson was referring to his decision to release David Mbutu, the prime suspect in the Livvy Tweedsmuir homicide case, at my urging. Livvy was a news anchor, beloved across Australia, who was violently murdered at home in front of her two young children. I still believed we'd done the right thing in releasing Mbutu, her pool cleaner, but the media – especially Bonnie Chambers at the *Sydney Morning Herald* – had crucified the Homicide Squad for that 'woke' decision, especially when Mbutu returned to Kenya. To this day, the case remained unsolved.

'I'm just saying, sir, that we shouldn't be discounting Cody White's evidence so quickly.'

'How can you trust anything Cody White has to say?' Wilson asked. 'Where has he been for the past week?'

'Off the grid, with his friends.'

'Getting high as a kite on horse tranquillisers and acid.'

'Sir, just let me execute a warrant on the Turner brothers, so we can officially rule them out. I've already had a warrant to search Duncan Turner's home and workplace signed off by the judge, so we can apply to expand it to cover Jamie and Hugo Turner, based on Cody White's statement.'

'I had that warrant revoked when Tamara Baruch was arrested. We no longer have cause.'

'Yes we do. Cody White's statement is—'

'O'Connor! Enough. This is where you always let yourself down. You're so bloody stubborn. You can't admit to being wrong.'

'I'm not wrong. I'm doing my job, sir. You taught me to keep all lines of inquiry open and not to cling to an early hypothesis. It's entirely possible that Tamara has been set up. Why won't you listen to me?'

'I'm listening, but all I'm hearing is that you have a gut feeling and no reliable evidence. Don't let your emotions get the better of you like they did with David Mbutu. We have the right person in custody.'

'Bullshit. You're taking the easy option because you don't want to risk your promotion.'

Wilson glared at me. I'd overstepped.

'Listen carefully, O'Connor. This evening, Tamara Baruch will be charged with two counts of using poison to endanger life, one count of attempted murder and one count of murder. That's final. Now get the hell out of here.'

•

I left the meeting room with an overwhelming urge to smack the crap out of something. Wilson had always been political, skilled at currying favour with the higher ranks, and a sexist dinosaur. But he'd crossed a line. Sure, maybe he was right and I had stuffed up on the Tweedsmuir case – but this was different. Wilson just didn't want to take on the Turners, and that made me question his integrity.

There was no sign of Macca at his desk, so I grabbed my gym bag and left the office. It was drizzling – and, according to that morning's *Sunrise*, the wettest, coldest April on record. The biblical floods that had succeeded the summer's bushfires could only be more depressing evidence of climate change.

I walked briskly until I hit Chinatown where I had to weave around bovine tourists posing for photos in front of the red arches. They were clutching bags of plastic boomerangs and stuffed koalas to commemorate their visit to this ancient Gadigal land. The air was pungent with fried egg roll and roast pork, and gulls patrolled for scraps outside restaurants strung with Peking ducks and tasselled lanterns. I split off down an alley, past the skips heaving with black bags of rotting fish carcasses and rounded a corner to Jakub's Boxing. When I stepped through the barrier, I inhaled the comforting perfume of leather and sweat. It was over a week since I'd last been to training, and my body was craving the release.

Jakub's was the antithesis of the slick franchise gyms with pop soundtracks and wellness programs that punctuated the city centre – the kinds of cheesy places that catered to the likes of Shaniah and the Ferret. It was a large concrete vault with rows of scuffed sparring bags strung up like hams from the exposed joists, a wall rack of barbells and a central ring. I could only just make out the whine of the ceiling rotor fans over the relentless crack of gloves on leather.

'Hey, Mei, we've missed you,' Jakub called when I passed him at reception. He was wearing his signature tight white singlet and glinting gold neck chain. 'When you gonna leave your boyfriend for me, baby? I'll cook you my world-famous pierogi.' He mimed stirring something in a pan and his veins rippled like lightning across his biceps.

I smiled and shook my head.

'You're breaking my heart.' He slapped his hands to his chest to signal heartbreak. It had been our routine exchange ever since I'd joined the gym.

After a short session with the jump rope, I gloved up and found a bag at the back. I began slowly and took time to hone my reflexes before starting the unload. The first round was for Wilson. The second round was for Nick. The third round was for motherfucking cancer. The fourth round was for Dad dying. The fifth round was for what happened to Grace. Before long, I was slick with sweat, my bag puckering like flesh with each blow.

My mind sharpened as the energy flowed back and forth between me and the bag. The Turner brothers were somehow complicit in the poisoning. They had to be. And there was no way I was going to let them get away with it. But without Wilson's support, my hands were tied. I couldn't afford to get demoted or to lose my job. My salary barely covered our living expenses, Mum's mortgage and treatment costs. There was no doubt about it: the situation was totally fucked.

It was dusk by the time I left the gym, and a handful of faint stars flickered like moths overhead. Office workers spilled onto the street, heading for trains, buses or one of the nearby bars. When Nick was still with the Homicide Squad, we always went for a drink after work on Thursdays. It was our unofficial date night – an opportunity to decompress before the weekend's blur of social events and life admin if we weren't on call. When Nick accepted his lucrative new job in private security, in a glistening high-rise near Bondi Junction, those date nights stopped. He left Jakub's and signed up with Bondi Gym, where Vanessa was a visiting physio.

It was tempting to believe that Nick's decision to change jobs was what caused our paths to fork and delivered him to Vanessa, but I realised now that there would always have been a Vanessa – a girl whose family was just like Nick's. A girly-girl who would love spa days and shopping with his mother and sister. A girl who wouldn't arrive at his family's spring barbecue with a gift of Chinese tea and moon cakes. A girl without the tragic shadow of a missing sister, and a father who'd killed himself over it.

•

When I returned to work, I saw a man I didn't recognise pacing up and down the lobby by the security turnstiles. He had dark skin, greying hair braided into cornrows, a battered satchel and the eccentric air of a maths professor.

I took the lift up to my floor. Many of the cubicles were empty, and the juniors were zipping their laptops into their cases and heading for home. While I was waiting for my computer to reboot, the HR manager, Ant Ruskin, materialised at the threshold to my cubicle. Ant had the perma-enthusiasm of a musical theatre kid. His relentless positivity was exhausting. He'd come to conscript me for his new 'offbeat' recruitment campaign, and sealed my non-participation when he used his fingers to put 'offbeat' in quote marks. These days, policing was a broad church – at least, it was on paper – yet somehow it was still always me who got rolled out as the face of police diversity. Ant could only have loved me more if I'd identified as non-binary and walked with a cane. I had to plead an urgent work matter to force Ant to leave, and it was true that my inbox was bulging – twenty-seven new messages since I'd left for the gym. Most were notifications that I could read and delete. There were also a few performance sheets to complete for our upcoming reviews. The remainder comprised a subpoena to testify at a court hearing, a request to speak at a school careers day and victim impact statements from the family of a teen killed in a hit-and-run. Nothing from Wilson or Macca. Nothing about the Turner case.

When I left forty minutes later, the maths professor guy was still hovering in the lobby with the expectant look of a relative at an airport arrivals hall.

'Can I help you?' I asked.

'I was hoping to catch Detective Chief Superintendent Wilson.' He had an American accent.

'He's left already.' Ordinarily, I would have kept walking, but there was something about him that piqued my curiosity.

'What about Detective Sergeant McKenzie?' he asked.

'No, he's gone too. Can I pass on a message?'

He gave a brittle laugh. 'I've already left plenty.'

'What's this to do with?' I asked.

'I need to speak to them about the Turner case. I'm an investigative reporter with the *New York Times*.'

This must be the guy who'd been hounding Shaniah on the phone earlier. 'Did you catch today's press conference?' I asked. 'All the relevant details were covered then.'

'That's not why I'm here. I've got important information. I really need to speak to them.'

I was intrigued to hear what he had to say, especially since Wilson had cut me out of the loop. 'Maybe I can help you.' I extended my hand. 'I'm Detective Senior Sergeant Mei O'Connor. I've been working closely with Detectives Wilson and McKenzie on the Turner poisonings.'

He returned a firm handshake. 'Abe Cohen. Is there somewhere we can talk?'

I made a quick calculation. Shaniah was working late and would alert Wilson if I brought the journalist through security and onto our floor. A safer option would be Fitzroy's, the seedy pub a few blocks over. They didn't serve Wilson's preferred lager, and Macca would be putting Jayden to bed under Saskia's beady eye; I could get first dibs on Abe's allegedly 'important information' without anyone running interference.

THIRTEEN

SKYE

THURSDAY

I didn't go with Cody to the police interview. I had too many conflicting thoughts churning in my mind, cresting and then dissolving before I could grasp them. The more I tried to calm myself, the more my breaths came in rapid gasps, like I was drowning.

In a section of the library where Duncan would never venture, I kept a tin of weed, an old pipe and a lighter inside a hollowed-out volume of *Healing Crystals*, anchored between *Abundance and Affirmations* and *You Can Heal Your Life*. This particular stash had been there for almost six months so had lost most of its potency, but it was better than nothing. I'd been desperate for a smoke all week, but this was the first time I could be sure that Duncan wouldn't interrupt me; he hated smoking of any kind. I stuffed the leaves into the bowl, snatched a blanket from the couch and headed outside to the pool.

The air was heavy, and a skin of mouldering yellow leaves had grafted itself to the surface of the water. I slumped into a lounger – one positioned with its back to the security cameras – and let the damp padding seep through my sweater until my spine itched. Overhead, bursts of starlings fired north like arrowheads into the colourless sky, and I yearned to join them. Anything to escape this hellish limbo. I lit the pipe, inhaling and exhaling until the dopamine dulled the sharp edges.

I sifted through the jumble in my head. Tamara had been charged. The detectives had screeds of evidence against her – not only of what she'd done to Tilly and Nina, but also of her stalking Jamie. Those were the facts, verified by the police.

So Cody had to be wrong, even if he was adamant that he'd seen Tamara and Jamie together on Friday night. He'd been away for days, injecting and inhaling God knows what into his body. I couldn't let him confuse me. No, Cody was just mixed up.

And yet.

What if Cody was telling the truth? What if Jamie was lying about his relationship with Tamara? He'd been unfaithful to Nina before. It would explain why he'd allowed Hugo to bring Tamara to Yallambee when the weekend was supposed to be family only. And what about Duncan's strange behaviour, and all the lies about where he'd been after Tilly's hospitalisation? Too many things didn't add up.

I picked up my phone. At some point I'd have to clear the thirty waiting voice messages, but I couldn't face them. Instead, I scrolled back through my photo reel until I found the picture from our security footage of Duncan climbing into the black ute. In the slurry of the past days, the photograph was a touchstone – unassailable proof that Duncan had disappeared on

Sunday morning and then lied to me about it. I tapped on the photo and zoomed in. I could make out the licence plate, so I entered the number into the Service NSW online database. It confirmed the registration was valid but didn't reveal the name of the owner. I tried some other websites but with no luck. There was no way to find out who owned the vehicle without the help of the police.

My phone buzzed, making me jump. It was Duncan. Was he somehow monitoring my phone searches? No, no. The weed was just making me paranoid.

'Hey,' he said. 'Everything okay?'

'Yes. Did you hear from Cody?'

'Not yet.'

'He was just here. At the house.'

I heard him pull his office door shut. 'What? How is he?'

'Devastated. He's only just heard. You were right. He's been up in the mountains with his mates, at a cabin, and his phone's been out of credit.'

'Can you put him on?'

'He went into the city to meet with the detectives.'

'Why's he done that?' His tone was sharp.

I thought quickly. I'd explain everything when he got home from work. In person, when I could see his reaction. 'He wanted to do the right thing. The police have been trying to get hold of him for days.'

Duncan didn't say anything.

'That's not a problem, is it?'

'No. Of course not. It's just, I wish I'd been able to talk to him first. It's a lot for a young guy to deal with.' Maybe Duncan was just concerned for Cody, but his tone was suddenly businesslike. 'I've got to go. I won't be too late home – probably around five.'

After he hung up, I couldn't shake the feeling that Duncan was worried about what Cody might tell the detectives. Why?

•

Betty arrived and fussed over me, chattering in broken English and then rapid Mandarin to convey her love and sympathy. She insisted that I rest, but I told her I had to run some errands. Betty tutted and shook her head. I promised I wouldn't be long. I had a vague idea that I'd nip out to the grocer to buy some fresh fruit and vegetables. But I made sure to leave my phone charging on the kitchen counter so that Duncan couldn't track me remotely on the app, just in case.

It was over a week since I'd driven my car, and the interior of the Range Rover smelled of stale chlorine. Tilly's regulation green school swim bag lay on the front passenger seat, bulging with her damp swimsuit and towel. We'd forgotten to take it inside last Thursday after school. She'd written her own name on the label, and I had a sudden memory of her at her desk before the start of the new school term, printing it out in her neatest handwriting. A fresh wave of anger thundered over me. It wasn't fair. None of this was fair. Why had this happened to my little girl?

I steered left out of the gates onto Victoria Road, my eyes blurred and stinging. The grocer was just a couple of blocks away but, instead of turning right at the top of the hill, I turned left. I couldn't explain why; it was as if a force were willing me to head south. I checked my rear-view mirror. It was clear, so I accelerated.

The tidy hedges and two-storey homes of Bellevue Hill gave way to modest bungalows and shopping centres and, before long, I was weaving through clusters of commercial buildings and warehouses, bound for the port. At the traffic lights, I switched on my car navigation and had it guide me to Hale Street. I slowed my speed to a crawl, looking for a building whose location and size fit my memory of where Duncan had been on the GPS app. Without Tilly's smartwatch, I couldn't be certain, but one of them looked vaguely familiar, so I pulled over.

The air was briny and thick, and trucks rumbled towards the nearby docks. Across the road, a man in a high-vis vest was stacking pallets into a commercial trailer. I couldn't see anyone else around.

The lot was set back from the road behind an L-shaped car park, squashed between an abandoned car repair workshop and a shuttered Balinese furniture import business. I tried opening the door to what appeared to be the reception area, but it was locked and the blinds were closed. No one answered when I knocked. I pushed again at the door, harder this time, and rattled the handle, but with no luck.

The reception connected to a large warehouse which was secured with a heavy metal grate. There were no logos or business names anywhere, and no signs of life.

I crossed the road. The high-vis man was locking up the trailer, preparing to leave.

'Hi. Excuse me.' He looked up, and I pointed across to the warehouse. 'Do you know what that business is?'

'No clue, sorry, lady,' he said. 'What place you looking for?'

'I'm not sure.'

He cocked his head, confused. I wasn't making much sense.

'Do you ever see any of the people who work there?'

He shrugged. 'Sometimes.'

'Can you describe them?'

'Nah, not really. I don't pay much attention.'

'What about the vehicles that come and go from there? Do they have a company name or a logo?'

'Not that I remember.'

'What about a black ute? Or a silver SUV?'

He shook his head. 'Sorry, lady, I have to get going. You sure you're okay?'

I nodded, but suddenly I felt ridiculous, standing in the middle of nowhere, interrogating this stranger. For a moment, I'd felt in control, like I was chasing down a lead that might explain everything, but now I wasn't so sure. Maybe Duncan was right. Maybe I was delusional and manufacturing a crazy conspiracy.

•

I went the long way back to Bellevue Hill, driving through Maroubra towards Coogee. On Malabar Road, a silver SUV crept into my rear vision. I accelerated slightly and turned right onto Arden Street. The SUV followed.

I took a deep breath and slowed down to let the SUV catch up, thinking I might be able to make out the driver's face, but the SUV matched my speed. I indicated left at Coogee Bay Road. The SUV also indicated left. At the last minute, I accelerated forward instead. Behind me, the SUV accelerated too. My heart seized.

I sped back to our house, running two stop signs. Only once the entrance gates had closed behind me and our garage door had clicked shut did I dare get out of the car, my heart thudding inside my rib cage. I ran down the hallway, past Betty vacuuming the library. My phone was still charging in the kitchen. No calls from Duncan or the hospital. I fumbled to unlock it and tapped on the Family Circle App. When I confirmed that Duncan's green GPS circle was pulsing over Chifley Tower, I headed straight to the workshop and slid the bolt across to lock it from the inside.

The filing case was still wedged at the rear of the locker where I'd left it on Monday. I had an overwhelming urge to open it, as though its contents would make sense of everything, as foolish as I knew that sounded. My chest was hammering when I lifted the case onto the steel workbench and prised open the latches, but the lid wouldn't budge. There was still no sign of a key.

While the other children at my primary school had been learning their times tables and spelling words, I'd been perfecting another skill with Davy Butler in his dad's caravan – and that was how to pick a lock. I returned inside and found a couple of bobby pins in a bathroom drawer. Once I was able to steady my hands, I straightened out the first one to make a pick and slid it into the lock's barrel. With the other one, I fashioned a lever using Duncan's pliers.

There was no time to spare, but haste made my hands clumsy. I had to manipulate the pins gently, deftly, applying just the right amount of pressure, but the harder I tried to control them, the jerkier and more unpredictable their motion became.

I was about to lose my nerve when the lock's pins settled into position, then clicked to release. I'm not sure what I'd expected to find when I opened the lid, but I was relieved to see sheaves of documents. No vials of poison. No secret keys or gloves or weapons. None of the most sinister imaginings my addled brain had conjured up. They were probably just hunting licences and warranty records for the workshop equipment. Still, for my own peace of mind I had to check.

Carefully, I lifted out the files and spread them across the workbench, papering over my pale reflection in the steel. I opened the first file and leafed through the documents. There were pages and pages of rows listing dates, and adjacent to each one strings of letters and numbers with no other contextual information. I had no idea what they referred to. Foreign bank account numbers? Passwords? Serial numbers? Or codes of some description? The most recent dates were from March of this year, so the file had been accessed recently. What could it mean that Duncan was keeping these documents hidden away down here?

The second bundle contained photocopies of non-disclosure agreements marked 'strictly confidential'. In each case, Turner Corp was one party to the contract, and the other party carried the honorific 'Ms', but the women's names, addresses and other identifying details had been redacted with thick black lines. Beneath the crust of legal jargon, the deal was depressingly simple. Each woman quit all rights in perpetuity against Turner Corp and 'Mr Turner' relating to any claim of workplace sexual assault in exchange for substantial payments – some in the seven figures. Each woman had to surrender to Turner Corp for destruction all copies of recordings in all media, all diary entries, emails and other written correspondence, and all digital devices that might contain copies of any recording of, or any other material connected to, the sexual assault. If she breached the contract at any time, then she would have to refund the settlement payment, and Turner Corp would release to the media a sworn, pre-signed statement from the woman stating the behaviour she had accused Mr Turner of had never happened, that she had fabricated all claims, and that she wished to retract all allegations unequivocally. What was left of my heart felt like it had caved in.

Every fibre of my body wanted to believe that Duncan was not the 'Mr Turner' referred to in the contracts – that it was Campbell or Jamie or Hugo – but I'd been wilfully blind for so long. If the contracts did not involve him, why would he be keeping them locked away down here, where no one would ever find them, instead of in the company vaults? His father was dead and there was no love lost between him and Jamie and Hugo, so it was unlikely he was safeguarding them for his father or brothers. In fact, he would have relished sharing with me what they had done. Besides, the agreements had all been prepared by a law firm called Harrod Schneider Wood. *Harrod* Schneider Wood. Jack Harrod was our lawyer's name.

It was hard to imagine that worse was to come. Inside the third folder was a large, sealed envelope of stiff archival paper. I peeled it open and drew out the contents – large-format photographs, grown gluey with age. At first, my mind processed the images in fragments to lessen the horror, but there was no escaping them. A stricken pubescent girl naked on a bathroom floor. Barely teenage girls forced to perform sex acts on one another in hotel suites, some overlooking cities I recognised from our travels. Each photograph in the series was a more depraved iteration of the one before. And on the backs of the photographs, in Duncan's handwriting, were names and dates of where these sickening events had occurred.

I clutched the workbench, overcome with nausea, while the room lurched towards me. My husband was pure evil.

Had Tilly seen or overheard something? Was that why he'd poisoned her? I had to speak to the police before he knew what I'd found. Before he could stop me.

My stomach fell when the workshop door handle jerked down as if wrenched by a ghost. Then there was a sharp rap.

'Miss Skye?' It was Betty, on the other side of the workshop door. 'Miss Skye? Hello?'

With shaking hands, I scooped up the documents and slid them back inside the filing case. There was no time to reverse pick the lock. Somehow I forced the case in behind the veil of hunting jackets, slammed the locker closed and then unbolted the workshop door.

When it swung open, Betty stepped back, her eyes wide – with relief or suspicion? 'I worry,' she said. 'Your car here but I can't find you anywhere. Mr Duncan ask me to look after you.'

She was spying on me.

'I just got home.' My voice was shaky. 'I heard a noise in the workshop, but it's nothing, so . . .'

She was unsmiling. Unconvinced. 'You need lunch. It is two o'clock and you eat nothing.'

'It's okay. I'm not hungry.'

She took my arm, her grip firm. 'Come.'

Betty led me down the hallway. Everything around me was slippery and distorted. She helped me onto a stool at the counter and prepared me a honey sandwich on the bread intended for Tilly's school lunches. Outside, the garden was cloaked in fog and the world seemed flat, with no perspective or possibility, and no escape. I was trapped. Betty presented a plate of white triangles, and hovered over me while I ate. The bread – now grown stale – stuck to my tongue and made me gag, but I forced myself to nibble at the corners. I needed time to think.

I was convinced now that Duncan was monitoring my phone. It explained why it had mysteriously disappeared and how he just happened to phone me when I'd taken Bo for a run. Was he also having me followed? And he'd had all of those new cameras installed around the property. In fact, he'd probably fixed a tracking device to my car. Just a fortnight ago, there was a news story about a Melbourne woman whose ex-boyfriend had stabbed her to death after he traced her car to her new partner's home using a cheap gadget he'd ordered online. The article explained how easy it was to install a compact tracker on a car's exterior with a wireless magnet mount. I remembered feeling horrified for the poor woman, but in that distant way of a person who believed it could never happen to her.

I thought about texting Ana and asking her to come over, but I couldn't rule out that she was another one of Duncan's spies. After all, she'd worked for the Turner family long before I'd met her and was still on their payroll. Who knew where her loyalties really lay? My phone was radioactive, pinging nonstop with messages from friends, but maybe Duncan had reached them too? Would they believe me, or think I was mad? I could just imagine Duncan phoning my girlfriends, asking them to alert him immediately if I displayed any sign of paranoia. They were probably all just waiting for me to relapse – after all, my mental health battle had been splashed all over the news. No, I couldn't risk confiding in any of them. I had to be smart.

I swept the remainder of the sandwich into the bin. 'Betty, I'm heading out to get a couple of things.'

'Let me get them for you, Miss Skye.' She wiped her hands on her apron.

'Thanks, but I need tampons. It's easier if I just pop down to the BP.'

She nodded, embarrassed, and stacked my plate in the dishwasher.

•

I drew into a parking space right outside the service station. Except for a glossy black Mercedes, the forecourt was bare. I tugged my cap down to shield my face in case someone inside recognised me from the media coverage. Beside the sliding entry doors, I glimpsed a newspaper rack. The front page of the *Daily Telegraph* screamed Nina's and Tilly's names above their photographs and my stomach fell away. *Don't look, don't look.*

Inside, I gathered up a large pack of Tampax and waited for the only other patron – a woman with a helmet of silver hair who belonged to the Mercedes – to pay for her fuel. When it was my turn to step up to the counter, the young attendant stared at me blankly with no sign of recognition. I scanned the store to double-check no one else was around, then took a prepaid mobile phone from the display beside the spool of scratchies and added it to my pile. I paid in cash. Before I left, I asked to use the restroom and discarded the receipt, phone packaging and half the tampons inside the wastepaper bin, covering the refuse with paper towels. Then I hid the phone inside the Tampax carton.

When I returned home, Betty was still there, and she trailed me around the house. There was no way for me to return to the workshop to lock the filing case with her hovering, but

I had to find a way to do it before Duncan returned home. If he checked it and found the case unlocked, God knows what he might do.

'Betty, thanks for everything, but it's way after five now. If you don't leave shortly, you'll hit terrible traffic.'

She checked her watch. 'You're sure, Miss Skye?'

'Absolutely.'

Betty's movements were agonisingly slow as she untied her apron and then tucked it away neatly in a kitchen drawer. Inside my head, I was screaming at her to hurry up. I steered her out of the kitchen and down the hallway, and ran straight into Duncan.

'What's wrong?' he asked, folding me into his arms. 'You don't look well at all.'

'I'm okay. Just tired.' I couldn't bear to be in the same room as him, to share the same air. Everything about him repelled me now. But I had to keep things as normal as possible.

'The DCJ finally filed the order, so Jack's pushing for a hearing tomorrow. Worst case it will be Monday. So not long now.'

'What's the medical update?'

'No material change, I'm afraid. Her vitals are stable but she's still on the ventilator and heavily sedated.' His eyes skimmed over me. 'Perhaps I should call Doctor Friel. You're so pale.'

'I think everything's catching up with me. I just need to lie down.'

'Good idea, babe. Let me show Betty out, and then I'll come and check on you.'

●

I lay in silence in Tilly's bed for hours, my mind cycling through the options. If Duncan had poisoned Tilly, then I couldn't allow him anywhere near her. Perhaps the DCJ's care order had been a blessing after all because it had kept him away from her. And if he harmed me, then Tilly would be all alone with him. That couldn't happen. A sharp pain lodged itself like a splinter behind my eyes. What the hell was I going to do?

FOURTEEN

MEI

Fitzroy's, the corner pub, was buzzing with weary tourists and horny office workers. The air stank of damp wool and fryer oil, and the jukebox was wailing Cold Chisel. I didn't recognise anyone.

Abe ordered our drinks at the bar, while I jostled my way through the crowd to secure a booth down the back. The table was ringed with condensation and discarded pistachio shells from the last patrons. Beside me, a few blokes were demolishing a bowl of potato skins and debating the footy, and in the next booth over, a young couple in matching blue parkas was arguing in rapid Italian.

I googled 'Abe Cohen New York Times'. Abraham Cohen was listed on the paper's website as a senior reporter, and the accompanying photo matched the guy at the bar. Not a loony true crime sleuth then.

Abe slid into the booth, bearing a vodka for himself and a Coke Zero for me.

'So, what's this information you have about the Turner case?' I asked.

He rattled the ice around his glass, exposing blue ink stains on his middle finger and along the base of his palm. An old-school journo. 'How much do you know about Campbell Turner?'

'I know that he died of a cardiac arrest in January, so he couldn't have poisoned Tilly and Nina Turner, which is the focus of our investigation. Am I wasting my time here?' I'd been foolish – this guy was just yanking my chain.

'Listen. We might be able to help each other. I know you've got a suspect in custody – I'm guessing a girlfriend or one of the hired help – but there's still time.'

'Still time for what?'

'To get the Turners. That family's rotten to the core.'

He had my attention. 'Can you elaborate?'

'Before I joined the *Times*, I was at the *Washington Post*. I've been investigating Campbell Turner for years.'

'Okay.'

'So, I'm guessing you know the official story – as in, Campbell Turner made his money in New York in the late eighties as an FX trader, before he built up Turner Corp's luxury goods empire.'

'Sure. I'm not across the specific details but that's pretty much what I've heard.'

'No one exactly knows how Campbell made his money in New York. There are rumours, and it certainly didn't all come from his trading career. That's another story. But I can tell you that the bulk of the family's current wealth is dirty money.'

'Dirty how?' I took a gulp of my soft drink.

'Have you heard of the Bratva?'

I shook my head.

'It's a chapter of the Russian mafia that spread into Eastern Europe after the fall of the Soviet Union. Since then, it's become one of the major players globally in illicit arms trading and human trafficking – mainly of young girls. Back in the early nineties, Turner started his buying spree with a Swiss jewellery brand and a German car manufacturer, and then added couture labels and an auction house dealing in fine art and antiquities. There was a huge buzz about this charming Australian financier who was taking the global luxury goods market by storm, so my editor had me write an in-depth profile on him. That's when I first heard about his connections.'

'To the Bratva?'

'Yes. A reliable source of mine in Washington told me that Turner was a fixer for them. Wouldn't go on the record, but he was adamant, so I dug into it. Long story short, he was right.'

Abe explained that Campbell Turner had used his businesses to launder hundreds of millions, possibly billions, of dollars for the Bratva over the past two decades. His acquisitions masked his criminal activities because trading luxury goods was an ideal way to shift large sums across territorial borders, and he could use his networks to recharacterise the proceeds as legitimate investments. Abe was convinced he also had protectors in the US Senate. They were massive allegations.

'Look, Abe,' I said, when he'd finished his spiel, 'I wish I could help you, but this stuff is way outside my jurisdiction. I'm with the state police here in New South Wales. You need to take this to our feds.'

'I have – but they won't touch it until they have legitimate grounds to investigate.'

They were gun-shy, Abe explained, because when the European authorities had launched an inquiry into Turner Corp, Campbell had successfully sued them for unlawful search, costing millions in damages and plenty of senior careers. 'I have a source who swears he paid off the judge in that trial.'

'What do you expect me to do about this?'

Abe leaned across the table and lowered his voice. 'Based on what I've heard about the Turner case, the family members must all be under suspicion for the death of Nina Turner and the poisoning of that little girl. So, for the first time ever, there's a bona fide legal reason – your homicide investigation – to search the Turners' homes and the corporation's records. I'm no expert in Australian law, but I do know that if you're searching under a valid criminal warrant in relation to Nina Turner's death, and you uncover evidence that implicates the Turners in other crimes, then that evidence will be admissible in the other trials. And I guarantee you'll find plenty of dirt.'

That made sense. Turner Corp's Sydney office was the global HQ, and Campbell's main residence and his sons' homes were all in New South Wales. If there was dirt to be found, at least some of it would be local. 'So you want us to find you a smoking gun?'

Abe nodded. 'Yes.'

I studied his face – the high, creased forehead, the bright eyes, the determined set of his jaw. I glimpsed the earnest cub reporter he'd once been.

'Why do you care so much?' I asked.

'What kind of a question is that?'

'Well, Campbell Turner's dead already, so you can't hold him to account. What's this really about? Your ego?'

Abe's face hardened and he set his glass down. 'Sure, Campbell's dead, but his sons are still running that business, and they're as guilty as he is. As long as the Turners keep washing dirty money, paedophiles will get away with trafficking little children, and corrupt regimes will keep murdering civilians. You might be okay with that, but I'm sure as hell not.'

Abe's impassioned plea seemed sincere, but of course the guy had his own agenda – a sensational story that would garner clicks, and perhaps a shot at a Pulitzer. Why should I put myself at risk? There were strict protocols that governed my interaction with reporters, and he was asking me to breach them.

'Abe, at the start of this conversation, you said we could help each other. How does any of this help me?'

'You don't really believe that the woman you have in custody is responsible for murdering Nina Turner, do you?'

I shrugged.

'I'm helping you to do your job properly, Detective.'

'Look, even if I wanted to take this further, my boss has zero appetite to investigate the Turners. The suspect in custody will be formally charged tonight, no matter what I say.'

Abe threw up his hands. 'This is the shit I'm talking about. The Turners always slip the noose. Someone else always takes the fall.' He sighed. 'We can't let them get away with it anymore. A woman is dead. God knows how many children have been abducted and hawked off to paedophile rings. The Turners are enabling it. What if it were your daughter?'

How about a little sister? God forbid that Grace had met that fate. Abe was right. I had to do something.

'Okay.'

'Okay, you'll help?'

'Yes.'

'Do I have your word?'

'Hi, Mei.'

I turned to see Bonnie Chambers smiling at me.

Shit. This was bad. Bonnie was a senior reporter for the *Sydney Morning Herald* and had been Wilson's nemesis since her unflattering exposé of our team's handling of the Livvy Tweedsmuir case. She resembled a Shih Tzu, with her petite figure, cutesy light-brown bob and button eyes, but the woman had the soul of a honey badger. 'Are you going to slide over?' she asked.

The nerve of her. Maybe she'd recognised Abe and had come to sniff out a story.

'It's not a good time,' I said.

Bonnie scrunched up her face at Abe. 'You didn't tell her?'

'Tell me what?' I asked.

'Bonnie and I are working on this story together,' Abe said. 'I invited her to join us. I take it you know each other?'

Bonnie smirked. 'We certainly do. Mei, maybe you didn't hear? I'm the new Sydney correspondent for the *New York Times*.'

This was a disaster. No one in the office knew Abe, so it was low-risk for me to be speaking to him. On the other hand, Wilson would go apeshit if he thought I was colluding with Bonnie Chambers. He'd rip me off the case immediately.

'Bonnie, you know I can't talk to you about this. Abe, this was a mistake. I have to go.'

•

Outside Fitzroy's, black umbrellas unfurled along George Street like a colony of bats, and the wet pavement glittered orange under the streetlamps. I hunched my shoulders against the sheeting rain and phoned Macca on my way to the car park.

'I hear you had a run-in with Wilson,' he said when he picked up. Jayden was whining in the background.

'Yeah, well, he was being a dick. He completely dismissed Cody White's statement. He's just not interested in investigating the Turners. It actually makes me wonder . . .'

'Wonder what?'

'If Wilson's protecting them.'

'Jeez. That's a pretty serious accusation, O'Connor.'

'I know, but why else would he be so resistant?'

'Because he genuinely believes Tamara is guilty.'

I heard the squeak of a bathtub and the sound of sloshing water through the receiver.

'Good boy, Jayden,' Macca cooed.

'Anyway,' I continued, 'I've just been speaking to a journalist from the *New York Times*.' It was best not to mention Bonnie Chambers. 'He's been researching Campbell Turner for years and made some very serious allegations. If he's right, it may shed light on alternative motives for the poisonings. I'll come over now and take you through it.'

I'd reached the car park stairwell, which was rancid with stale urine. I checked over my shoulder to make sure no one was following me.

'It's not a good time. I need to get Jayden down to bed. Saskia's not feeling well.'

'It won't take long. It's important.'

'O'Connor . . .'

'Yes?'

'Wilson's made it very clear that it's time to move on. Tamara's been charged.'

'Weren't you listening to what I just told you?'

'Look, I know you're upset that you weren't there when we arrested Tamara, and you're pissed Wilson didn't acknowledge you at the press conference, but—'

My skin prickled. 'Macca, I don't give a shit about that, and you know it. I don't believe Tamara is responsible. You don't either. We need to find out who is. Are you in or not?'

There was a long silence at the end of the line. 'O'Connor, you know we have the new baby coming soon, and Saskia's already started her maternity leave.'

'So, you're out then?'

'I need this job.'

'I don't believe this.'

'I knew you wouldn't understand.'

'What does that mean, Macca?'

'Just that it's different for you.'

'Different in what way?'

'It's easier. You can afford to take more risks.'

'Because?'

He paused for a moment. 'Because you don't have a family.'

His words cut like spears. 'You know what, Macca? You can go to hell.'

FIFTEEN

SKYE

I feigned sleep while Duncan showered and then clattered around the bedroom, opening and closing the armoire and tugging out drawers while he dressed. When he leaned in to kiss my cheek, I moderated my breathing and tried to keep my eyelids from fluttering. I was counting down the seconds until I could get back to the workshop. I hadn't dared attempt it while Duncan was in the house.

Overnight, I'd begun to formulate a plan. I had to stop Duncan getting access to Tilly when the DCJ order was lifted. To do that, I had to share the contents of the filing case with the detectives. But how? I was certain he had me under surveillance. Besides, I wasn't convinced that I *wanted* to pass everything over. It was feasible that Duncan had contacts in the police, given his family's network of connections, and if the documents and the photographs went missing, it would simply be my word against his. The word of a woman who'd been committed to psychiatric care. A woman with no family of her own to vouch for her. I wouldn't stand a chance. I needed an insurance policy, so the smart thing would be to photograph everything with my burner phone and share the electronic versions with officialdom at first. That way I could keep the originals secure until I was certain that the police were genuinely investigating him, instead of whitewashing the whole process.

●

It wasn't until Duncan's car tyres scuffed the driveway that I rose from bed. I went straight to the downstairs cameras to check the gates had closed behind him and that I was alone.

Everything had to seem as normal as I could manage in case Duncan was watching me remotely. First, I fed Bo his breakfast. I left my mobile in its usual spot on the counter, beside the fruit bowl, and switched on the kettle. While it was boiling, I returned upstairs to our bedroom ensuite and retrieved my new burner phone from inside the box of Tampax. It still had some pre-loaded battery charge. I slipped the phone into the pocket of my robe before returning to the inevitable surveillance of the bedroom and kitchen. The entire time, I had an out-of-body sensation, watching myself perform these paranoid, irrational acts, and yet – as ridiculous as I knew my behaviour was – my gut told me I had no other choice. Bo shadowed me with doleful eyes, in tacit agreement.

This time, when I stepped over the threshold into Duncan's workshop, the soles of my feet burned with the guilt of my transgression. The space was as spotless and orderly as it had been the previous afternoon, with no sign of any cameras, but that didn't mean they weren't concealed in the light fixtures or among his tools, recording my movements. Still, I had to take the risk.

I unlatched the end locker and opened the door to retrieve the filing case – but there was a black void on the shelf where I'd stowed it. With rising panic, I elbowed the hunting coats aside and groped into the darkness until my hand grazed the back wall. It was gone.

The earth pitched and slid away. Desperate, I tried the next locker, and then the next, in case I was misremembering where I'd left the case, until they were all gaping open like slack mouths. Still nothing. Duncan had taken it. Not only had I lost my evidence, but I'd left the filing case unlocked, so he would soon discover – if he hadn't already – that I had opened it and seen the contents. And then what would happen? How much time did I have?

A disturbance in the hallway set Bo barking. I realised belatedly that it was the gate buzzer. The security camera showed my friend Vicky's anxious face peering into the screen from the driver's seat of her Discovery. Then another face loomed towards the gate intercom's screen from the passenger seat – another friend, Bridget.

'Skye, honey, we just want to check in on you,' came Bridget's voice through the speaker. 'We're so worried about you. Please let us in.'

Duncan had sent them to check on me, of course. I had to escape. I left the intercom ringing and stumbled out to the back garden. My garden studio was my usual refuge, but Duncan would expect me to head there and would surely have had it wired with cameras. I scrambled through the hedgerows until I reached the furthest terrace, where there was the least chance of being monitored. Today, the harbour was dark silver and in low relief, like beaten metal, and clouds gusted across the sky, obscuring the sun. In only the thin fabric of my robe, I began shivering uncontrollably and braced myself against the damp bark of a copper beech while I keyed Detective O'Connor's number into the burner phone's keypad.

She answered on the third ring. 'Detective O'Connor.' Her tone was impatient.

'It's Skye Turner.'

There was a pause, then a softening. 'How can I help you, Mrs Turner?'

When I tried to explain, the words came out all sticky and broken. The more I tried to correct course, the more incoherent my story became. A deep sob sharpened in my chest. What if the detective didn't believe me? What if she dismissed me as crazy too? She was my only hope.

There was rustling at the other end of the phone and the faint drone of other voices before Detective O'Connor spoke again. 'Whose phone are you calling from?'

As steadily as I could manage, I told her about my new prepaid mobile, about the documents in the workshop (I couldn't bring myself to mention the photographs yet), about Duncan's secret meetings at the warehouse in Hale Street, and about the vehicles that had been following me. Detective O'Connor asked me to come into the station so she could take a statement, but I explained that Duncan was having me watched and followed. That I was worried about him having access to Tilly once the DCJ order was lifted. And then the phone battery died.

When I returned to the house, Bridget and Vicky were scouting around the outside. They had their backs to me, their faces pressed against the glass panes of the bifold doors. They must have sensed me approaching, because they both swivelled around at the same time, clasping their hands to their mouths in horror at the sight of me.

'My God, Skye,' Bridget managed.

'It's freezing out here. What on earth are you doing?' Vicky asked. The look she exchanged with Bridget was so full of concern that I checked my reflection in the glass doors and saw myself as they did – wild hair, in a flimsy white robe, rising out of the garden like a ghoul.

'How did you get through the gates?' I asked.

Bridget glanced at Vicky then back at me. 'Duncan gave us the code, honey.' She spoke in a treacly tone, as if I were a child. 'Let's get you inside. Jesus, you're ice-cold.'

They wrapped tentacles around my waist and shoulders, and steered me back towards the house. I feared they would notice the burner phone bulging in my pocket and report it back to Duncan, so to distract them I asked for a blanket. The tactic worked. Once we stepped inside, they swaddled me and forced me onto the sofa.

'We've been so worried about you,' Vicky said. 'You haven't replied to any of our texts or calls, and your voice mailbox is full.'

Bridget shot her a warning look. 'Not that we *expect* you to respond. The last thing we want to do is pressure you. It's just . . .' She trailed off, then recovered. 'It's just that we want to make sure you're okay – we love you, you know. We want to be here for you. You can't do this alone.'

For the next hour they fussed over me, making tea I didn't drink and filling the silence with a mixture of awkward reassurance and pointless observations ('It looks like you're running low on almond milk.' 'Can we make you something for lunch?' 'This weather is so vile, but the forecast for tomorrow looks good.') They were edging around the only subject that mattered – Tilly's prognosis – terrified to initiate a real conversation. I couldn't bring myself to utter more than a word or two in response.

Bridget and Vicky must have sent Duncan an SOS, because he arrived home early.

'I just spoke to Tilly's lead doctor,' he said. 'They've taken her off the ventilator.'

'What does that mean?' I asked.

'She's breathing on her own, and the swelling around her brain has subsided, so they're weaning her off the sedatives.'

Hope fluttered in my chest.

'Well, that's good news, isn't it,' said Bridget.

'The anaesthesiologist is optimistic she'll regain consciousness in the coming days as the brain synapses re-establish,' Duncan continued, 'but she was very clear that there's no guarantee that will happen. Many patients who've experienced a prolonged period of intubation and heavy sedation don't make it.'

The plummeting sensation returned. I couldn't just sit here in this huge house, waiting, waiting, waiting. I had to get away from Duncan. I had to find a way to be with my daughter.

SIXTEEN

MEI

FRIDAY

When the unknown number flashed up on my phone, I was en route to Macca's cubicle to have it out with him. During the night, I'd mentally replayed our phone conversation until I was so incensed that I'd had to knock back a couple of Mum's Temazepam to fall asleep. I'd bent over backwards to indulge his desire to be father of the fucking year to pacify Saskia, yet he had given zero consideration to my situation with Mum. That was what made parents like him so insufferable – they constantly bemoaned their sleep deprivation, the cost of nappies and formula, their children's ailments and the interruption of their precious routines, without once contemplating the equivalent burdens borne by their childless peers with infirm parents: also sleeplessness, financial ruin, persistent worry and thankless servitude.

I'd answered the phone call half-heartedly, still feeling a little drowsy, and it took me a while to register Skye Turner's tremulous voice at the other end. She sounded frantic, claiming that her husband had her under surveillance, and she gave an incoherent account of secret documents and meetings. I couldn't determine whether she was referring to a potential cover-up of the poisonings, or the Bratva connections Abe Cohen had alleged, or something else entirely. She was worried about Tilly's safety, and insisted that she couldn't come into the office and that I must not come to her, so I did my best to rein in the specifics. By the end of the call, I'd managed to extract two pieces of verifiable information: the licence plate number of a vehicle owned by a security company that she believed had transported Duncan Turner to a secret location the day after Tilly was admitted to hospital, and an approximate location of where the meeting had taken place. At least it was a start. She promised to call me again soon.

I ran the plate first. The database spat back a Ram Laramie 3500 which matched Skye's description of the black ute. It was registered in New South Wales to a company called HEI Services Pty Limited. A search of that entity on the government's business registers led me on a merry dance through an opaque and multilayered structure of trusts, partnerships and foreign companies, all using professional services firms as fronts for their operations. This was no ordinary security company.

There was only one individual associated with HEI Services Pty Limited and its holding company – an Adrian Yanus – but there was no further record of him in any police databases. According to the Companies Register, the resident address for Adrian Yanus was an apartment in Rouse Hill, but further inquiries revealed the apartment building had been abandoned by its developers pre-completion during the pandemic. Another dead end.

Next, I searched the property file of the address of the warehouse that Skye alleged her husband had visited in the HEI Services ute. The Hale Street property was owned by a trust, so I tracked its shell trustee company up the corporate chain until I arrived at its holding company – also HEI Services Pty Limited. Bingo.

It was time to call in a favour from Cyrus, my contact in the intelligence unit at the Australian Federal Police. Cyrus was also Yvette's ex-boyfriend. I'd always found them a bizarre match – Yvette was supermodel tall and loved hardcore house, while Cyrus was a diminutive blond of German origin who favoured camel-toned chinos with suspenders and belonged to an a cappella group. They had been the oddest couple, but whenever Yvette hit the single malts, she'd rabbit on about his sexual agility, sharing all the grisly details. Consequently, whenever I had to deal with Cyrus at work, I was distracted by vivid mental imagery, despite my best efforts to block it. I knew that the only reason he helped me out was in exchange for scraps of information about Yvette. He still had a thing for her, two years after they'd split for indeterminate reasons.

Cyrus sounded irritated when he picked up but absorbed my download and promised to phone me back. As I was ending the call, I spotted Macca sauntering out of Wilson's office, followed by the NSW Police Commissioner. The Commissioner was saying something now, and patting Macca's shoulder, which caused Macca's ruddy face to contort into a goofy smile. By this point, Wilson had joined them and the smug triumvirate was guffawing. Wilson and Macca's faces simultaneously dropped when they clocked me approaching. Wilson edged closer to the Commissioner and squared his shoulders to create a physical barrier.

I greeted the Commissioner then turned to Wilson. 'Sir, do you have a minute?'

He glared at me. 'Detective, I'll let you know when I'm available.'

'It's urgent, sir.'

The Commissioner raised a comical eyebrow at Wilson. 'I see the fun police have arrived. My cue to leave.' He gave Macca a final pat on the shoulder on his way to the elevator – 'Keep up the good work, DS McKenzie' – and Macca glowed while the world drained of justice.

Wilson turned to me, his face thunderous. 'Go on then, O'Connor.'

'Skye Turner just called me. She's found some new evidence.'

'Of the poisoning?' asked Wilson.

'Not of the poisoning, no. But she's found a cache of hidden documents and Duncan Turner has been behaving suspiciously. He secretly met with a security firm the day after Nina's death, when their daughter was in the PICU, and she believes he has her under surveillance.'

'So, the guy wanted to beef up security. Sounds entirely logical. Perhaps Mrs Turner is a little paranoid? She's been under a huge amount of stress, and we all know that she has some mental health issues.'

'Sir, with respect, you don't understand.'

'Has Duncan Turner threatened his wife?'

'Not as such, no, but—'

He cut me off again. 'And has Skye Turner made a formal complaint against her husband?'

'No. Well, not yet. But – look, can we speak privately, sir?'

Wilson sucked in his cheeks to signal his exasperation. 'I thought I'd been clear, O'Connor. The Turner case has been resolved. Althea will be in touch when she needs your input into the legal documentation. Until then, I am ordering you to move on. We have a huge backlog of other cases. Now, excuse me. I have a meeting upstairs.'

Before I could respond, Wilson had muscled past me to the elevator, and I was captured by two colleagues wanting advice on a gang-related homicide that had come in overnight. By the time I had freed myself and made it over to Macca's cubicle, he'd disappeared from the floor. Shaniah told me he'd been assigned to a domestic shooting in Blackett. It was news to me that Macca was being assigned to cases without my supervision. Yet again, I was being penalised for doing the right thing – and Macca was being rewarded for his cowardice.

True to his word, Cyrus phoned back before lunchtime; he was nothing if not Teutonically efficient. 'I have the information. You ready?'

I scrambled back to my cubicle to take notes as he spoke.

'Adrian Yanus is ex-Mossad. In 2016, he befriended a British intelligence officer called James Chapman in Iraq. A year later, they quit their jobs and established Hawk Eye Intelligence, which now has offices in Tel Aviv, New York and Singapore. Hawk Eye provides corporate intelligence services.'

'What exactly does that mean – corporate intelligence services?'

'Officially, things like assisting multinationals with litigation research, investigating employee fraud, undertaking due diligence for potential acquisitions – you get the idea. Hawk Eye has some legitimate operations, but they also serve some bad actors, and their methods can be quite unsavoury.'

'Unsavoury how?'

'They rake through executives' garbage, stalk sexual assault complainants to deter them from testifying, impersonate law enforcement officers. Also wiretaps and hacking. That's probably not the worst of it.'

'That's not unsavoury – that's illegal. How do they get away with it?'

'Well, they're experts. They know how to operate under the radar, and they have a vast network of assets to protect them.'

'So, is Adrian Yanus here in Sydney?'

'No. As far as we're aware, neither he nor his co-founder James Chapman have ever set foot on Australian soil. However, they have recruited a local operative – a former Wagner mercenary. I need to do some more digging to get the details.'

'Thanks, Cyrus. I know you're busy, but this is urgent.'

If I could prove that Duncan Turner had engaged Hawk Eye, this could indicate that the poisonings were part of a broader conspiracy. It was feasible that both victims had stumbled across information about the family's activities.

There was a pause. 'So, how's Yvette?' he asked.

I had expected this question. Cyrus would withhold further information about Hawk Eye and Adrian Yanus's connections to Duncan Turner until I'd furnished a nugget of information about my friend. I didn't feel great about it, so I kept it to the bare minimum. 'Yvette?' I said casually. 'She's great.'

'She seeing anyone?'

I'd learned from experience that my response had to be non-threatening yet also substantial enough for him to ruminate on for a few days. It was a delicate balance. I'd never really gotten to the bottom of why Cyrus and Yvette had split up, and there remained a mutual fascination between them. I loathed being piggy-in-the-middle.

'She's been on a few dates recently,' I said, milking the pause before admitting, 'But there's no one serious.'

'What happened to the doctor?'

'Daniel? He moved to Victoria in March. New rotation.'

'Oh, I see.'

He was satisfied. I didn't mention that Yvette and Daniel, a handsome orthopaedic surgeon, still had energetic sex whenever they met up.

'So when do you think you'll have something more for me?' I asked.

'By close of business today, I hope.'

'Thanks. Appreciate it.'

•

The afternoon dragged. I struggled to concentrate on the raft of new cases urgently requiring my attention. Had I been foolish to take Skye Turner's information at face value? I had no actual proof that anything she'd told me connecting Duncan Turner to Hawk Eye was true. I hadn't seen the security footage that showed Duncan stepping into the black ute. She could have been leading me into a trap, or intentionally misleading me to protect herself. It was essential to take possession of the GPS tracker watch and the home security camera footage that Skye had referred to on the phone so that I could verify their authenticity. Until then, there was no way that I could take her revelations to Wilson without him laughing me out of his office.

There was also another angle to explore. Someone had to have entered and exited Tamara Baruch's apartment prior to the police search to plant the evidence and doctor her laptop. I located her home address on the digital case file – a Surry

Hills apartment block called The Mirage. A quick online search showed that her building was managed by Porters, a professional property management firm that I'd dealt with on previous investigations. I knew it was their company policy to install CCTV at the entrances and exits of the buildings they managed as part of their security function. Even better, I'd previously dealt with the bloke who ran Porters' security division – a retired cop called Rex Howard who'd taken a shine to me because I reminded him of his daughter. It wouldn't be too hard to get hold of the footage quickly, and Rex wouldn't insist on the usual documentation that would otherwise alert Wilson to my inquiry. I left a phone message for Rex and followed it up with an email. He usually turned my requests around within twenty-four hours.

I fired off the email and flushed with imminent triumph. It would be so satisfying to see Wilson and Macca's faces when I served all my evidence to them on a platter. For a moment, I imagined their humiliation and allowed myself to wallow in the prospect of their apology. I made an imaginary speech at an imaginary briefing of my peers, explaining how important it was to persevere in the quest for the truth and not take short cuts. Of course, when the time came, I would be humble.

At five o'clock on the dot, the floor began to hum with the cheery banter that heralded the weekend. A few of the youngsters were trying to shepherd everyone down to the pub. I'd made a decent dent in my to-do list by then and was sorely tempted by the prospect of a drink. But I was determined to return to Rebecca White's place before I knocked off. I had to find out what she knew about Duncan Turner.

It was almost dark by the time I rolled into Rebecca's driveway. Rain was lashing the cabbage trees and thundering out of the gutter in front of the house. The interior lights were on, but Rebecca's Datsun was gone, and parked in its place was a tomato-red Toyota coupé.

I spread my jacket over my head and dashed up the path onto the front porch. A pit bull rushed at the slanting fence on the boundary line, barking with such ferocity that I envisioned it stripping the flesh from my bones on the water-logged lawn before I reached the buzzer. There were brisk footsteps before a man in his late twenties with a gold tiepin and shiny suit opened the door. He had a furious red pimple on his chin and looked annoyed. I wondered if he was Rebecca's flatmate; I didn't pick him for her toyboy.

The man narrowed his eyes. 'Yes?'

'Is Rebecca in?'

'No. She's not in.'

'Will she be long?'

'Ms White isn't out. She's gone.' He brushed the palm of his hand over his crisp gelled hair. 'I'm the letting agent.'

Shit. 'When did she give notice?'

'She didn't. Dropped the key off yesterday, no explanation. The lease doesn't expire for another two months.'

'Did she leave a forwarding address?'

He scowled. 'What do you think? She sure as hell won't be getting her bond back.'

It couldn't be a coincidence that Rebecca had fled just after our visit. What was she so afraid of?

I dialled Cody White on my way out of Azalea Street – surely he would know where she'd gone. When he didn't answer, I left a voicemail asking him to call me urgently. If only bloody Macca had done what I'd asked and put Rebecca's house under surveillance, we would have intercepted her before she disappeared.

On the route home, my phone bleated with messages. The first one was a voicemail from some minion in the Porters security office advising me that Rex was away on a cruise and that she wouldn't process my request until I'd provided a sworn statement justifying why the footage was required. For fuck's sake. That would require me to register the statement on the case file, which would alert Wilson.

I'd hoped the other messages were from Cyrus or Skye, but when I glanced at my phone screen at the traffic lights, it turned out to be the WhatsApp thread for Lena's hens' party. In the fog of the past days, I'd forgotten it was tonight. Lena's two younger sisters (also her bridesmaids), Tania and Kylie, had organised it, so it was bound to be a cringe-fest of screeching women tottering through Darling Harbour swinging handbags while Lena performed smutty dares in a sparkly sash and tiara. It was the absolute last thing on earth I could tolerate tonight, but I had no choice. Lena was one of my oldest friends, and despite having almost nothing in common these days, our friendship had endured because of our shared history. In Year 8, we'd snuck communion wine and invented unkind nicknames for the cruellest nuns. I'd held Lena's hair back when she puked tequila shots into her mother's rose garden on her fifteenth birthday. She'd accompanied me to the Family Planning clinic for the morning-after pill when Billy Barlow's condom split after the St Bede's formal. At a minimum, I had to show my face at the hotel drinks. I would head home before they hit the bars.

•

Tania and Kylie had booked a deluxe suite at the Novotel, which they'd loaded with bottles of cheap sparkling rosé and inflatable penises. The room stank of booze and floral perfume. There was a balcony with a harbour view, but it was too wet outside to use it, so about forty of us were crammed around the bedroom furniture like livestock at a freezing works, while Taylor Swift blasted from the speakers. Lena was already half-cut, trussed up in an AliExpress bachelorette costume and gyrating against Kylie's backside. When Tania spotted me, she bailed me up in the nook between the wardrobe and the minibar.

'I've got something to confeth,' she slurred.

'What's up?'

'Vanetha's here. She'th on the other side of the room.' She opened her eyes wide, then burped a cloud of pink fizz into my face. 'You know: Vanetha, as in Nick and Vanetha? Lena wanted to tell you but she chickened out.'

Tania's blush dress was two sizes too small and matched with trotter-like blush heels. I was in no mood for Miss Piggy's sympathy.

'Vanessa and I were bound to bump into each other sooner or later,' I said charitably. Preferably later.

When Tania moved on, I tipped two tiny bottles of Absolut from the minibar into the dusty bar tumbler. Fucking Lena had invited fucking Vanessa to her fucking hens' do. What the fuck? Then I remembered that Lena's fiancé owned the physio clinic at Nick's gym. Vanessa worked for him. That's how Lena and Vanessa knew each other. Lena would have invited Vanessa weeks ago, before news of her affair with Nick came out. I'd have to suck it up. This was Lena's night, and I'd simply avoid Vanessa. But then again, Lena should have uninvited Vanessa as soon as she found out about Nick's affair. In her shoes, I wouldn't have thought twice. No matter how I looked at it, Lena was a disloyal cow.

With the vodka roaring down my oesophagus and into my empty stomach, I pushed through the crowd, chatting briefly with old schoolfriends and promising to return for a proper catch-up. Emboldened by the spirits, I decided I'd find Vanessa and catch her off guard. That way I'd have the upper hand.

I spotted her in the far corner of the suite. I had to admit she looked annoyingly radiant in a skin-tight blue dress. She was chatting to a mousy girl whom I recognised vaguely as Lena's cousin. Before I had a chance to address her, Vanessa pre-empted me.

'Mei,' she called out in a husky voice.

'Vanessa.' I straightened my spine.

'I hope this isn't too awkward for you – you know, me being here,' she added, as if it needed clarification.

The mousy cousin studied the swirls on the brown carpet.

'Not at all,' I replied, and was irritated that my voice came out louder than I'd intended. She was the one who should have felt awkward, but in the moment I couldn't formulate a sufficiently cutting reply.

Kylie, sensing an imminent catfight, came barrelling up with a bottle of pink Jacob's Creek. 'Top up, ladies?'

I shook my head, as did Vanessa. 'I'm not drinking,' she said. Then she smiled expansively at me and tapped her belly. 'You see, we're expecting.'

SEVENTEEN

SKYE

On Saturday morning, the rain finally stopped. When I drew back Tilly's curtains, the brash blue sky and sunlight that tumbled in felt like a violation. I'd slept overnight in Tilly's bedroom, both to feel closer to her and to escape from Duncan. When I woke, for a magical moment it was a routine school morning and I waited for Tilly to crawl into bed to wake me. But then shards of memory sliced through – tubes, alarms, flashing red lights, my baby's limp body – and I was slammed back to the ER.

A week had passed since Tilly had fallen ill, but I no longer experienced time as I had done before. The distance between me and Tilly felt at once interminably vast and also non-existent. Her bedroom was a palimpsest of her at every age. I saw the baby in her Moses basket, surrounded by nursery walls I'd hand-painted with woodland animals in my final trimester. I'd spent hours perfecting those murals, dreaming of soon meeting the little soul budding inside me. And I saw the toddler with a halo of dark curls, staggering around the room hurling her dolly and pushing her wagon over-stuffed with plush toys – a rabbit, a bear, an elephant, a cat and a mouse that was the most beloved of all. Eventually Mouse became Tilly's dearest, grubbiest companion. And then that Tilly was overlaid with the kindergartener, sitting on the wooden chair flipping through books while I corralled her wild curls into pigtails. And, finally, I saw the schoolgirl working industriously at her desk, which was cluttered with reams of coloured paper, stickers, pencils and felt tips. Last year, the woodland was superseded by pastel shapes that we'd painted together to Tilly's design.

It killed me that I was not at her side, but in this room she was present in every splotch on the carpet, in every scuff on the skirting boards, in every smudge on the windows. God, I missed her so much. I craved her presence with a ravenous hunger that could never be sated.

Tilly was my life. My purpose. There was no path ahead for me without her. And a dark, long-buried truth awoke. Hadn't I always known who had the greatest reason of everyone to hurt Tilly?

•

I found Duncan drinking coffee at the kitchen island. A slab of sunlight cut across him, and Bo was lolling at his feet. When he heard my footsteps, he raised his eyes and smiled. 'Did you get some sleep? I didn't want to disturb you.'

I stood there, motionless.

'Would you like tea?' he continued. 'I could poach you some eggs?'

Duncan rose and guided me onto a stool opposite him. I sat like an automaton. He set a saucepan on the hob and cracked eggs into white ramekins, then he added vinegar and salt to the water. He hummed softly as he worked.

'I have to make some work calls soon – all the media attention has unsettled some of our offshore partners, so I just need to reassure them the business is on track – but it will only take an hour or two, max. Then I'm free for the rest of the day so I can take care of you.' He was draining the eggs, trimming herbs, choosing cutlery, and my hatred for him in that moment was so intense that I thought I would combust. This was a farce. He didn't care about anyone but himself.

He served me the eggs I didn't want, and kissed my cheek.

'I'll be in my study if you need me.'

I waited until I heard his door close then fetched my burner phone from our ensuite. I messaged Detective O'Connor to say I had to meet her urgently.

She responded right away. *Where?*

I didn't want to risk heading into the police HQ – Duncan would be sure to have spies there who would tip him off – nor anywhere else in public where I might be recognised, and she couldn't come to Thornfield. I needed somewhere under the radar. Somewhere safe.

How about your place? I replied.

She messaged me her address. It was on the other side of the city, but only about a twenty-minute cab ride on the weekend. I replied that I would come right away, and dressed quickly in a t-shirt and leggings. I switched off the burner, in case its signal could be tracked, before sliding it into a small bag, along with a fistful of banknotes I'd stashed in my underwear drawer. Leaving my usual phone on my bedside table,

I snuck downstairs to the laundry. Bo shadowed me, watching intently, as if he could sense my plan.

'Good boy,' I said and gave him a cuddle. 'Be quiet when I leave, okay?'

I slipped out through the laundry door, on the far side of the house from Duncan's study, in case he was watching from the window. Hopefully, he would be too engrossed with his work calls to check the security cameras.

I kept close to the boundary and snuck around the back of the tennis court. When I was safely out of view of the house, I sprinted past the helipad and down the driveway. I pressed the button to open the pedestrian gate, but the red light blinked. I tried again, but it wouldn't budge. The release button for the vehicular gates wouldn't open either. Duncan's security guy must have put some kind of lock on them.

There was no other way out. The high boundary walls were reinforced with dense hedging, and the locked gates before me were an impenetrable screen of wrought iron with spiked finials running across the top. At any minute Duncan could discover me gone. This was my last chance. My only choice was to climb. I scanned the garden and driveway for anything I could use as a platform to gain height, to propel myself to the top of the gate, or for a hose or coil of rope to loop over the spikes, but there was nothing at all. It would take too much valuable time to return to the house in search of a stool or a ladder.

I had to find a way. The ledges on the gates' horizontal bars were too shallow for me to grip with my feet or my fingers, but the gates arched up to meet in the centre, so my best shot would be to climb up one of the vertical posts that secured the gates on either side at the lowest point of the curve.

The sun was intensifying, and sweat was erupting along my brow. I steadied my left foot on the hinge, at knee height, but my sneaker slipped and I lost my footing when I tried to raise my right leg. It was hopeless. I still wasn't anywhere near high enough to get traction. There were small narrow gaps above the hinges – the first at around my knee height, and the second just above my hip. I wrenched off my sneakers and hurled them over the top of the fence, then raised my leg and jammed the ball of my left foot into the lower gap in the iron. It hurt like hell, but I had enough stability to push up and tuck my right foot into the higher slit. From there, I bent my knees and sprang as high as I could with my arms outstretched, but my fingertips still only brushed the top rail. I kept at it, my face pressed tight against the gate, dragging myself up, using the tiny toeholds to get higher. My feet were aching and tender, but I couldn't give up. I was so close now. Finally, my hand gripped a spike, and I gathered enough momentum to hoist myself up.

The spikes tore the flesh of my right cheek and palm, and snagged on my t-shirt, grazing my stomach when I vaulted over, but I'd done it. I dropped down to the footpath, burning with adrenaline, and jammed my sneakers back onto my throbbing feet. My plan was to run the three blocks to the taxi rank outside the grocer. I couldn't risk using the burner phone or waiting for a cab to find me.

I flew past the weekend joggers and the strolling dog walkers. In the distance, a neighbour shouted my name, but I forged on until a cluster of shops appeared around the bend. An elderly lady with a grocery bag was approaching the lone cab in the rank, but she reared back when she saw me, her face appalled, and motioned for me to take it. It wasn't until I was inside the taxi that I realised my white t-shirt was blooming crimson, and blood was trickling down my face and hands. Only after I thrust a wad of crumpled bills at the driver did he agree to edge out into the road. I peered out the back window for any sign we were being followed.

My chest thumped as we drove west, skirting the city centre. Eventually, we reached a cul-de-sac lined with brutalist apartments and rows of brick walk-ups. The driver stopped outside a two-storey block of flats with a tidy garden out front, and burned off as soon as I closed the door.

Alone on the footpath, I had the sense I was being watched. There was no one around, except for a little girl of about Tilly's age with big spectacles and long dark hair. She was standing across the road holding a skipping rope. When I met her eyes, she smiled, as if to urge me on.

Was I really going to do this? Once I told the detective what I knew, there would be no turning back. Was I really going to take on the Turners?

EIGHTEEN

MEI

SATURDAY

I woke on Saturday morning with the remnants of a kebab mashed against my cheek and Laifu kneading my thighs. The tip of his tail was flicking back and forth like a metronome, in time to the throb of my brain inside my skull. Holy Mother of God. I rooted around for my phone and found it under a soggy kebab wrapper on the floor and out of battery. On my way to the kitchen to charge it, I had a flashback to dancing on a table in an Irish pub with Lena, and then to drunk texting Nick, and immediately flushed with regret.

Laifu streaked across the room to join me and butted his head against my calf until I topped up his biscuits. Mum had taped a note to the fridge to say she was feeling well so Sandy was taking her on an outing to the garden centre and then to the Saturday markets to make the most of the sunshine. I washed down one of Mum's Tramadol to settle my head.

There were no clean glasses, so I chugged water directly from the tap.

The kitchen was a disgrace. In fact, the whole flat was filthy. I had a sudden urge to Marie Kondo the whole place to temper the metaphysical shame of my hangover. I stacked the dishwasher, wiped down the bench and found a dusting cloth in a drawer. Then I set to work on the cupboards and blinds. The windowsill was a joyless mise en scène: a mushy cactus in terracotta; Dad's pewter stein, engraved with a shamrock, that held lint and a box of matches; and a chipped Virgin Mary ornament. At the end of the ledge was a silver photo frame embossed with *Memories* in a jaunty black font.

I picked up the frame and studied the faded photograph. I hadn't looked at it properly in a long time. It had been taken in the overgrown garden of my childhood home when the huge fuchsia rhododendron was in full bloom. I was squinting up at the camera in a yellow tie-dye pantsuit. I must have been about to turn five years old because my mother stood beside me with a tiny muslin-wrapped Grace in her arms. Mum was exquisite in a cornflower blue sundress, with dark, shining eyes and long black hair dripping over her shoulders. Dad towered beside her in a faded Nirvana t-shirt, his pale freckled face beaming, with one arm around Mum's waist and the other resting on my narrow shoulders. Mum and Dad had always seemed so solid and reassuring, but now I was struck by how young they were – both barely twenty-seven when that picture was taken. Six years younger than I was now.

You could see the hope on my immigrant parents' faces in that picture – hope for their children and for the future – and I was overwhelmed by sorrow. Dad's bones were resting in a churchyard in Parramatta. Who knew what had happened to Grace? And now Mum didn't have much time left. A year at best. Soon I would be the only one left of the four of us. As if that fact had only just occurred to me, all the possible paths that I'd ever imagined might lie ahead of me suddenly curled back on themselves like withered vines, until all I could envisage was myself, alone at the end of a blank cul-de-sac.

My phone shuddered back to life on the bench. I braced myself before examining it to see what drunken messages I'd sent during the course of the hens' night. A surprisingly coherent message to Wilson at 9.32 pm saying he should rethink his position on the Turner case in light of new information I'd received about the family. Then at 10.43 pm I'd texted Macca that he was a pathetic, pussy-whipped coward, followed by the black cat emoji and the hockey stick emoji (a whip?). Oh my God. He had read it immediately but had not replied.

I'd reserved my real vitriol for Nick. Between 11.15 pm and 3.03 am I'd sent him five text rants, the gist of which was that he had an unusually small penis. I felt an irrational hatred of Lena's sisters Tania and Kylie, and of Lena herself, for luring me into a situation where I had to face Vanessa, which, in turn, had compelled me to scull chilli margaritas at a Darling Harbour meat market. Then I remembered that Nick and Vanessa were having a baby, and whether it was that thought, or the memory of the margaritas, or the Tramadol burning my stomach lining, or all three, I heaved white foam into the kitchen sink.

I wiped my mouth with a tea towel to answer my ringing phone. It was Cyrus.

'Mei, sorry I didn't get back to you last night. I had another situation to deal with.'

'Has anything else come up?'

'Yes, as it happens, it has.'

I squeezed my eyes closed and clenched my fists – the closest I came to praying for a miracle.

'Hawk Eye's local operative is a man called Viktor Utkin. He's an Australian citizen, born in Victoria in 1972 to an Australian mother and a Russian father. He split his childhood between Melbourne and Moscow. We know he worked for Wagner Group in Crimea, and then in the Central African Republic.'

'Go on.'

'Some of the information is classified, but I can tell you that Utkin returned to Australia in 2020. We believe that's when he joined Hawk Eye and became their man on the ground here, although he regularly travels back to Russia.'

'Is there any connection between him and the Turner family?'

'Yes. I just spoke to an asset who confirmed Viktor Utkin met regularly with Sir Campbell Turner over the past three years. They were associates of some sort, although I don't have any more details yet.'

Holy shit. This was huge. A direct link to the old man.

'Cyrus, can you send me your file on Utkin?'

'No.'

'Well, how about a photograph of Utkin at least?'

'You know I can't. I shouldn't even be talking to you until you've sent me the authorisation paperwork.'

'Look, I understand, I really do. And I wouldn't be asking you if it wasn't essential. It's a delicate situation.' I hated begging. 'Please, Cyrus.'

He sighed expansively into the speaker. 'I'll send a picture. That's it. Don't forward it on. And promise me you'll submit the authorisation as soon as you can.'

'Okay. I promise.' I couldn't file the paperwork without Wilson signing off on it, and that wasn't going to happen, so what choice did I have? I had to do Wilson's job for him. It was just a little white lie.

Cyrus hung up. Shortly afterwards, he pinged through a WhatsApp with a photograph of a man taken with a long-lens camera. The man was striding across a busy road dressed in a fitted black t-shirt and skinny black jeans. He was white, middle-aged, bald and wiry. Mean-looking, with thin lips and a bloodless complexion, but not someone you'd take any notice of if you passed him in the street.

I saved the picture to my reel as a second WhatsApp message came through, but this time it wasn't from Cyrus – it was a message from Skye Turner. She wanted to meet urgently, and when I asked where she suggested she could come to my home. Figuring she must have something important to tell me, I messaged back with the address and then headed for the shower to wash off the previous night's excesses before she arrived.

NINETEEN

SKYE

Detective O'Connor's flat was on the second floor of a red-brick walk-up. I vaulted up the steps in case someone was following me, but the only person I could see was the little girl with long dark hair, skipping on the verge across the road. A huge black cat was collapsed on the mat outside number two. I knocked.

I didn't recognise Detective O'Connor when she opened the door. She looked like a teenager, in a black singlet and jeans, her eyes glazed and her damp hair scraped into a messy bun.

'What happened to you?' she said, pulling me inside. 'You're bleeding.'

'I'm fine,' I said, suddenly conscious of my stinging wounds.

She double-bolted the door and ushered me into a cramped open-plan kitchen and living area that smelled like boiled vegetables. 'Do you want to change your t-shirt?'

'It's okay. I'm fine. Really.'

She rinsed a cloth at the sink and dabbed at the congealed blood on my neck. Then she rolled a bunch of paper towels over the cuts on my hands to stem the flow.

'Take a seat while I get you some water.' Detective O'Connor motioned towards a settee. It wasn't until she handed me the glass that I realised I was shaking uncontrollably.

'Before we get started with your statement, look at this photograph.' She held up her mobile phone screen to me. 'Do you recognise this man?'

I only had to glance at the image. 'Yes. He's our security guy. Why?'

'You're certain?'

I peered closer. 'Yes, I'm sure that's him. Duncan's had him installing cameras around our property. He drives that ute I told you about on the phone. Who is he?'

Detective O'Connor pulled up a chair to sit opposite me. 'His name is Viktor Utkin. He's an operative for a commercial intelligence service called Hawk Eye. Have you heard either of those names before?'

'I don't think so.'

'Did you ever see him with your father-in-law, Sir Campbell?'

'No. But Duncan said he helped with security for his company, so... perhaps?'

'Viktor Utkin and Hawk Eye are also connected to the property that you believe your husband visited in Botany.' She paused for a moment. 'I believe your husband and Hawk Eye are implicated in criminal activity – although I'm not yet sure how this relates to the poisonings.'

I couldn't believe it. For days I'd been convinced I was losing my mind, and now here was the detective saying that my instincts had been right all along. But my relief almost instantly dissolved into panic as I tried to absorb the gravity of what she was telling me.

Detective O'Connor reached forward and laid her hand over mine. 'I know this is a lot to digest. Do you want to take a break?'

I shook my head. No. It was now or never.

'Are you happy for me to record this conversation?'

'Yes.'

She laid her mobile phone on the coffee table between us and opened her laptop. 'On the phone yesterday, you mentioned you had some concerns about your husband's behaviour. I'm going to ask you to take me through everything you have observed.'

I downloaded everything – Duncan's disappearances, his lies, and that I was convinced he'd bugged my mobile phone. I explained how I'd tracked his location with the GPS app on Tilly's smartwatch, and reluctantly handed it over to her in a zip-lock bag. She asked me about the cache of hidden documents I'd mentioned, with the dates and alpha-numerical codes – she agreed they sounded like offshore bank account numbers and passwords, or maybe codes for cryptocurrency wallets – and I told her how the file had vanished before I could copy the contents.

'Is there anything else?' she asked.

I nodded.

'Okay. Please go on.'

'In that file, there were also some photographs. Horrible photographs.'

The detective looked up from her screen. 'Skye, for the purposes of the recording can you please describe what you saw in the photographs?'

'Girls. They wouldn't have been any older than twelve or thirteen, maybe younger. Some were at Yallambee, others in what looked like hotels. They were—' My stomach was roiling. 'They were—' I had to tell her, but I couldn't.

'Were they pornographic images?'

'Yes,' I whispered.

'Skye, did you recognise any of the girls in the photographs?'

'No. I'd never seen them before. But—' I stalled.

'What is it?' she asked.

'My husband had written on the backs of the photographs. Dates and locations.'

'You're certain it was your husband's handwriting?'

I wiped my eyes with the heel of my hand.

She nodded gently, soberly. 'Skye, have you ever heard your husband or any other member of the Turner family mention an organisation called the Bratva?'

'No. What is it?'

'It's a powerful branch of the Russian mafia. They're involved in the sex trafficking of children. We have reason to believe the Turner family has a long association with the Bratva, both as a front for its money laundering and as a logistics partner in its trafficking operation.'

A kick of nausea. It was so much worse than I could ever have imagined. How had I brought a child into this viper's nest? I couldn't allow Duncan or any of his family anywhere near Tilly.

'Do you think . . .' Saying the words aloud risked it being true, but I had to ask. 'Do you think Duncan poisoned Tilly and Nina?'

The detective raised her eyes so that she was looking directly at me. 'It's possible, based on the circumstantial evidence, especially given what you've just recounted. But we have no obvious motive, so it's difficult to say at this stage.'

'What if I told you that there is a reason that Duncan might have done it?'

Her eyes widened. 'You need to tell me everything, from the beginning.'

And so I did.

•

The year 2016 had been challenging. Duncan was frustrated that Campbell had kept him as Turner Corp's treasurer and hadn't moved him into a broader commercial leadership role in the family business. It wasn't really the job that Duncan resented; it was that he was playing understudy to Jamie. Our relationship was also under pressure after a failed fifth round of IVF, and our mutual despair that we might never conceive was amplified when Nina gave birth to her and Jamie's third child – an adorable baby girl they named Arabella.

Campbell requested that we join him at Yallambee for the week after Christmas to attend his annual New Year's Eve party, along with four hundred of his most glamorous and influential friends. We'd attended Campbell's New Year's Eve parties for as long as we'd been dating, but that year I put my foot down. I was in no state of mind to tolerate Hugo's puerile antics, nor to be cooped up with Nina and Jamie and their perfect brood.

I wanted to join friends who were skiing in Aspen, but according to Duncan our presence at Yallambee was non-negotiable. He said Campbell would perceive our absence as a slight, and that would backfire on him. He needed to stay in Campbell's good books if he was ever going to be promoted out of finance. We could ski Aspen any time, Duncan said. He would hire out the Little Nell for the following week if I would just do him this one favour. He pleaded and pleaded until I relented.

We arrived at Yallambee on 28 December, but I didn't encounter Campbell until the afternoon of New Year's Eve, when I overheard him tearing strips off some poor staffer on an upstairs balcony. He'd been sequestered away in his private quarters in the main house attending to business while a battalion of workers dashed around preparing for the party.

When I returned to the guesthouse after a swim, Duncan announced that there had been a work crisis. He had to take the jet to Singapore immediately as Campbell's delegate for a meeting – something to do with securing credit lines for the East Asian businesses before an anticipated liquidity crisis. Surely it could wait a few days, I said, or perhaps I could go too? But Duncan said that it was urgent, and that it wouldn't be appropriate for me to join him. In that case, I told him, I wanted to return home to Sydney, but Campbell wouldn't hear of it. He insisted that I stay on at Yallambee for the party. There was a famous art dealer from Manhattan attending who was desperate to meet me, he said. And so, reluctantly, I stayed.

In the early evening, I watched on from the terrace with gathering resentment as the party warmed up on the lower lawn beside a vast fairy-lit marquee. The air was sweet with frangipani and sparkled with the chatter and laughter of the first arrivals. An orchestra played lively jazz while helicopters whirred through the pink sky, delivering guests from the flotilla of superyachts moored on the horizon. Waiters in crisp uniforms flitted about offering canapés and vintage champagne beneath a canopy of hand-painted paper lanterns. To any other observer, the scene would have been picture-perfect, but I was furious that Duncan had abandoned me. After everything I'd been through – the months of IVF injections and procedures, the late miscarriage, and the toll it had taken on my mind and my body – how could he have left me here alone, especially when he had known that I desperately didn't want to be there? He cared more about staying onside with his father and his pathetic rivalry with Jamie than me.

That year, the guest list was as impressive as ever. Football stars, pop princesses, supermodels and actors, including the Australian A-list, had flown in from Los Angeles, New York and London, along with the tech billionaires, economists and money men who would assemble again in a fortnight in Davos. Campbell presided over the swelling crowd like a shaman. In the early years, my proximity to such extreme affluence and celebrity had been electrifying, but now I was exhausted at the prospect of making small talk with so many strangers. There were only a few guests I knew well, and none whom I counted as friends. Even Ana hadn't made the cut this year. I was contemplating faking a migraine when Campbell spied me standing alone at the top of the steps and beckoned me down.

When I reached his group, he pressed a chilled flute of Cristal into my palm. 'Skye, darling, let me introduce you to some of my friends.'

No one could have guessed from his warm welcome that we hadn't exchanged a single word in the past three days, but I'd grown accustomed to his quicksilver changes. For his role as the consummate host, Campbell had filed away his gruff business persona and dialled up his full-octane charm.

That night, he was cosplaying a relaxed James Bond. His greying hair was artfully tousled, and his shirtsleeves had been rolled up to reveal deeply tanned forearms. I was expected to segue seamlessly into his act.

He introduced me to his circle as 'my ravishing daughter-in-law and an important Australian sculptor'.

A man with a huge diamond stud and a black goatee settled his eyes on my chest, while his wife – a skeletal woman with sad eyes – nuzzled a Pomeranian. It transpired that he was the famous Manhattan art dealer. He promised to contact me after the holidays and make my dreams come true.

Even after the sun slid away, the heat remained stifling, and I was conscious of damp patches forming under my breasts and at my nape. Hugo draped himself over me, his eyes dragging over my body. I twisted away from him, but he pulled me closer and slithered his hands down the back of my dress.

'Leave her alone.' It was Jamie over my shoulder. He pushed Hugo off me.

Hugo sneered at his brother. 'Well, if it isn't Saint Jamie of Vaucluse to the rescue.'

'Don't be a child, Hugo.'

'Don't be a cunt, Jamie.' He sauntered away into the crowd.

Jamie turned to me. 'Are you okay?'

I nodded.

'Can I get you anything?' he asked.

'I'm going to get some water.'

'Good idea. I'll keep you company.'

We cut our way to the nearest bar through the swathe of bodies. Jamie ordered two tall glasses with ice.

'How are you really holding up?' he asked. 'You're not yourself.'

I shrugged, and took a long pull of water. I could feel the prick of tears. He handed me a starched white square from his trouser pocket.

'You're the only man I know who still carries a handkerchief,' I said, and pressed it to my eyes.

He smiled. 'I'm old-fashioned.'

'You're a gentleman.'

'My brother's a fool.'

'He's just wasted.'

'I'm talking about Duncan.'

I was taken aback. 'Why do you say that?'

'After the year you've had, I can't believe he's left you here alone. I know it's not your scene.'

I didn't disagree, but I had to defend my husband. 'Duncan didn't have a choice. Campbell ordered him to go to Singapore.'

Jamie raised his eyebrows. 'Is that what he told you?'

'It's not true?'

Jamie sighed. 'Dunc's trying to prove himself to Dad. He wants more responsibility. I don't want to overstep, but' – he forked his fingers through his hair – 'well, he needs to get his priorities right.' His face was etched with concern. 'He shouldn't take you for granted.' He searched my face for a reaction. 'I'm sorry. I shouldn't have said that.'

'It's fine,' I said.

'It's just . . .' He paused.

'What?'

'If you were mine, I wouldn't have left you.'

He held my eye, and a flush climbed up my neck. I had to change the subject. 'Where's Nina tonight?' I asked.

'She's shattered,' he said. 'The twins, and now the new baby. It's a lot. She turned in early.'

What a lousy excuse, I thought, given she had a nanny and a night nurse in tow.

'So you have to soldier on alone too then?' I asked.

A waiter appeared at Jamie's elbow with a methuselah of Cristal. 'Sir?'

Jamie grinned at me. 'I think that water needs a champagne chaser.'

I nodded, and accepted a flute.

'To soldiering on together,' he said.

We raised our glasses.

•

By nightfall, the full moon hung huge and low in the sky, and golden light spilled onto the terraces and the lawns from every window of the residence. The champagne kept flowing, and soon my head was swimming. A DJ who'd touched down fresh from Ibiza hit the decks. Child acrobats and fire eaters arrived, and models in gold metallic body paint discreetly dispensed tiny parcels of coke and molly. When the sugar rush hit, beautiful girls with glistening flesh swayed alongside older men. Everything felt overripe and dangerous.

Shortly before midnight, the DJ announced a fireworks show. The pyrotechnics would be activated from a pontoon in the bay, so the party relocated to the top terrace for a better view. Instead of joining them, I drifted towards the water. A security guard tried to stop me at the perimeter, but I said I'd left my mobile phone on the beach in the afternoon. He let me pass. I stowed my sandals at the edge of the lawn and wandered along the sand towards the boathouse. The peals of laughter and pounding bass from the party grew distant.

Inside, the boathouse smelled of oiled teak and salt, and the timber was still warm underfoot from the afternoon sun. Moonlight poured through the dormer windows, and the only sound was the gentle thud of the jetboats and tenders butting against the dock in the black water.

I slumped into a deckchair and checked my phone. No word from Duncan. The fireworks cracked to muffled cheers down the bay. I was flooded with self-pity and with the shame of not belonging. Of never belonging. I fumbled through my purse for a lighter and a clumsily rolled spliff.

Then someone was opening the door. I turned as their silhouette moved towards me. I stood up slowly, somehow already knowing, already ready. His breath was hot on my neck, his hands firm around my waist. He peeled my dress over my shoulders. We didn't speak. It would have broken the spell. We collapsed into one another, as if there had been an inevitability to it that was too great to control. In that moment, I was free of worry and disappointment and failure. And there was something pure about it too, in the purging of my anger and grief.

Afterwards, we shared the joint in silence and made our separate ways back to the party. The next day, when Jamie came to my guesthouse to check on me, we agreed that it must never happen again.

I should have felt terrible about betraying Duncan and Nina. I didn't. What I felt was vindication. And when Duncan returned from Singapore a few days later, I shed that night like a dead skin, just as I'd done when I left my old life behind. I convinced myself it had never happened.

We kept our word. Jamie and I never spoke of our time together at Yallambee. Not even when I discovered in early February that I was finally pregnant. And not even after Tilly was born in late September. Duncan never suspected a thing. But now, I couldn't help wondering if somehow he had found out. If maybe Jamie had confessed.

If Duncan had known all along and had simply been biding his time.

TWENTY

MEI

SATURDAY

I hadn't seen Skye's bombshell coming. She sat on Mum's sofa with her elbows on her knees, her eyes fixed on the carpet as she spoke, braced for impact. She was oddly calm, which I recognised as both the resignation and relief of confession. I couldn't grant her the absolution she sought, but I'd sure as hell ensure Duncan Turner was held to account.

While Skye was speaking, I missed two call from Wilson, so I phoned him back right away.

'DSS O'Connor, we need to talk. Can you come into the office now?'

There was a hint of apology in his voice, and an urgent Saturday meeting could only mean one thing: Wilson had finally seen the light and wanted to investigate the Turners. I suspected Cyrus had given him a heads-up about Viktor Utkin as a courtesy.

'Of course, sir. Skye Turner's here at my flat, so she'll join us. There's a lot to catch you up on. I think we're getting close.'

'Wait – you're with Skye Turner now?' He sounded surprised – and impressed.

'Yes. I'll explain everything when we arrive. We're on our way.'

My headache eased instantly and my body flushed with relief. Skye's admission of her affair with Jamie Turner was a game changer for the investigation.

Before we left the flat, I responded to a text from Bonnie Chambers; she had been hounding me for an update on the investigation.

Gd news. DT had motive. Mtg Wilson shortly. Will get back 2 u this afternoon.

Bonnie responded immediately with a thumbs-up emoji.

•

The sunshine had made a boisterous return to Sydney, bouncing with alacrity off car fenders, bridge struts and the scoops of temples as Skye and I made our way into the city. The weather suited my newly buoyant mood. We passed joggers heading for the harbour, and shoppers swarming towards the Saturday markets. Mum had never adjusted to the splashy confidence of the sun here. She said it overwhelmed her senses, bleaching out sound and smell; so different from the tentative sunshine of her childhood village in Luanping. Today, the sandstone architecture was a Disney confection of honeycomb and caramel. It could fool you into believing that Australia was still the lucky country.

Before we were absorbed into Wilson's formal process, there was one more question I had to ask Skye. 'Do you have any idea where Cody's mother might be? She's moved out of her rental. I thought Cody might have mentioned something.'

Skye jerked her head to face me. 'Why? Do you think Rebecca's involved?'

'I think she knows something about your husband's past. It might help the investigation.'

She swivelled back to watch the road ahead. 'Why would she help?'

'I thought if you asked Cody, he might convince her to talk to us about what she knows. Why she left Duncan, why she disappeared.'

A moment passed. 'It's worth a try.'

I put a call through to Cody, and this time he picked up right away.

'Hi Cody, it's Detective Senior Sergeant O'Connor. I'm here with Skye Turner,' I said. 'You're not with Duncan, are you?'

'Huh? No. Why?'

I indicated to Skye that she should speak.

'Cody, I think it was Duncan,' Skye said, her voice wavering. 'I think he's the one that poisoned Tilly.'

'What? You don't mean that, do you?'

'I do.' She swallowed a sob, and I nodded at her to continue. 'There's a lot I need to tell you when it's safe to do so, but for now, I need a favour. Please ask your mum if she will talk to us. We think she can help.'

'She's got nothing to do with this,' Cody objected.

'But she knows what Duncan is capable of. He's dangerous, Cody. You can't trust him. Promise me you'll talk to her. Please.'

There was a long silence on the end of the phone line.

'Cody? Are you still there?'

'You really think Duncan could have done it?'

'I do. I really do.' She had begun to cry, and I felt a flicker of shame. I'd become so intent on being right, and on proving Wilson wrong, that I'd lost perspective. A woman's life had been taken, and a little girl might yet die too. I reached out and touched Skye's hand.

Another long silence, then Cody sighed. 'Okay, fine. I'll talk to her.'

•

Wilson was waiting for us outside the elevator, as sombre as I'd ever seen him. He shook Skye's hand.

'Mrs Turner, thank you for coming. I'm going to ask you to wait with my colleague, Detective Sergeant Stuart McKenzie, while I have a word with Detective O'Connor.'

Macca was striding towards us from his cubicle, his hand extended towards Skye in greeting. Typical. Of course he'd managed to muscle in on the action after my hard work.

'Skye, it's okay,' I reassured her. 'We won't be long.'

She nodded uncertainly.

'How about a cup of tea, Mrs Turner?' Macca asked, and guided her towards the kitchenette while I followed Wilson across the floor to his office.

When I stepped inside, I was surprised to find Ant, the head of HR, hunched over his laptop beside Wilson's desk. Was he seriously here to bang on again about his bloody recruitment campaign? But when he glanced up at me, there was no sign of his signature grin. Something else was on the agenda.

'Please take a seat,' Ant said in a weirdly formal voice, not quite meeting my eye. 'I'm present because Detective Chief Superintendent Wilson has called this disciplinary meeting.'

'*Disciplinary* meeting?' I glanced at Wilson.

He stared back at me, his left eye twitching.

'We're here to discuss some extremely serious allegations that have been made against you,' Ant continued.

'What allegations?'

'Sit down, DSS O'Connor,' Ant ordered.

I lowered myself into a chair, burning with disbelief, and looked directly at Wilson. 'Sir, are you just going to sit there?'

Wilson focused on a spot on the wall over my shoulder. 'Oh, I *see*,' I went on. 'This is just about you being pissed that I'm doing your job for you. Ant, I don't know what Wilson has told you, but Tamara Baruch has been set up and Wilson has made a hash of the investigation. I've got a pile of material here that—'

'Stop it,' Wilson cut in. 'This has nothing to do with the Turners, although your behaviour this past week has compounded the misconduct we are here to discuss. Mrs Turner is in an extremely fragile state, and it's deeply irresponsible of you to have raised her hopes and misrepresented the status of our investigation.'

'What the hell is this about then?'

'Nick has made a complaint,' Wilson said.

'*Nick*? As in my lying, cheating, former fiancé Nick? What's he got to complain about?'

Ant crossed his arms. 'Are you really going to play this game?'

'What game? Guys, I genuinely have no idea what you're talking about.'

Ant's eyes cut to his screen. 'Nick Lynch registered a formal complaint with Detective Chief Superintendent Wilson early this morning in relation to your campaign of harassment of him and his partner, Vanessa Freeman. He has forwarded the abusive email you sent to him early this morning, which threatens to publicly expose Ms Freeman's father for tax fraud.'

Before I could respond, Ant continued, 'Detective, we have authenticated your email with police IT. Mr Lynch and Ms Freeman allege that, in order to acquire the information about Ms Freeman's father, you must have abused your access to confidential police databases. Consequently, we ran a check with the database custodian and the results are unequivocal. As you can see from this feed' – he swivelled his screen to show me a list of search inquiries – 'you have repeatedly abused your restricted access to undertake searches on Mr Lynch, Ms Freeman and their family members on confidential state and federal databases.'

I stared at him, dumbfounded. 'Ant, this is crazy. I didn't search any databases, and I didn't send that email. I didn't even know Vanessa's last name.'

'I'm not done,' Ant said, raising his palm like he was halting traffic at an intersection. 'Mr Lynch also supplied copies of abusive text messages that you sent to his mobile phone last night, as well as security camera footage of you attempting to break into Ms Freeman's home early last Sunday morning.'

My head was spinning. 'Jesus Christ. Okay, fine. Yes, I sent Nick some drunken text messages in the early hours of this morning. Petty stuff – I'm not proud of it. And last weekend, I was jogging past Vanessa's house when Nick just happened to come outside with her dog. It was completely random. I didn't know where she lived. I didn't go there on purpose. I certainly wasn't breaking in.'

Wilson shook his head. 'Stop bullshitting, Mei. You expect us to believe you were out jogging at half-past five on a Sunday morning in jeans and a leather jacket? I've seen the footage myself. You were inside the entrance gate, for God's sake.'

Fucking Nick and that fucking puppy and his stupid fucking security cameras. 'Fine. I was on my way home after a night out. I'd crashed at a friend's place. But I swear to God that this stuff about me checking the police databases and emailing about tax fraud is total bullshit. I'd never do that. Ever. You know that.'

Wilson leaned forward and rubbed his flickering eyelid with the back of his hand. 'Mei, we've worked together for a long time. You're a very talented detective. But enough is enough. You're out of control. Look at you – your eyes are bloodshot, you stink of booze. I know you're going through a tough time on the personal front with your mum, and it won't be easy to see Nick moving on so quickly. But I can't keep making excuses for you. This time you've pushed things too far. It's out of my hands now.'

'DSS O'Connor,' Ant said, 'your misuse violations and the threatening behaviour you've exhibited towards Mr Lynch and Ms Freeman amount to very serious misconduct. Consequently, you are suspended from duty with immediate effect for a period of one week while we undertake further investigation. You will need to surrender your badge, access card and laptop to us immediately and cease all involvement in your investigations. However, Detective Chief Superintendent Wilson has agreed that, because you are your mother's primary caregiver, you may keep your work car and mobile phone until our disciplinary investigation is complete.'

A heatwave ripped through my body. 'This is a fucking outrage!'

'Detective, if you don't willingly surrender those items to me now, they will be forcibly removed.'

Blood was roaring in my ears. I couldn't hear anything else they said as they steered me into the elevator. Either Nick was lying and had faked the evidence, or someone had set me up. Had Viktor Utkin somehow hacked into the police computer system to run those searches and send that email to get me off the case? But how would he have connected me to Nick and Vanessa?

When the elevator opened in reception, Macca was waiting by the security turnstiles.

'Macca, where's Skye?' I asked.

'Mrs Turner is in safe hands,' he said, a smile curving his lips.

'What the fuck does that mean?'

'It's not your concern now.'

And then it rushed at me like a freight train. In all my years on the force, I'd only ever shared my login credentials and password with one person. I wished I was wrong, but I knew in my heart that it was him. Macca.

That son of a bitch had fucked me over.

TWENTY-ONE

SKYE

SATURDAY

Detective McKenzie was kind. A gentle giant with freckles and a warm smile. He asked lots of questions about Tilly while he swished tea bags around two steaming mugs. His son loved *Paw Patrol* and *Bluey* too, and like Tilly he was obsessed with the dodgems at Luna Park. The detective squeezed the tea bags against the side of the mugs with a spoon and then dropped them into the rubbish bin. He asked me if I followed the NRL – he was a lifelong Rabbitohs fan, he said – and chatted away about his hopes for the team to make the play-offs. Even though my mind kept drifting, I was grateful for the distraction. We hadn't even finished our tea when his phone rang, and he said, 'Okay, we're on our way,' and bustled me back down the corridor. I expected we were heading to Detective Chief Superintendent Wilson's office at the end of the floor, but instead he steered me into the elevator.

'Where are we going?' I asked.

'They need you downstairs.'

There would be some formalities to complete at the front desk, I assumed, or perhaps a police counsellor to meet – but when the elevator door opened into the lobby, the last person on earth I'd expected to see was standing right there, flanked by uniformed police officers. The ceiling clamped down on me and, before I could process what was happening, Duncan had his arms around me.

'Thank God you're okay.'

'No,' I screamed, but the word choked in my throat. I couldn't breathe. I was paralysed. Where was Detective O'Connor? Duncan and Detective McKenzie were conferring in hushed tones, and then the uniformed officers were manoeuvring me out of the building.

When the two of us were alone inside Duncan's car, he pressed the lock button then bowed his head towards the steering wheel. 'Babe, what were you thinking, running away like that?' He turned to face me and his eyes were wet with tears. 'I couldn't bear it if anything happened to you.'

We drove left out of the building, towards the city centre. I balled my hands into fists and pressed them as hard as I could into the soft leather of my seat to feel something solid.

'Duncan, stop pretending. I know everything.'

'Huh?' he said, his profile to me. The lights turned green and we surged across the intersection.

'I know everything.'

'What are you talking about now?'

'You and that security guy – what's his name? Viktor? You've been having secret meetings, spying on me. I know about the Russian mafia. And I saw those documents you were hiding in the workshop with all the numbers and the secret codes. And those awful photographs.'

He glanced at me quickly before returning his eyes to the road ahead. 'Oh, babe.' His expression was pained. 'This is all starting to make sense.'

'What is?'

'Doctor Friel warned me about this. Your new medication can cause hallucinations, especially after such a major trauma.'

'This isn't in my head.' I tried to keep my voice steady, but I couldn't stem the rising hysteria. 'I've told Detective O'Connor everything. You won't get away with it.'

I'd expected him to react with shock or anger, but he didn't flinch. He indicated and calmly rounded the corner towards Hyde Park. When the traffic slowed to a halt, he turned to face me. His expression was one of pity.

'Babe, you're unwell.' He spoke in a gentle voice. 'And you need to know that Detective O'Connor has been suspended for misconduct.'

'Stop lying.'

'It's true, I swear. It's not your fault. She preyed on your vulnerability. Tamara's been charged. The police investigation is closed. I'm so sorry she's planted these ideas in your head.'

'I don't believe you.'

'Superintendent Wilson phoned and told me to come and collect you. How else would I have known where you were? He's in a disciplinary meeting with Detective O'Connor right now.'

'Stop it! You're gaslighting me.'

'Gaslighting you? For God's sake, look at the state of yourself. You're covered in blood, muttering about vanishing documents and secret codes and the Russian mafia. Please tell me you understand how crazy that all sounds!'

'I saw your file. The contracts, and the codes, and those photographs. You disgust me.'

He slid across a lane of traffic and pulled the car into a parking bay. 'Look at me, Skye. I have no idea what you're talking about. You're delusional.'

My eyes stung with tears. 'Don't say that,' I screamed. 'I am not! You tried to kill our daughter!'

'You know I'd never hurt Tilly.' There was steel in his voice. 'This is all in your head. You're having another breakdown.'

I couldn't bear to listen, but he wouldn't stop. 'You know I'm right. Vicky and Bridget found you running around half-naked in the rain yesterday. And how do you think I felt to get a call half an hour ago saying you were being held at police headquarters in a distressed state, when I'd thought you were safe at home with me?'

He reached for my hand, but I yanked it away.

His voice reverted to caramel. 'Skye, my love, it's not your fault. It's no wonder your mind is playing tricks. You're stressed out about Tilly. You're on new meds. You've eaten almost nothing all week. You've barely slept. And now this troubled cop has brainwashed you with her conspiracy theory.' He paused to wipe tears from his eyes. 'I love you so much. I'm trying to support you as best as I can. But – I'm suffering too. I have to get you and Tilly well.'

I couldn't look at him. I bit down on my lip until I could taste blood. Outside the car, shoppers were spilling out of the Westfield Mall, laughing and chatting. I wanted to scream out at them to help me, to claw at the window and to thrash my body against the door. But what was the point? There was no escape.

We didn't speak for the rest of the trip home. When the car rolled through the entrance gates and Thornfield loomed up ahead – the windows cast in shadow despite the bright sun overhead – I felt the full force of my defeat.

Bo was scratching on the other side of the garage door and greeted me with exultant barks and pawing, as though I'd been gone for months instead of hours. I pressed my cheek into the comfort of his warm coat. Duncan suggested I clean myself up while he made me some lunch.

Upstairs, I dropped my bag on the bedroom floor and shucked off my clothes. Stepping into the ensuite, I wrenched the shower up to full pressure. The hot water rushed over me, coating my cut and bruised body like a salve and clouding the glass with steam. I didn't know what to believe anymore. I'd lost my bearings. I was in a labyrinth of blind turns, with no thread to help me retrace my path and no star overhead by which to navigate.

Was it really all in my head? It was terrifying to be back at this point, not knowing whether or not I could trust my own mind. I'd convinced myself that Duncan had found out about what had happened between me and Jamie all those years ago at Yallambee. But how could he possibly have known? Jamie had no reason to have told him – especially not all these years later. Maybe my guilty conscience had gotten the better of me, and my mind was fabricating a new reality to help me cope, like it had done after Tilly's birth. It felt as though my innermost self was bleeding away, like dye into water, and I had no way to stem the flow.

And did that mean Duncan was also right about Detective O'Connor? I thought back to her grimy flat. Her bloodshot eyes. The jumble of medicine bottles and pill packets. Something had definitely been off-kilter. Had I been a fool to trust her?

After my shower, I pulled on a robe and went downstairs. Duncan was in the kitchen. He dressed my injured hand in a bandage and dabbed cream onto the cuts on my face. He'd fixed a plate of Vegemite toast, cut up into soldiers the way I prepared Tilly's, and a strawberry milkshake.

'Is this okay?' He was apologetic. 'I thought you might like something plain.'

I took a few sips of the milkshake. It tasted gritty and oversweet, but I forced some down to placate him. I glanced at the countertop where I'd left my phone charging that morning. It was gone, along with my car keys.

Duncan followed my gaze. 'I called Doctor Friel while you were in the shower. He thinks it's best that you stay off your phone and other devices – just until you're back to your normal self.' He spoke with concern. 'Just in case you do something you regret.' He placed his hand on mine. 'And try hard to finish the milkshake – you really need the calories.'

I did as I was told. I had no strength left to fight.

•

I woke with a start on Tilly's bed in the hazy, late-afternoon light, with Bo tucked into the hollow of my hip. For a while I lay in silence, trying to assemble the surreal events of the morning. My mouth was dry, my head ached and my insides crawled with dread. At this time a week ago, Tilly had been admitted to the hospital – although time had lost all meaning since then. It had loosened and billowed back over itself so that the nightmare of the emergency room ran in parallel with every present moment.

When Bo grew restless, I got up and crossed to the window. Bronze leaves were fluttering down from the trees and settling on the lawn, and the sun hung low in the sky. Craving a burst of the crisp autumn air, I unlatched the sash window and tried to pull it up, but it was stuck. No, not stuck, I realised when I tried again. Locked. We'd never locked the windows up here. It hadn't been necessary. They were far too heavy for Tilly to lift, so posed no danger, and I always liked to have a breeze in the upstairs rooms during the day.

I checked our bedroom windows next, as well as the windows in the study and the guest rooms along the hallway, but they were all locked too, along with the windows in my attic studio on the third floor. It would be a death wish for anyone to attempt to climb down from that distance. Did Duncan really think I would risk it? That I'd abandon Tilly?

I couldn't live like this, a prisoner in my home. I had to talk to him. This had to stop.

When I reached the bottom of the staircase, I heard Duncan talking in the library. I crept along the hallway and strained to listen through the gap in the door. From the intermittent silences, I realised he was speaking on the phone.

'Yes – severe delusions, hallucinations, irrational behaviour.'

A long pause.

'She had two of the diazepam with lunch, which calmed her enough to sleep this afternoon, but what would you recommend for overnight? She'll need something stronger.'

I presumed he was talking to Dr Friel, but I was confused. I hadn't had any tablets with lunch. Unless he'd ground the medication into the milkshake. No wonder he'd been so concerned about me finishing it. No wonder I felt so drowsy.

He said something else, but it was too muffled to hear, and then: 'I hate to say it, but I agree, especially given what happened this morning. I'm extremely concerned that she'll harm either herself or Tilly.'

Another, shorter silence.

'No, she wouldn't go willingly, so it would be best if you prepare the paperwork on that basis.'

Any residual hope that I could trust Duncan shattered in that moment. Not only had he sedated me without my consent, but it was clear he was planning to have me sectioned again. If he had Dr Friel's support, I wouldn't be able to stop him, and once I was in hospital they could apply for a mandatory treatment order to medicate me against my will. And God only knew when I'd get to see my daughter again.

I was immobilised with panic. I had to stop him, but I was trapped in an impossible vortex. He'd taken away my phone and my laptop, so he thought I had no way of reaching the outside world. I was powerless. If I unleashed on him, or tried to escape again, he'd use it as further evidence that I was irrational and unstable. And the more he treated me that way, and severed my connection to the outside world, the more irrational and unstable I was becoming. He was driving me to madness.

Thank God for the burner phone. It was still tucked inside my small bag. I crept back upstairs, careful not to make a sound, and along the hallway to our bedroom.

The clothes I'd left pooled on our bedroom floor before my shower were gone, and my bag had been placed on the bed. I knew it had been emptied before I even picked it up.

My despair at that moment was so violent I feared I couldn't go on.

TWENTY-TWO

MEI

SATURDAY

Wilson and Macca marched me through security and cast me off into the lobby.

'You bastard,' I hissed at Macca.

'Just go home, Mei,' Wilson said. 'And clean yourself up while you're at it. You're only making things worse.'

'Fuck you!' I yelled, but they'd already turned their backs on me and were striding towards the waiting elevator, the clip of their shoes on the tiles ringing out like pistol shots. The two police officers from the Central Sydney division stationed at security – presumably to stop me from scrambling back over the turnstiles – wouldn't meet my eye.

I streaked out of there with a chemical burn in my chest. What the fuck was I going to do now? Skye wasn't answering either of her phones. Macca had said she was in safe hands, but what did that mean? I could only hope they hadn't sent her back to Duncan Turner.

I had to pull myself together and think. I needed air. Instead of taking the car, I strode up Market Street, trying to shut out the raucous symphony of revving engines and rising sirens. The only person who could help me now was Cody White, but he'd be spooked if he learned I'd been suspended from duty. I had to find some way of skirting over that detail.

This time, when I dialled his number, he answered on the second ring.

'Cody, there have been some developments since we spoke earlier. Have you had a chance to talk to your mother?'

'Yeah, I called her. She really doesn't want to get involved.'

I kicked a rusted can into the drain and silently cursed Rebecca White. 'Look, this is really serious. We'll give her all the protection she needs if she comes forward.' I was struggling to keep the desperation out of my voice.

'I'm sorry,' he said. 'I've tried, but she won't change her mind. How's Skye doing?'

I paused for a moment. There was no way to fudge it. 'I'm not sure. I think she's with Duncan.'

'What? I thought she said—'

'I don't think she went willingly. That's the other reason I called. Could you check on her, see if she's back at the house with him?'

'This is messed up. How come you don't know where she is?'

'It's complicated. Just check on Skye – go around to the house to see if she's there and if she's okay. And try your mother again. Please.'

'My shift's about to start. I can't go until tomorrow morning. And I'm telling you, Mum won't change her mind.'

I hung up and turned into George Street. A silver Prius ran the red light and almost clipped me as it rounded the corner. The shock of the near miss, combined with the shrill blast of the driver's horn, made the rage inside me boil over, and I folded outside a Chemist Warehouse in a hectic current of pedestrians and Lime scooters to release great heaving sobs.

The next step was inevitable. I couldn't go home to face Mum and her disappointment. This wasn't just a failure. My whole life had imploded. And what was there to do now, other than to seek erasure? A woman was opening up a pub on the next block. It was a sign.

The inside stunk of vomit, despite the cleaners' best efforts to scrub it down. I was relieved that the bartender made no effort to converse when I ordered a vodka soda, even though I was her sole patron. I chose a table facing the street and took perverse pleasure in watching a couple trying to wrangle flailing twin toddlers into their stroller on the pavement in front of me.

I messaged some friends to see if anyone was free to meet up before I spiralled out of control. Lena and the others who'd been at the hens' party were too hungover to venture out, and I'd forgotten that Yvette was at a linguistics conference in Canberra. Everyone else sent the usual excuses – children's swimming lessons, visiting the in-laws, a working bee in the garden, but they'd be happy to meet up later for an early dinner with the kids. When had they all become so boring?

Sandy messaged to say she and Mum were back home after a lovely morning but Mum was a bit tired, so they were going to binge-watch last season's *My Kitchen Rules*. I liked her text and ordered another drink, then another, as people shuffled in and out of the bar. Abe and Bonnie messaged separately, asking for an update. I ignored them and turned my phone to silent. Soon, the remaining free tables were swamped by bloated, dead-eyed men. One of them, with craggy *Game of Thrones* features, sidled over and offered me a glass of Prosecco.

'You look lonely.' His teeth were yellow.

'I'm fine.' I returned to my phone.

He ran his palm down the back of my t-shirt and leaned in so close I could smell the sour tang of his breath. 'Don't be like that.' His other hand gripped my shoulder.

I tried to shrug him off, but the grip tightened.

'Could you just piss off?' I said.

'So rude after I bought you a drink. I should wash your mouth out with soap, you ungrateful Asian cunt.' He reached his hand down between my legs and grabbed at my crotch, so I launched an uppercut to his jaw, toppling the Prosecco. Before he could retaliate, his stocky friend seized his arms, and I grabbed my bag and slipped past them into the street with my heart thundering in my chest.

I found another bar a few blocks up, opposite Hyde Park – this one was overpriced, with a European menu and an ibis poking at crumbs under the sidewalk tables. I took an outside seat. Across the road, a busker was performing an energetic cover of 'Riptide', collecting coins from the tourists flocking towards the fountain to take selfies. Beside him, some poor bastard was dancing around in an inflatable orange cow suit to promote a new online brokerage firm. Life could be worse, I supposed.

The waiter suggested a tequila-based cocktail, which seemed a good idea, as did agreeing that the handsome Norwegian backpacker at the next table could join me. His name was Aksel, and with his pretty face and blond topknot he reminded me of a young David Beckham. He was travelling around Australia with the bartender, Thomas, until August when they would return to Oslo to finish university. Another couple of cocktails materialised at our table, and Aksel and I chatted until Thomas finished his shift.

'So, what are your plans for tonight?' Aksel asked.

'I'm not sure. My only plan is not to go home.'

'Who's at home? Your boyfriend?'

'Actually, no. My mother.'

He grinned. 'You still live at home?'

I nodded.

'So, you and your mother must be close?'

'Not exactly. It's a pragmatic solution, for now.'

'Okay.' He studied my face. 'So, why aren't you close?'

'Why the interrogation?'

Aksel laughed. 'I'm sorry. I'm just interested. Women are so complicated.'

'It's not complicated. I disappoint her.'

He leaned back in the booth, frowning. 'I find that hard to believe. What is she disappointed about?'

'That I'm not my sister.'

'What's so great about your sister?'

He was staring at me with those wide blue eyes. I felt a stab of irritation, but I wasn't sure if it was with him or with myself. Why had I brought up Grace? The alcohol had loosened me, made me careless. But fuck it. I'd never see him again.

'My sister went missing – a long time ago now. She disappeared on the way home from school when she was six. They never found her. And Mum blames me.'

'Why would she blame you?'

'Because it was my fault.'

And so the whole tragic tale gushed out like projectile vomit. I told Aksel about how, on the day Grace disappeared, Molly Brennan, the most popular girl in the class, had invited me to have a go of her Tamagotchi. Molly had made my life a misery when I'd started at St Dominic's, teasing me about my lunchbox of wontons and telling everyone half-Chinese people could not be Catholics; the Pope had said so, according to Molly. But I'd won Molly's grudging respect when I blitzed the field on athletics day, and then when I bore a brutal strapping from Sister Berthilda rather than dobbing in Molly for chatting in class. So, the invitation to try the Tamagotchi was significant. It marked a turning point in my social status. I couldn't risk Grace annoying Molly – or, worse, breaking the Tamagotchi. That was why, when Grace appeared in Sister Edith's classroom to meet me for the walk home, I sent her outside. She pleaded to stay, but I hissed at her that she was annoying and to get lost. I'd expected her to wait for me in the playground, but instead she'd set off for home by herself.

Later, when Mum and Dad and then the detectives had asked me why Grace might have walked home alone – something so out of character – I'd said I had no idea, even while my stomach roiled with guilt. And somehow, even though I'd never told a soul what had happened, Mum knew I was lying.

Aksel took my hand. 'You were just a kid. You can't blame yourself.'

He ordered another round, which Thomas made extra strong and didn't charge us for.

As the alcohol cut deeper, and we kept trading stories – Aksel about his travels and plans for the future, me about my work and break-up with Nick – I realised how much I'd sacrificed for my career. How much life I'd missed out on.

And for what? To end up single and childless, with my reputation in tatters and my job in peril, betrayed by my closest work colleague? Nina Turner was still dead. Tilly Turner was still on life support. Duncan Turner was still a free man. In the end, money and power always triumphed. I'd been a fool to think I could ever win against the Turner family.

TWENTY-THREE

SKYE

SUNDAY

Overnight, wild thoughts had infected my mind. Duncan had been careful to lock all the doors on the ground level before he'd retired to bed. I'd sat on the landing listening to his footfall on the old oak boards, and the click and whir of the bolts sliding. I still hadn't been able to locate a phone or laptop, and even the desktop computer in Duncan's study was newly password-protected. I was trapped, a bird in a cage.

If I couldn't leave and had no way of communicating with anyone, then I had to find a way to summon others to the house. In the depths of the night, my anger raged, white-hot. I'd contemplated setting fire to the bedlinen, or slicing myself deeply with a kitchen knife, so that Duncan would be forced to call emergency services and they could rescue me. But those were the violent, unreasonable acts of a madwoman and would only serve to seal my fate. They'd never allow me anywhere near Tilly again.

Where was Ana? Where were my other friends? Why hadn't anyone come to the house? They'd promised me steadfast support. The only explanation was that Duncan had turned all visitors away, but they should have insisted on seeing me. How had they all been so easily derailed? And where was Detective O'Connor? After all that I'd risked, had she turned her back on me too?

The jagged pain at my temples wouldn't cease. I paced in loops around Tilly's room in the darkness. I opened her wardrobe and buried my face in her soft clothes, inhaling her scent. I flipped through her favourite books by lamplight, hearing her voice reciting her favourite lines. All the while, the house spoke to me through the deathly silence in rattling pipes and the whoosh of running water. I was in that bardo between wakefulness and sleep, where everything is at once hazy and lucid. Through the gap in the curtains, the moonlit birches in the garden below vibrated and revealed themselves as a cloud of atoms pulsing in tune with the universe. Tilly was part of me, her heartbeat thudding within me.

I found myself drawn up the narrow staircase to my attic studio, where strange shadows stretched and quivered on the walls. The windows had no curtains, and I caught a glimpse of myself floating, grotesque and haunted, in the darkened pane. Had my mad, dead mother carved this fate into my bones?

I took a notebook and a pencil, and curled up on the sofa. I had the idea that I would sketch something, but instead words spilled onto the page as I expelled the feverish thoughts from my mind. Tilly was there, at my shoulder, urging me on. I wrote of my disgust for Duncan and all he represented. I wrote of my fear of what he might do to me and, most of all, to our daughter. I wrote how I'd rather die than live without her.

•

Then Sunday delivered a miracle. Around noon, Cody arrived. When I looked down from the locked studio window, he was standing beside Duncan on the patio. They had their backs to the house, and both held their hands up to shield their eyes from the glare. Somehow I had to find a way to get Cody alone. I wasn't sure if I could trust him, but at this point I had no other choice.

I slipped on a dress, washed my face and brushed my hair and teeth. I covered my cuts with concealer before heading downstairs to make coffee. I was determined to appear sane and purposeful in front of my husband. I switched on the espresso machine and turned the oven on to grill some slices of a banana loaf left by a visitor, and scanned the room for potential distractions that might give me a few minutes alone with Cody. I could burn the loaf to trigger the smoke detectors, or leave the kitchen tap running so it would overflow. But that would make me appear distracted. Incompetent. I couldn't give Duncan any more ammunition to use against me.

I scooped a spoonful of butter into a little ramekin and laid the grilled loaf out on a tray with a knife and a milk jug. Next I poured the coffee. I'd bought the espresso machine for Duncan's last birthday. It had cost a fortune and was insanely complicated to use, but what else did you buy for a man with more than everything? I'd spent hours fiddling with the controls to program the perfect brew. And that gave me an idea. I entered a test code into the machine that would set it beeping in a few minutes' time.

Bo shadowed me outside with the tray.

'Hi, Cody.' I forced a bright smile and ignored his strange, searching look. 'What a nice surprise.'

Duncan did a double take. For the first time in over a week, I was well-presented and behaving normally.

'I thought you boys might like some coffee,' I said.

'How are you feeling?' Duncan asked.

'So much better after a decent night's sleep.' I placed the tray down on the outdoor table and handed each of them their espresso. 'You have to try some of this banana bread. It smells delicious.'

Duncan was watching me closely. Suspiciously.

A loud beeping sound came from inside. I sighed. 'The coffee machine must be faulting again.'

As I'd predicted, Duncan offered to look at it for me. When he was out of earshot, I turned to Cody, my heart beating like wings in my chest. 'Listen to me carefully. We don't have long.'

'What the hell is going on? Are you okay?'

'Duncan's trying to get me committed to a psych facility.'

'What?' His face paled.

'He's told the doctor that I'm delusional. He's confiscated my phone and laptop, my car keys too. He won't let me leave the house. I'm scared. I'm scared of what he might do to Tilly. She's not safe. You have to help me.'

Cody shifted his weight, looked at the ground. I was asking him to doubt his father; the father he had longed for his whole life.

'Please Cody,' I tried again.

He sighed. 'What do you want me to do?'

'Duncan can't think we're conspiring. Call Detective O'Connor. Tell her what he's planning to do. And Cody, your mum has to tell the police what she knows.'

'I've tried. She won't do it. I'm sorry.'

'Tell her what's going on. She might change her mind.' I glanced over my shoulder, back towards the house. 'I'm not asking for my sake; I'm begging – for Tilly's.' Tears tugged behind my eyes but I couldn't afford to cry.

The beeping sound had stopped and I heard Duncan's footsteps behind me.

'All sorted,' he said. 'It must need a service. What did I interrupt?'

I froze, my mind blank, and looked to Cody.

'We were talking about Tilly. About the court process.'

'We're up against socialist bureaucrats,' Duncan huffed. 'The system's broken. It's a disgrace.'

Soon enough, it was time for Cody to head off. He had an afternoon shift at the bar, he told us. We walked him back through the house and out to his rusted car in the driveway. Cody shook Duncan's hand.

He promised to visit us again soon. I tried and failed to catch his eye one last time, to remind him what he needed to do. Duncan and I stood side by side and waved him off.

•

That afternoon, Duncan came to join me in my studio. I was at the window, looking out over Bellevue Hill towards the harbour.

'I've got good news,' he said.

'Yes?'

'Jack called. He's just been on the phone with the judge. The care order will expire tomorrow morning and the court won't renew it.' He cupped my cheek in his hand. 'We'll be able to see Tilly.'

TWENTY-FOUR

MEI

SUNDAY

I woke with Aksel naked beside me and sunshine blasting through the gap in the curtains. My head throbbed, and the sight of my underwear twisted up on the floor alongside an empty blister pack of Mum's fentanyl filled me with existential dread. What had I done? Had Aksel drugged me? No – as I thought back to the rounds of cocktails and handful of pills, this was surely all my own doing. I cringed to think that Mum would have heard us through the paper-thin walls. The last thing I could remember was dancing at a basement club with Thomas and Aksel, but I had no idea where or what time that had been.

I shot out of bed and rooted around under our clothes for my bag. Thank God I hadn't left it in a bar or club somewhere with all that sensitive evidence inside it. My phone had four per cent battery remaining. There were several missed calls and texts from Bonnie and Abe. I left them unopened. Nothing from Cody or Skye.

Aksel rolled onto his back, almost capsizing the tiny bed, and opened his eyes. He was beautiful, but barely twenty years old. Within one week, I'd become a recidivist cougar.

'Hey,' he said in his lilting accent. 'What a fucking great night.'

I realised I was starkers, and grabbed a throw off the bed to shield myself.

'You know it's too late for that, right?' He grinned.

'Jesus, Aksel.' I clutched my head. 'I'm old enough to be your mother.'

'If my mother gave birth at twelve years old. More like a sexy young aunt.'

'Don't be gross.' I hurled the throw at him. 'You have to get out of here before my mum sees you.'

'Your mum's not so scary.'

'What?'

'You don't remember?' He was enjoying my misery.

No. No. No. I withered inside. As far as Mum knew, I was engaged to Nick; I'd told her some cock-and-bull story about him being away on a work trip to explain why he hadn't been over to the flat. What had I been thinking bringing a man back here – let alone a young, wasted backpacker? She would be horrified. The only upside was that I was still woozy with drink and pills, so that when the reckoning came I'd be somewhat numb to it.

'You have to get out. Now. Really.'

'I feel so used.' It was all a big joke to him.

He pecked me on the lips, pulled on his clothes, and left. I waited until I heard the click of the front door before I ventured out into the kitchen.

'Meiying Han Lu.' Mum appeared like an apparition. The morning light illuminated her bald pate and the delicate network of veins running across it. She was frail but there was no mistaking the force of her disgust.

'Hi, Mum.' I was determined to pretend Aksel had never been here. 'How are you feeling?' I drew a glass from the cabinet and filled it with water.

'How am *I* feeling?' Her eyes travelled over my slovenly appearance, accusation writ large across her face. 'You are engaged to be married.'

'Actually, Nick and I broke up.' I sculled the glass of water and immediately refilled it.

She braced herself against the doorframe. 'What are you talking about?'

'It's over. There's not going to be a wedding.'

'When did this happen? Why didn't you tell me?'

There was silence for a moment as I tried to find the words. Why hadn't I told her? Was it because I didn't want her to worry, as I'd assured Yvette? No. It was because I couldn't stand to face her judgement.

Mum was shaking her head now, mistaking my hesitation for guilt. 'Oh, *lè lè*, what did you do?'

'What did *I* do?' I laughed then, a strange, tight laugh. 'Because of course this must be *my* fault.'

'Relationships need work. You must work hard to find happiness.'

'Is that right? Well, I'd say I've worked pretty bloody hard, and in the end, what do I have to show for it? Not much.'

'Stop this. You should count your blessings. You have every chance to succeed, every chance to have a wonderful life. Others are not so lucky.' She was talking about Grace now, and the fact she would dare to go there sparked the furnace inside me.

'What do you want me to say, Mum? That I'm sorry?' I was screaming like a banshee. 'Sorry that I'm such a disappointment to you? Sorry that Nick doesn't want me? Sorry that I'm not a doctor with three children like Paula fucking Wong? Sorry that I can't afford private medical care for you?' I met her eye as I delivered my final salvo. 'Sorry that Grace disappeared instead of me?'

I watched my words hit their target.

'Oh, *lè lè*,' Mum said. She reeled as if I'd struck her. 'How can you say such a thing?'

I couldn't stop the tears then. Great, ugly, snotty sobs.

Mum swept across the room and clasped me to her tiny frame. I let her lead me to the sofa where, like a child, I crumpled in her lap. 'Nick has someone else. And she's going to have his baby.' I dragged the sleeve of my sweater across my face to soak up the tears. 'He doesn't love me.' And then it hit me: nobody loved me. My whole body convulsed.

Mum cradled me and rubbed my back. I realised then how much I'd craved her touch. When I had calmed enough to speak, I sat up and faced her. I had to confess if she was ever going to forgive me. 'That day, when Grace came to my classroom, I told her to get lost and to leave me alone. That's why she walked home by herself.' I paused to steady myself. 'It's my fault she never came home.'

But Mum was shaking her head. 'No.'

'It is, Mum. I lied to you and Dad, and to the police. I'm sorry.'

Tears were running down Mum's face now. It was the first time I'd ever seen her cry. Even when Dad hurt himself, even when he died in the hospital, even at his funeral, her face had been impassive. 'No. No. You must not say that.' She clutched her head in her hands.

'What's wrong?' I asked.

When Mum lifted her face, she wore an unfamiliar expression – one of vulnerability. 'The school told us about a strange man loitering near the park. He had approached another girl the week before, but she was older and she ran away. I should never have let you girls keep walking that route. Your father wanted to collect you from school himself, but I told him he needed to work. We both needed to work. We needed the money. But we should have made other arrangements.' She drew a wobbly breath. 'If you had been walking together that day, perhaps both of you would have been taken.' She swiped her tears away with the back of her hand. 'Your father never forgave me. And I didn't trust myself with you. You were better off without me. But I have had this burning feeling here' – she pointed to her stomach – 'ever since. It is my burden.'

I thought back to all the arguments she'd had with Dad behind their closed bedroom door or in the kitchen late at night when I should have been asleep. I'd thought they were arguing about me.

'Mei,' she continued, 'you make me so proud. I'm sorry that I've never told you that before. Your father would be proud too.'

'Proud of what?' In all facets of my life, I was a failure.

'You are so brave, so strong. You need to find justice for that little girl and that lady. You must not give up now.'

●

260

When I returned to my bedroom, my phone was rattling on the bedside table. It was Rex Howard of Porters' security team, probably calling about the CCTV footage from Tamara's apartment building that I'd requested in a former lifetime.

'We docked yesterday,' Rex said, 'and I'm back in the office. I was calling to check you'd received my email?'

'No, actually I haven't.' I couldn't exactly admit that I'd been suspended and no longer had access to my work account.

'Ah, I'm glad I followed up then. I thought it was odd you hadn't responded.'

I straightened myself up and rubbed my eyes. I ought to have told him to send the footage to Wilson. 'I've been having some problems with my work account – some sort of storage issue,' I fibbed. 'IT's trying to resolve it but it may take a while, especially given it's a Sunday.'

'I could send the link through to one of your colleagues?' Rex suggested.

'Unfortunately, the email glitch is affecting the whole unit and it's essential I get underway today, given the urgency of the case. Why don't I pop down to your office to view the reels on site?' I'd have to Uber to his office, but better that than the tapes get into the wrong hands.

'Hmm.' Rex was wavering, so I embellished the situation a little further. 'Also, Rex, between us' – I paused for dramatic effect – 'there's a rather sensitive aspect to this matter. I know I can trust you with this, given your professional history.' Rex loved it when I alluded to his distinguished police career. 'I can't name any names, but let's just say that there are some internal conflicts of interest on this one.' Rex would recognise this as code for a tantalising internal scandal within the State Crime Command. 'That's why I need to review the tapes myself. Also, please don't disclose this conversation if anyone else from the Homicide Squad contacts you, no matter how senior that person might be.'

'Ah, I see,' Rex said. 'Well, I'm on this afternoon, so I suppose you can come down now and get underway.'

•

Rex was waiting for me in the reception of Porters Property Management. He was a bull of a man, with a boxer's flattened nose, and had served at the King's Cross Area Command for forty years before a botched hip replacement forced him to retire. He launched into a cheery review of his Pacific highlights cruise as we crossed an open-plan office scented with Glade air freshener. The control room was in the basement with no cell reception. Live feeds of the CCTV cameras from Porters-managed properties in the CBD and inner east played on large wall-mounted video screens.

Rex had queued up synchronised footage from all four of The Mirage's cameras from the previous Monday. The playback began at 8.15 am, just prior to when Tamara had left The Mirage that morning, according to her statement. At 8.19 am, the cameras had caught Tamara stepping out of the elevator into the lobby and continuing out of her building, heading south. The exterior camera recorded her opening her umbrella and walking briskly along the pavement until she merged into a crowd of commuters.

Onscreen, buses hauled themselves along Crown Street against the snarl of morning traffic. Couriers and residents of The Mirage scuttled back and forth through the lobby. Over the years, like most senior officers, I'd developed a knack for identifying suspicious activity on CCTV reels, which enabled me to speed up the footage. Some called it a sixth sense, but it was simply recognition of dodgy behaviour patterns – loitering, facial concealment, individuals moving at an unusually fast or slow speed.

At 11.03 am, two tradesmen in navy blue trousers and polo shirts entered The Mirage with toolkits. They wore caps and bowed their heads so the street cameras didn't capture their faces, but the lobby camera caught their profiles when they signed in at reception. I paused the tape and zoomed in. I didn't recognise the shorter one, but the tall, wiry one had sharp features and bore a resemblance to Viktor Utkin. The image was too pixelated to be sure, though.

'Rex,' I said, 'how would I find out which company these tradesmen work for?'

He rolled his chair over to take a closer look at my screen. 'They're fellas from Conroy Electrical, I think. I can check the maintenance schedule if you like?'

'Yes, please.'

Rex swivelled back to his computer and tapped to pull up a file. 'Let's see. An electrical fault was logged with Conroy Electrical at quarter past nine.'

'Which apartment logged the fault?'

Rex scrolled along the screen. 'Huh. That's odd.'

'What is?'

'External maintenance requests can only be lodged by an authorised staff member once they've completed a request form. But somehow this request was lodged without a form or a sign-off. The system shouldn't allow that.'

'Do you recognise either of these Conroy staff?'

He studied the image of the tradesmen on the screen and shook his head. 'No, but they do have relatively high staff turnover. I'll request an ID from Conroy's head office.'

I pressed play. The receptionist handed the shorter man a security pass, and they both disappeared down a hallway.

'Are there any other cameras within the building – in the elevators or floor lobbies?' I asked.

'No. Too difficult to get those approved these days with all the privacy hoo-ha.'

I fast-forwarded ahead – only a handful of people passed through the apartment building's lobby during the following hour. At 12.20 pm, the two tradesmen returned the security pass. The shorter one exchanged a few words with the receptionist while the taller man hung back with his head down, as if intentionally screening his face from the cameras. I was convinced it was Viktor from Hawk Eye Intelligence.

But what did I do now? I couldn't access police facial recognition software while I was suspended. My only option was to forward the footage to Wilson for analysis. But then he'd know that I'd misled Rex and continued investigating after I'd been ordered to stand down, and that would be a sackable offence. I couldn't risk losing my job permanently, not with Mum's medical bills rolling in. And even if the footage did prove that Viktor Utkin had been in Tamara's apartment building on the same day that police found incriminating evidence in her apartment, would Wilson do the right thing? He seemed to be hell-bent on shutting down the investigation before any connection to the Turner family and their associates could be established. And now that Duncan Turner knew Skye was talking to the police, there was even more of a chance that this footage would inevitably be doctored or mysteriously vanish before Tamara's defence lawyer could access it during the legal discovery process. I couldn't risk that happening either.

I had to go with my gut. If Viktor Utkin was the man in the footage, it substantiated a conspiracy between him and Duncan Turner to frame Tamara Baruch for the poisoning of Tilly and Nina Turner. It also connected one of Campbell Turner's sons and a senior executive of Turner Corp to a Hawk Eye operative, and that could help prove the Turners' alleged connection to the Bratva. It would be immoral to ignore this tape, no matter what the personal cost to me.

Then I realised I had a third option. Cyrus didn't know I'd been suspended. It would be unorthodox to bypass Wilson, but if Hawk Eye and Turner Corp were associated with global organised crime networks, then the feds would have jurisdiction, and the poisoning of Tilly and Nina could fall under their remit as a related offence. Once the footage was in their hands, they could take it forward without me. I'd be off the hook, and Wilson need never know that I'd been involved. Brilliant. I asked Rex to send the footage on to Cyrus, and to tell him that we needed an ID on the tradesmen.

When I stepped out of the basement control room and regained cell reception, I saw four missed calls from Cody. When I phoned back, he explained that Duncan was trying to get Skye sectioned.

We had cut close to the bone. Duncan was starting to panic. Unfortunately I was powerless to do anything until I was reinstated. Goddamn Macca, that lying fuck. I told Cody I was chasing up a lead, and that he had to keep tabs on Skye.

What I really needed now was a Hail Mary. Surely all those years at a Catholic school had to count for something.

TWENTY-FIVE

SKYE

MONDAY

Early on Monday morning, we drove into the underground car park at the Randwick hospital campus, and wound our way down the ramps. The wait to see Tilly had been agonising, and although I was elated to be reunited with her, I was anxious about how I could break away to seek help. In the end, I'd written a note on a scrap of paper that I'd concealed in my pocket. I planned to slip it to a PICU nurse. The note said that my husband was keeping me against my will, that I was convinced he'd hurt Tilly, and asked the recipient to call Detective O'Connor immediately to seek help.

Duncan had arranged for us to meet a patient liaison who could whisk us through a back entrance of the connected Prince of Wales Hospital to spare us from the media scrum camped outside the Children's Hospital. We chugged up in the elevator and advanced through the maze of walkways. At the meeting spot, a woman with a soft face and a helmet of silver hair greeted us warmly and introduced herself as Dr Maria Vanderlind. She handed us each a blue surgical mask and shepherded us down a long corridor, scanning her key card each time we arrived at a set of double doors. Eventually, we arrived at windowless room with pale blue walls. It smelled faintly of lemon. The room was empty, aside from three white upholstered chairs arranged in a triangle in the middle. A woman in a grey suit was sitting in one of the chairs with a clipboard. She rose when we entered. Her name tag read *Dr Susie Bairstow*.

'Grab a seat,' said Maria. 'I'll hand you over to Susie here.'

I pulled up a chair opposite Susie. It took me a moment to realise that Duncan had left the room with Maria. There was no handle on the metal door they had exited through.

A gust of panic. 'What's going on?' I asked. 'Where's my husband?'

'Come sit with me, Mrs Turner,' said Susie in a soothing voice. 'Or may I call you Skye?'

'I'm here to see my daughter, Tilly. She's in the PICU.'

Susie smiled. 'This is the Safe Assessment Space, Mrs Turner. I understand you have been having a difficult time, which is understandable given what your family has been through. I'm going to ask you some questions.'

'No. No!' There was a rushing in my head. 'I don't agree to this.'

'Mrs Turner, there's no need to get upset. I'm here to help you. Please sit back down.'

'You have to listen to me. I need to get to my daughter. My husband is dangerous. He wants you to think I'm insane, to have me locked away. He and my doctor, they're in it together.'

Susie was watching me, a patient expression on her face.

'Look, I can prove it,' I continued. 'There's a detective. Detective Mei O'Connor. She knows everything. Here.' I thrust the square of paper from my pocket at her. 'This is her phone number.'

Susie's mouth formed a thin line as she read the note then placed it down on her clipboard.

'You have to listen to me! This is very important.' I felt anger rising. 'The Turner family is corrupt. They're in league with an organisation called the Bratva, which is part of the Russian mafia. My husband is behind the poisonings. My daughter isn't safe.'

'Mrs Turner, do *you* also feel unsafe?'

'Yes, I feel unsafe! Aren't you listening? That's why you need to call Detective O'Connor.'

Susie had picked up a pen and was starting to take notes. 'What makes you think that your husband is trying to harm you?'

'He's extremely dangerous. He can't be trusted. He's turned the house into a prison. He's trying to silence me.'

'Silence you?'

'He wants to stop me from talking to the police.'

She scribbled on her clipboard again, then looked back up at me. 'Have you thought about harming yourself?'

'There's no time for this. You need to call the police, right now.'

'Mrs Turner, can you tell me how you sustained those injuries?' She indicated the bandage around my left hand and the cuts on my face.

'It was an accident.'

'Can you describe the nature of the accident?'

The metal door shuddered open. It was Maria returning. This time she was wearing reading glasses and carrying a file.

'How's it going in here?' she asked with a fake smile.

I rushed towards her. 'Maria, I need your help. It's an emergency. There's a detective you need to phone. She can explain everything.'

Maria smiled. 'You mean Detective O'Connor?'

'Yes.' How did she know?

'Detective O'Connor has been suspended from duty,' said Maria.

'That's a lie. Duncan told you that.'

'Mrs Turner, I've verified that information myself with Detective Chief Superintendent Wilson. You're here because your husband and your GP are extremely concerned about your mental wellbeing. We know you've suffered a significant trauma. Doctor Friel has updated us on your clinical history, so he and your husband are right to be concerned. They only want what's best for you.'

I was sobbing now. 'It's not true. They've fooled you.'

Maria opened her file and pulled out a sheaf of papers. 'Is this your handwriting, Mrs Turner?' She turned the pages around to face me.

It was the rambling note I'd written two nights earlier in my attic studio, when I hadn't been able to sleep. Duncan must have found it.

'Do you remember writing these words?' the doctor asked.

I didn't answer her.

'The content of this document indicates that it was written within the past week. You write about wishing to harm your husband, your belief that he is involved in a conspiracy against you, and also of a desire to self-harm.'

'Why aren't you listening to me?' I shouted.

She ignored me. 'Your husband has also given us a detailed account of your recent behaviour and your regular marijuana use, which can exacerbate your symptoms. On that basis, we recommend that you stay here to receive appropriate treatment for your mental health. I'm proud to say that this hospital has the best inpatient psychiatric unit in the state.'

Terror swept through me then, like wildfire. I'd walked into this trap. How could I have been so stupid? Once you were assessed as mentally disordered, everything you said was presumed to be insane. There was no way to prove otherwise. My theories about Duncan's family would sound absurd to these doctors, who would only know the Turners by their reputation as business royalty and renowned philanthropists.

'My clinical opinion is that you need to be treated as an inpatient here until you have stabilised. I recommend a short course of intravenous haloperidol with reassessment in forty-eight hours.'

That's when the laughter began. Peals of manic laughter. I couldn't stop myself. I knew what they meant by stabilised. They were going to torch my mind with antipsychotics.

Susie tried to hand me a letter. 'This sets out all the information about dosage and side effects. It contains a sedative effect that will help you relax. Take your time to read the letter before we continue.'

'No, I do not consent. I'll never consent.'

The doctors exchanged a look.

'You do understand that the treatment we are recommending will help you?' Maria said. 'That it's in your best interests?'

'Don't you see what's happening here?' I replied. 'My husband's clever. He's worked this out perfectly. I don't need treatment. I need to speak to the police. I need to be with my daughter!'

'Mrs Turner, under the Mental Health Act, I can order you to receive treatment, without your consent, based on my clinical finding that you do not have sufficient capacity to understand what is in your best interests,' Maria said. 'But that is my last resort. Before I exercise that option, I am going to ask you one more time to read the letter so that you can provide your informed consent to our recommended treatment plan.'

I lunged at her then. 'Why aren't you listening?' I raged. 'Are they paying you off too?'

That's when Susie pressed an alarm and two orderlies arrived with restraints. The four of them moved me into a side room with a single bed and cuffed my hands and feet together. They held me down while Maria pulled up my skirt and jammed a needle into my thigh, and then everything turned white.

TWENTY-SIX

MEI

MONDAY

Cyrus rang first thing on Monday morning. I was already sitting cross-legged on the sofa eyeballing my phone screen with mounting desperation. When he confirmed that his software had identified Viktor Utkin in Tamara's apartment block on the CCTV footage, I actually fist-pumped the air like Mackie McDonald crushing Nadal at the Aussie Open. I shared my theory – that Utkin had entered The Mirage to frame Tamara, and that the motive for the Yallambee poisonings was somehow linked to the Turner family's criminal activities alleged by Abe Cohen.

'The problem is,' I continued, 'Wilson's not taking my theory about Duncan Turner's role in all of this seriously.' I omitted to mention that Wilson had suspended me, and that I was dangerously close to losing my job; it would distract Cyrus, and I needed his help. 'It's a federal matter now. Can you have a word to Heather about the tape?' Heather Dixon was the senior officer in the Australian Federal Police's investigations team, and Cyrus ultimately reported to her.

'No,' he said.

'What? Why not?'

'You know why not. Heather won't get involved in a state homicide inquiry. She'd only have grounds to intervene if you brought her evidence of a link to organised crime or another Commonwealth offence. The picture of Viktor Utkin in Tamara's building might make him complicit in the poisonings, but that's not within the AFP's jurisdiction.'

'Yes, but Skye Turner can testify to the codes and photographs she saw in Duncan's hidden file – they're bound to be connected to the Turners' money-laundering and trafficking racket – and Abe Cohen from the *New York Times* can share his research. Those crimes are all within the AFP's remit.'

'All of that's hearsay. Heather won't touch the Turners until you produce some solid evidence. You know that. Do you have anything?'

'Not yet.'

'Then you need to deal with this within the State Crime Command.'

Goddammit. He was right. And that put me in an impossible situation.

•

My Hail Mary was answered in the form of a phone call from Cody an hour later. He was trying to find out where Skye had been committed. Duncan was avoiding his calls.

'Keep me posted,' I said.

'There's something else. I spoke to Mum again. She's agreed to meet you. Just you, though. None of the other cops, and not at the police station.'

The relief made me so light-headed that I had to sit down to finish the conversation. We agreed that Rebecca and I would meet that afternoon at a women's refuge drop-in centre in Redfern. It was a safe, neutral space and Lou, who ran it, was a good sort. She'd find us a private space to talk.

•

I arrived at the centre at midday, half an hour early, and chatted to the hulking security guard, Tavita, who was a former prop for the Manly Sea Eagles. One factor I'd considered when choosing our meeting place was that if Viktor or another Hawk Eye henchman followed us, they'd never get past Tavita. He was accustomed to dispatching aggressive partners who'd tracked women to the refuge.

Lou gave me a warm welcome and agreed to lend me her office for the meeting. I waited in the reception room for Cody and Rebecca to arrive. The walls were painted in cheerful citrus hues, and the room was furnished with an eclectic assortment of donated chairs and artwork. There was a pervasive aroma of cottage pie from the volunteer kitchen down the hall. The women bustling in and out of the refuge spanned all ages and ethnicities. In the chair to my left was an exhausted teen mum with orange-streaked black hair jiggling a mewling infant on her knee. To my right was a woman in her mid-sixties in a pastel pink cardigan, a string of pearls at her neck, and her blonde bob coiffed to conceal a nasty black eye. Policing had taught me that the business of domestic violence was staunchly equal opportunity.

I spotted Cody first, striding up Renwick Street. Rebecca followed, her shoulders hunched and her long hair whipping behind her. I'd dealt with hundreds of reluctant witnesses in my career, but never before had the stakes felt so high to get one onside. I took a deep breath. This was my last chance. I couldn't afford to fuck it up.

I met them in the hallway. Rebecca was fidgeting with her bag strap and looked like she might bolt at any moment. Her face was hidden behind a curtain of dark hair. She wore no make-up, no jewellery, and a penitential-grey sweater and jeans. Everything about her was ordinary. I couldn't picture her with Duncan Turner. Cody took my seat in the waiting room while I ushered his mum down to Lou's office.

'Thanks for coming, Rebecca. I know this isn't easy for you.'

She scratched at her jumper. Her eyes reached for the door. I stiffened. *Don't leave. Don't leave.* A long moment passed, and then she met my gaze. For the first time, I had a clear view of her pale face – the high forehead, the wide-set eyes, the fine features. She was an old-fashioned beauty.

'My son convinced me. He adores Tilly. I don't know if I can help with your case, but I'll tell you what I know.'

'Can I record our conversation?'

'I'd prefer that you didn't.'

I swallowed my frustration. 'Okay. Why don't we start at the very beginning. How did you first meet Duncan Turner?'

When Rebecca began to speak, her voice was surprisingly clear and firm. She'd been waiting for this for years. Her chance to tell her story, in her words. I realised that hers was a calculated drabness – she strove for anonymity. But behind that facade was a woman of quiet strength.

She explained that she'd been the first person in her family to attend university. After qualifying as an accountant, she joined Deloitte's graduate program in Sydney in 2000. A couple of years later, she was seconded to Turner Corp's finance team. It was a huge professional opportunity. As she spoke, I saw a glimpse of that aspirational young woman, before whatever demons she was fighting had taken their toll. What the hell had happened to her?

'That's where I met Duncan,' she continued. 'There was a lot going on in the office – late nights, work events. We became close. Within a few months, our friendship turned romantic. Around the time we got together, Duncan's father started giving him more responsibility, and Duncan began travelling a lot with Campbell on business too. Over the months, I saw a shift in him. He seemed tense, unhappy even. I put it down to stress, not wanting to let his dad down, that sort of thing, but whenever I asked him about it, he'd clam up. I figured he'd open up eventually, so I didn't press him too much.

'As time went on, I was sleeping over at his place most nights – even when Duncan was away for work – because my flat was so far away from the office. One night, when I was there alone and Duncan and Campbell were in Singapore, I was having trouble logging on to my laptop, so I used Duncan's home computer to finish my work. I wasn't meaning to snoop, but I came across some spreadsheets and charts on his hard drive that involved Turner Corp entities. They made no sense to me at first.'

She paused to make sure I was following. I had so many questions, but I didn't dare interrupt her flow, so I nodded at her to continue.

'The transactions were incredibly complex and involved a whole range of jurisdictions – mainly Russia, Eastern Europe and Panama. Since there were such huge sums involved, I spent some time studying them. I didn't want to look ignorant in front of Duncan and my colleagues when the deals eventually came across my desk. But I still couldn't work out how they fitted into the corporate structure, so I started hunting around some of Duncan's other files.

'Pretty soon I realised these files were not meant for my eyes. Turner Corp was laundering huge sums of money. I'm talking hundreds of millions of dollars. And although I couldn't piece together exactly what the underlying transactions were, it was clear that there was a criminal element. I was horrified. It was completely corrupt. I couldn't believe Duncan would have had any part in it.'

My heart was racing. This was exactly what Abe Cohen had talked about. Even though these transactions had happened two decades ago, there was no limitation period on money-laundering offences. The feds would have grounds to obtain a fresh search warrant if Rebecca signed an affidavit testifying to what she had seen. Who knew what else might turn up?

'Rebecca, do you remember the names of any of the Turner Corp entities or individuals mentioned in the documents you saw?' Any scrap of detail would help to substantiate her claims.

'Not off the top of my head.'

I sighed inwardly.

Rebecca unzipped the small bag slung across her chest and drew out a bundle of floppy disks sealed inside a plastic sandwich bag. 'But it's all here.'

I didn't dare even hope. 'What are those?'

She held out the sandwich bag, and I understood this was both an offering and a sacrifice.

'Copies. I copied everything that night so that Duncan wouldn't be able to deny it when I confronted him.'

At that moment, the knot of pressure that had been coiling tighter and tighter inside me released, and the relief almost brought me to tears. After all of the Turners' evasions and manipulations, Skye, Rebecca, Cody and I were going to bring them down. Our luck had finally turned.

Booyah. We had our smoking gun.

•

I farewelled Rebecca and Cody, then sprinted to my car, dialling Cyrus on the way. This time he relented and said to bring the disks straight in. My heart was clattering in my chest as I crawled around interminable roadworks and orange cones towards the AFP's Eastern Command centre on Goulburn Street. My cargo was a grenade, and there was nothing the Turners might not do to sabotage its delivery.

Cyrus met me in the lobby and told me he'd secured a meeting with his boss, Senior Constable Heather Dixon. We passed through security and rode the elevator to Heather's office on the thirteenth floor. Her assistant waved us through, and Heather rose when we stepped inside. She was physically huge, tall and big-boned, with strong features and a pelt of grey hair. Her hand crushed mine when she shook it. She was impressive. Powerful.

'DSS O'Connor,' she said, 'you have five minutes before I head to my next meeting. Shoot.'

As succinctly as I could, I summarised what I'd learned about the connection between the Turners, Hawk Eye and the Bratva. Then I handed over Rebecca's computer disks and explained how she'd uncovered proof of the Turners' involvement in serious financial crimes when she worked for Turner Corp in the early 2000s.

Throughout my spiel, Heather's face remained expressionless. When I finished, she continued to stare at me in silence, and my earlier conviction that Rebecca's information was a crucial breakthrough began to waver. I looked to Cyrus for support, but he had his eyes fixed on his boss.

It dawned on me that I'd just admitted to a senior federal officer the multiple ways I'd violated the terms of my suspension. What if Wilson had already briefed her? Had I just fucked myself over royally? When she picked up her desk phone, I was convinced she was phoning Wilson to dob me in.

'Cancel my afternoon meetings,' Heather said. 'And get someone from digital forensics here ASAP.' Then she hung up and turned to me. 'Let's hope those files prove what Ms White says they do.'

Heather explained that the Turner family and Turner Corp had been on the radar of both the AFP and the Australian Secret Intelligence Service for many years, but they hadn't had enough reliable information to commence a formal investigation. 'Viktor Utkin could be an important asset for us if he's willing to testify against the Turners. I take it you have his arrest in motion?'

I had to come clean. I inhaled and looked her straight in the eye. 'DCS Wilson suspended me from duty on Saturday.'

Cyrus spasmed in my peripheral vision.

'I haven't done anything wrong,' I rushed to add. 'It's a mistake.'

Heather squinted across at me. 'You'd better explain yourself.'

I told her about the false allegations of unauthorised database searches and threatening emails to my ex-fiancé. Given my credibility deficit, I omitted my inflammatory drunken late-night texts and my accidental visit to Vanessa's house.

'The only explanation,' I continued, 'is that my colleague, Detective Sergeant Stuart McKenzie, used my login details and set me up.'

'Why would he do that?' asked Heather.

'I don't know, but he's the only person who had access to my credentials, and he knows about Nick's new girlfriend.'

'Well, if that's true, the allegations against you can be easily disproved,' Heather said. 'Isn't that right, Cyrus?'

He nodded. 'It will be straightforward to track the origin of the email and search requests to the IP address of the computer that was used,' he said. 'Even if your colleague masked the IP address via a proxy server or VPN, I should be able to find a workaround.'

'How will you get access to the email and the search information?' I asked Cyrus. 'They didn't give me copies of anything.'

'Leave that with me,' Heather said. 'I'll sort it out with the Commissioner. Now, excuse me, I have important work to do.' She bundled us out of her office before my relief had a chance to land.

•

When I pulled into the driveway of Mum's apartment block, Sandy was heading out in her blue Daihatsu Charade. She braked and rolled down the window, so I did the same.

'You just missed your gentleman caller,' she said.

'Sorry?'

'A young man stopped by for you. Foreign. Handsome. He only just left.'

Christ. What had I been thinking, bringing Aksel back to the flat? He'd probably run out of money and was looking for a place to stay.

I jogged up the steps. Mum's front door was ajar, and I had a fleeting sense of unease, but inside everything seemed perfectly fine. I set my bag and jacket down on the kitchen bench. Mum was reading in her armchair.

She looked up and smiled. 'Your friend was here,' she said. 'He brought me flowers.' She pointed to a vase of white lilies on the mantelpiece.

'Wow. Aksel's really turning on the charm.'

She frowned. 'No, not Aksel. Someone else. He brought you a gift. It's in your bedroom.'

My heart clenched. Who else could it have been?

I stumbled through the lounge and along the hallway. There was a large red giftbox on my bed, tied with a golden bow, and an unmarked envelope on top. I slid my finger inside to open it.

On plain white paper was a typed note: *Detective O'Connor, we were sorry to learn of your mother's fragile health. We know you will not want to do anything to put her at further risk. Please accept this gift from us as a warning with our best wishes.*

I should have waited, used gloves, followed my training, but I couldn't help myself. I ripped open the wrapping paper with my heart in my throat. Inside was a plain black cardboard box. It was lighter than I'd expected. I peeled off the sellotape with my fingernails and lifted the lid. The interior was packed with black tissue paper. I reached my hand inside and encountered something soft and firm. I lifted it from the box.

It took me a moment to realise I was looking at Laifu's severed head. I vomited all over the floor.

•

Mum was distraught when Laifu didn't come home that evening. The truth would have destroyed her, so I went with the lesser of two evils and let her believe he was missing. On Tuesday morning, I made a poster of Laifu and told her I'd stick up copies around the neighbourhood, despising myself for lying to her. The whole thing was my fault. If I hadn't been staying with her, Mum wouldn't be in danger and Laifu would still be alive. But it wouldn't deter me from the Turner investigation. I wouldn't rest until I'd dispatched the piece of shit who killed Laifu on a long vacation to Goulburn Supermax with the Turner brothers.

When I reported what had happened to Heather later that night, she said I wasn't the only one to receive a nasty surprise. Hawk Eye had mounted a counteroffensive as soon as news broke that there was a warrant out for Viktor Utkin's arrest, and all the senior members of her team had arrived home to death threats in their letterboxes, slaughtered pets or bullets on their children's pillows.

•

On Tuesday afternoon, Heather summoned me back to her office. She wouldn't be drawn on the reason for the meeting, so I wasn't sure whether I was about to be exonerated or fired. When I arrived, she and Cyrus were both hunched over his laptop.

'Cyrus will explain what he's found,' Heather said by way of salutation.

He swivelled the screen around to show me rows of unintelligible code. 'I looked into the database searches and emails that form the basis of your suspension,' he said. 'We ran diagnostics and identified two separate users behind them. As you suspected, one IP address was trackable past the proxy to the home of your colleague Detective Sergeant Stuart McKenzie.'

'You're sure?' I asked Cyrus.

'Yes. One hundred per cent.'

I felt like I'd been punched in the stomach. Even though Macca had been the obvious culprit, the confirmation of his betrayal was a blow. We'd been work partners for years. What on earth had led him to betray me?

'You said there were two people. Who was the other one?' I was desperate to pin the blame elsewhere.

'The second user was more difficult to unmask. They were concealed behind a VPN with advanced encryption protocol, but eventually we traced them back to Hawk Eye.'

My head was aching. Did that mean . . . ?

'Your colleague was working with an associate of Viktor Utkin,' Cyrus said.

No. Surely not. Macca had made a stupid mistake, setting me up like this, but at some level I understood. He was under pressure, with another baby on the way, and his wife had been on his case ever since I was promoted above him. But cooperating with Hawk Eye? That involved an unfathomable degree of corruption – and to what end?

'I see you doubt me,' Cyrus said, 'but the money never lies.' He scrolled through a series of windows on his screen. They showed how, the day after Macca and Wilson executed their warrant on Tamara's apartment at The Mirage, US$50,000 was wired from an account connected to Hawk Eye interests in the Cayman Islands to Macca's wife's bank account.

'Besides, Utkin admitted it,' said Heather. 'We arrested him yesterday and he squealed like a stuck pig. Our officers found a load of materials on Hawk Eye's premises relating to the arsenic poisoning. He must have realised the game was up; this morning, in exchange for a plea deal, he confirmed he was acting on the instructions of the Turner brothers when he framed Ms Baruch.'

'Did he admit to any involvement in the poisoning itself?' I asked.

'No. He still flatly denies that, but as part of the deal he's going to testify against the Turners and provide evidence of some of their illegal activities.'

'So, what will happen to Macca?' I asked. Seeing their blank faces, I clarified: 'I mean, DS McKenzie?'

'His employment has been terminated with immediate effect,' Heather said. 'He'll face serious criminal charges.'

Jesus Christ. It was unbelievable. 'What about DCS Wilson?' I asked. 'Is he involved too?'

'He's been stood down pending further investigation,' Heather said, 'although at this stage there's no evidence that he's been complicit in any wrongdoing.'

'Where does all this leave me?'

'The Commissioner has reinstated you. However, since we're now running the investigation into the poisoning as well, I've asked for you to be seconded to my team. Is that okay with you?'

•

I rushed home to tell Mum the good news, and found her pouring tea for DCS Wilson, who was settled awkwardly on the sofa. When he saw me, Wilson stood and clasped his hands together like he was about to pray.

I lobbed my bag into the armchair. 'What are you doing here, sir?'

'I want to apologise.' He appeared on the verge of tears, which was satisfying and mortifying in equal measure.

'Okay.'

We both glanced at Mum, who showed no inclination to leave the room. Instead, she shuffled closer to me in solidarity.

Wilson cleared his throat. 'Mei, look, I've been trying to keep my head above water. My job – it's not easy. I got talked into taking the easy route.'

He looked at me expectantly.

'That's not an apology,' I said.

His face coloured. 'I should have listened to you. You were right.'

'And?'

'And I'm sorry.'

'Thank you. Apology accepted.'

Wilson's whole body loosened with relief. 'Will you put in a good word for me when you speak to the Commissioner?'

TWENTY-SEVEN

SKYE

TUESDAY/WEDNESDAY

I opened my eyes to white light. Distant voices. The drag of
something within me. My own breath? A whir of blue shot
across my vision. I raised my neck, swivelled my eyes. A web
of wires streamed from my body to a blinking machine. Then
I remembered.

•

Hours ticked into days. White light into darkness. Nurses
bustled in and out to check on me. When the tranquilliser
wore off, I was moved into a new room with white walls and
a single bed made up with starched white sheets. In the corner
was a desk and chair. The only other item in the room was a
jigsaw puzzle of a cottage with a garden by the sea. With the
sedatives, my fury dissolved into apathy.

•

A man I hadn't seen before knocked on the door. 'Mrs Turner, I'm Doctor Patel, the lead psychiatrist here. May I come in?'

I shrugged. Like I had a choice.

He settled into the chair, so I leaned away from him against the bed.

'How are you feeling?'

'How do you think?'

'Mrs Turner, when my colleagues assessed you on Monday, they were acting on the information provided by your husband and GP, including your clinical history. The staff who assessed you here are very experienced practitioners.' Dr Patel adjusted himself in his seat, pulled at his shirt cuffs. He was working up to something. 'However, while you've been under observation, you haven't presented with any of the described behaviour or symptoms. We've also received further information from the police suggesting your husband's account may not be reliable.'

My heart stammered. 'What information?'

'You have some visitors waiting outside. They can fill you in after I discharge you. The nurse will be in shortly with your personal effects.'

•

Detective O'Connor was waiting for me in the reception area with Cody. They both hugged me hard. She handed me my mobile which Duncan had confiscated.

'What's going on?' I asked. 'Detective O'Connor, how did you—'

She cut me off. 'Call me Mei. We're past formalities.'

'A lot of shit's gone down,' Cody said. 'Mei had to get the feds involved.'

'How's Tilly?'

'She's breathing on her own now,' Cody said. 'But still unconscious.'

'Can I see her?'

Mei smiled. 'Yes. They're expecting you.'

The relief coursed through me like a current. I ran, not caring that people raised their phones to photograph me when I passed. Let them splash my face all over the news. Let the trolls work themselves into a frenzy. It was all white noise to me now. With Cody and Mei in my wake, I wheeled down the corridors, through the hydraulic doors, until I pushed through to the Children's Hospital. We took the elevator up to the PICU.

My memory of Tilly's hospitalisation the week prior was grainy and incomplete. I recalled chasing the stretcher up from the emergency department, Tilly blue-lipped and breathless, the sets of sober eyes above surgical masks, shiny surfaces. This time, a police officer was guarding the door. On Mei's instruction, he admitted us to the reception, which was festooned with balloons and bright murals. An administrator tried to divert me with paperwork, but I only wanted to see Tilly. Soon, I was masked and sanitised, and a nurse led me to my daughter.

I'd been anticipating this moment for days, but it was still a shock to see her. Tilly's tiny form, cloaked in a hospital gown printed with cartoon bunnies and kittens, barely made a swell under the stiff sheets. Her eyes were closed, and a heavy oxygen mask was strapped across her mouth. Wires snaked from her chest, her arms, her fingertips – tenuous threads connecting her to life. Under the bright lights, machines and pumps bleeped and wheezed, bins slammed, instruments clattered and alarms shrieked, but Tilly didn't startle.

When I kissed her forehead, her skin was as cold as stone. 'Baby, it's Mumma.'

The nurse peeled back her eyelids and shone a torch into them. Her amber irises were dull, as if her internal light had almost been extinguished.

'I'd encourage you to talk to her,' the nurse said. 'Even though she's unresponsive, there's a chance she might understand. I'll leave you to have some time together.' She swished the teal curtain around our bay and bustled off to the next bed.

The enormity of what had occurred during the past twelve days crashed over me then. I held Tilly's tiny wrist and begged her to wake up. I found Mouse in a box and tucked him under her arm so she could feel his worn plush fur against her flesh. I told her that Bo missed her so much, and we needed her home. I sang her lullabies and recounted the bedtime stories we both knew by heart. As much as I willed her to, she didn't open her eyes. She didn't move at all. But I had to believe she was listening.

Then came the cycle of specialists – the anaesthesiologist, the pulmonologist, the cardiologist, the neurologist, the interventionist – speaking of EEGs and CTs and MRIs. The good news was that Tilly's brain structure was well-preserved, but it was too early to determine whether she would ever regain consciousness – and, if she did, what the long-term effects might be. I asked for copies of everything and scoured the reports, trying to divine her future in the medical jargon. But in the end, there was nothing to do but to wait and to trust, the two hardest things.

•

A nurse announced that Cody was waiting for me in the reception. He'd brought coffee and a stale muffin from the hospital cafe, bless him, as well as a phone charger. Ana would be coming later with fresh clothes and toiletries.

We sat together beside Tilly, and Cody updated me on what had happened while I'd been shut away. After all of Duncan's lies and my self-doubt, I'd been right the whole time. But the vindication was bittersweet. I still didn't know who'd poisoned Tilly, and in spite of everything, I didn't want to believe Duncan was responsible.

There was one person who might hold the answer.

'Cody, do you think your mum might be willing to talk to me?'

His eyes searched mine. 'Why? She's already told Mei everything.'

'I know. But there's something I have to ask her. Could you try? Please?'

•

Rebecca came to see me that evening. For privacy, we were allowed the use of an office behind the nurses' station. She was far from the temptress I'd mythologised when I'd first heard her name – the calculating woman who'd scarred Duncan's heart and robbed him of his only son. The person before me was so fragile, it was as if she'd been rendered in the most delicate glass and could shatter at any moment. And she had the saddest aura of anyone I'd ever met.

'Skye, I'm so sorry. How's Tilly doing?'

'She's fighting hard.'

We faced each other in the small, windowless room crammed with file boxes and containers of medical supplies.

The flat white light cast deep shadows under Rebecca's eyes. She shrank back into her chair like she was afraid to take up space.

'Thanks for everything you've done,' I said. 'I know you've been a huge help to the investigation, but the thing is, we still don't know what happened at Easter. We don't know who gave Tilly and Nina the poison, or why. It has to have been either Duncan or one of his brothers. I've driven myself crazy going back over everything.' I dug my hands into my eyes to stop the tears. 'There's so much I don't understand. May I ask what happened between you and Duncan? Why you disappeared?'

Rebecca didn't respond. As the silence stretched, I feared that she would change her mind and leave. She twisted away from me towards the door, as if she were considering it. But then, turning to face me again, she asked, 'What did he tell you?'

I thought back to that conversation. The shock of it. 'The first time Duncan mentioned you was when Cody made contact. He said you worked together, years ago. That you had a brief relationship, and that you vanished without telling him you were pregnant. He seemed really hurt. Maybe that was part of the act.'

Rebecca hesitated for a long moment. When she spoke, her eyes were glistening. 'I've never told anyone.'

I nodded at her to go on.

Her face creased as she considered where to begin. 'Things between Duncan and his father were strained, but he wouldn't talk about it. I put it down to Duncan resenting the attention that came with the Turner name. And the pressure, too. He wasn't like his brothers. Jamie played the game. He was ambitious, desperate to succeed his father. And even as a kid, Hugo loved the money and the celebrity.'

This was all familiar. Nothing had changed in twenty years.

'One night, Duncan was away on business,' she continued, 'and I was staying over at his apartment. That's when I found the documents on his computer – the ones I gave to the police.

'I also found an email thread between Duncan and Campbell in his deleted items. Duncan had told his father he wanted to leave to do his own thing, but Campbell demanded that Duncan stay on to run Turner Corp's finance division as his lieutenant. When Duncan resisted, Campbell said that if Duncan ever tried to leave, he'd regret it. Duncan called Campbell's bluff then, and threatened to go to the police, but Campbell had it all planned out. He'd ensured that Duncan had fronted Turner Corp in most of the illegal transactions, so that Duncan would go down before Campbell if there was ever an investigation. He'd set up his own son. He was effectively blackmailing him.'

Everything Rebecca was saying made sense. It explained Duncan's simmering resentment towards his father, and his refusal to open up to me about it. It explained why Duncan had stayed at Turner Corp all those years, even though he was so unhappy. 'So what did Duncan say when you told him what you'd found?' I asked.

'I never got the chance to tell him.'

'Why not?'

'It wasn't a conversation we could have over the phone. I texted him to say I had something important to tell him when he arrived back in Sydney. We agreed to meet at his place the next afternoon. He was supposed to come straight home from the airport.'

'He didn't show up?'

'No.' Her face changed then. 'When I let myself into his apartment, Campbell and Jamie were waiting for me. I realised then that I'd made a terrible mistake. Somehow they knew. They asked me why I'd been looking at confidential information. Who I was working for. I said it was an accident, and pretended I didn't understand what they were talking about. But I'm a bad liar.'

'Did they threaten you?'

'They said if I ever told another living soul what I'd seen, there would be consequences for my family. I asked them what they meant by that, and they laughed and said that I was a clever girl, I could work it out. They knew my sister's name, the names of her best friends. That she was in her last year of high school. They knew my mother's address. Where she worked. I was terrified. I kept waiting for them to search my handbag and find the disks, but for whatever reason, they didn't. I kept promising them that it was an accident, that I was telling the truth, but Campbell said he needed to be sure I'd learned my lesson.' She paused then, and tears began to fall.

I couldn't bear to hear what was coming.

'Campbell left. On his way out, he told Jamie to take care of me. Then Jamie held me down, with his hand over my mouth, and he raped me. The things he did – he was cruel. He humiliated me. I tried to fight, but he was too strong. In the end, I just went limp. I thought he was going to kill me. For a long time afterwards, I wished he had.'

I thought I was going to be sick. I couldn't believe what I was hearing. And yet I knew that every word Rebecca uttered was true.

'The last thing he said was that if he ever laid eyes on me again, or if I ever told anyone what had happened, then he would come for my little sister. I was to leave right away, and tell no one. I was never to speak to Duncan again. Jamie made me write him a letter saying I wanted to end our relationship. Afterwards, I somehow managed to clean myself up, go back to my flat and pack a bag. Then I left.'

'Why didn't you go to the police?'

'I was in shock. All I knew was that I had to disappear. Besides, if I'd gone to the police, they would never have believed me. My word against Jamie Turner's? Come on. He would have told them it was consensual. And I couldn't risk him being anywhere near my family.'

'Where did you go?'

'I caught a bus south. Looking back, I don't know how I functioned, but I had the idea to head to our neighbour's caravan where our family had stayed one summer. I knew it would be empty. I figured I'd just stay there until I worked out a plan.'

I thought of that young woman, traumatised and pregnant, and all alone. 'How far along with Cody were you at the time?'

She lowered her eyes. 'I wasn't pregnant then. By the time I realised, it was too late.'

I finally understood, and my heart broke for her, and for Cody.

'Does Detective O'Connor know any of this yet?' I asked.

She shook her head.

'You have to tell her.'

'No. It would destroy Cody. His life has been hard enough already.'

'Then why did you tell him that Duncan was his father?'

'I didn't. I never wanted him to have anything to do with that family.'

'I don't understand. How did he find out about Duncan?'

'We were watching the news together when it flicked onto Campbell's funeral. And I suppose the shock of seeing their faces after so long – well, I just lost it. I broke down. Cody worked out there was some history there. And he's so obviously a Turner – he looks exactly like them. When he asked me about it, I denied it, but like I told you, I'm a bad liar. He managed to get out of me that I had a relationship with Duncan. He put two and two together and guessed Duncan was his father because of the timeline. I begged him not to make contact, but he went ahead anyway. He was furious that I'd denied them a relationship. I couldn't tell him the truth. I was worried sick that once Jamie found out about him there would be terrible repercussions.' She bowed her head. 'And there were.'

My mind was whirring. Did she mean the poisonings?

'Jamie has to be behind what happened to Nina and Tilly,' she said. 'And I'm sure some of it was meant for Cody. Somehow his plan went wrong.'

'Jesus, Rebecca, you have to tell the police. And if you don't, then I will.'

TWENTY-EIGHT

MEI

WEDNESDAY

I joined Heather and Cyrus in a long conference room packed with around thirty people. Heather introduced them all to me – a range of senior duty officers, intelligence analysts, lawyers and members of the asset confiscation team, as well as officers from the Australian Secret Intelligence Service.

'You're all here,' Heather began, 'because we've established a multidisciplinary taskforce for this investigation. As some of you know, on the back of Viktor Utkin's statement and the other evidence unearthed by DSS Mei O'Connor, we have applied for covert warrants to search the offices and records of Turner Corp, the homes of Jamie, Duncan and Hugo Turner, and also the property of the late Sir Campbell Turner. Those warrants have just been approved in court, and I'll be dispatching federal officers shortly to detain the Turners in custody.'

The room buzzed, and a pleasant warmth spread through my chest. Cyrus raised his chin at me from the other side of the conference room, and I savoured the moment of victory. What I would have given to be alongside those officers when they tracked down the Turner brothers. I wondered where the officers would find them – perhaps reclining in their oak-panelled offices, or dissecting crayfish at an inner-city bistro. With any luck, there would be a crowd of spectators when the moment came. And soon enough, they would be charged with a catalogue of crimes. The only inequity was that Campbell Turner couldn't be brought to justice as the architect of their malignant dynasty.

When Heather finished speaking, she invited me to brief the room on the Homicide Squad's investigation into the poisonings.

I was peppered with questions from the floor. How did I know Rebecca and Cody White were reliable? What information did we have about Skye Turner's psychiatric history? Why had we been so quick to arrest Tamara Baruch on such obviously phony evidence? What was Tilly Turner's health status?

I did my best to answer the questions as accurately as I could. Then Heather allocated tasks and sent everyone off to work. She asked me to wait behind.

'Detective O'Connor,' Heather said, 'a tip came through from the general inquiries line from a guy who says he's a lawyer in England with information about Nina Turner. No idea if he's legit. I've forwarded the details to you. Can you follow up?'

•

Heather's assistant had organised me a temporary workstation that backed onto the utilities bay. The desk vibrated whenever the printers were going, which was constantly, despite it being a paperless office.

The latest email in my overloaded inbox gave the contact details of a Martin Fairhurst of Fairhurst & Gleeson Solicitors in Kent, England. Google led me to a legitimate-looking website. The firm specialised in conveyancing, family law, estates, and wills and probate, and the staff were introduced with small biographies beneath lawyerly black-and-white portraits. Martin Fairhurst was the senior partner – a rotund bloke with bushy grey eyebrows and a bulbous nose. The likelihood that he had any helpful information seemed remote. Nina had grown up in England, but she'd lived in Australia for more than fifteen years. According to Skye, Nina had rarely returned to the UK since her children were born and, aside from her invalid mother, had no other family there.

I checked the clock. It was 5.30 pm Sydney time, which made it 8.30 am on Tuesday morning in the UK. I rang the number on the website.

Martin Fairhurst answered in a posh accent that conjured up visions of bow ties and smoking jackets. I introduced myself and asked whether it was a convenient time to speak.

'Yes, indeed,' Martin said. 'I'm relieved to hear from you. The last fellow I spoke to – a Detective McKenzie, I believe his name was – never followed up.'

'I apologise, Mr Fairhurst.' What other leads had Macca let slide? 'I understand you have some information that might help our investigation into Nina Turner's death?'

'Yes, I do.'

'Did you know Nina personally?'

'I've been Nina's parents' solicitor for many years. When her father died and her mother, Pamela, became unwell, Nina asked me to be her man on the ground, so to speak. I still manage Pamela's affairs.'

'I see. Are you calling on behalf of Nina's mother then?'

'No. I'm phoning because of a conversation I had with Nina – it was almost exactly a year ago.' There was a rustling sound, and then a couple of thuds. 'I have the file note right here.'

'What did you and Nina talk about?'

'Well, Nina had set up a video meeting, ostensibly to discuss an updated power of attorney. But then, when it came to it, she wanted to talk about something else entirely.'

'And what was that?'

'A custody matter.' He cleared his throat. 'Nina asked me what legal steps would be required to resettle her children in England if she were to leave her husband. I must confess that I was shocked by her question. Until then, I'd understood Nina was happily married. She rather put me on the spot. I explained that the Geneva Convention prohibits either parent moving a child outside their place of habitual residence without the other's consent, so her children would have to remain in Australia – unless, of course, her husband agreed to the move. If she were to bring the children to England without his consent, they'd be repatriated to Australia under international law. She didn't seem very happy with that advice. She said she'd never be able to leave him if she couldn't bring the children.'

What had happened a year ago that made Nina want to flee her marriage?

'Did she give any context?' I asked.

'No, I'm afraid not. I have to say, she was very agitated. Not at all herself – she's usually so composed. She believed she was under surveillance. That she was in danger. To be frank, it sounded as though she was having some sort of episode.'

'What do you mean by *episode?*'

'Just that it was all a bit dramatic. Hysterical. And it was most unlikely. Her husband and his family are so well-regarded. I should also mention that Nina and I corresponded quite regularly after that conversation, in relation to Pamela's affairs, and she never revisited the matter. I suppose, until I heard the news reports of her death, I put the whole thing out of my mind.'

I let a silence sit between us. I wanted Martin to reflect. A clearly distressed woman had sought his help and, instead of taking her seriously, he assumed she was having some sort of mental breakdown. Because the alternative – that she was telling the truth – didn't occur to him.

TWENTY-NINE

SKYE

THURSDAY

I hadn't stopped shaking since Rebecca shared what Jamie had done to her. The layers of abuse perpetrated by the Turners on so many women for so many years was almost too horrifying to accept. I'd spent my adult life trying to elude the darkness of my childhood, but somehow I'd ended up at the epicentre of this family, unknowingly but unarguably complicit in their crimes. And worst of all, I'd walked right into Jamie's trap. I'd been so weak and desperate for validation that I'd believed he wanted me that night at Yallambee, when in truth I was just a means by which he could humiliate his brother.

Under the pounding lights of the intensive care unit, there was no sense of progress – no rotation of day into night, or night into day. Time was a weight that pinned us down until chance freed us. I didn't speak to the other parents, and they didn't speak to me. Each of us was anchored in our own ocean of concern, secretly anxious that another child's luck might bring our own child's end, because the odds were in no one's favour.

Tilly was oblivious to the comings and goings around her while fluids pumped into and drained from her lifeless body. The boy who currently occupied the next bed had drowned at the beach. The nurses were discussing him in the corridor when I went to stretch my legs. His family had recently immigrated from India and he didn't know how to swim. The hollow-eyed parents held hands and murmured to one another softly in Hindi. The girl in the bay to the other side of Tilly was the only member of her family to survive a car crash. She arrived with a crust of dried blood across her swollen face. No one came to visit her. Who would tell her what had happened when she woke? If she woke. The newest arrival, a little boy, had experienced complications during heart surgery. His mother's occasional sobs punctuated the steady beat of the monitors and ventilators.

Doctors came and went, but at all times the children were under the nurses' steadfast supervision. They dashed from bed to bed, lanyards swinging, checking vitals, charting medication, emptying drains, resetting IVs. They addressed Tilly as they might a favourite niece: 'How are you today, my darling? Behaving yourself?'

I made amends with the head nurse, Sonia. I apologised for what I'd said on the phone, and she hugged me and told me she understood; that she was sorry for what I'd endured. Sonia had crocheted a blue butterfly toy which she hung above Tilly's bed. She said we could take it with us when we left, and I felt a surge of hope at this prophetic suggestion. I pictured Tilly waving goodbye to the nurses with the butterfly tucked under her arm. Only later did it occur to me that we would have to leave eventually, no matter what the outcome.

I would have given anything to know what Tilly was feeling, what she was thinking, what she could understand. Was she in pain? Was she frightened? Or was she cocooned in sleep, her last memory fastened to Easter at Yallambee, in the time before? The desperation to reach her, to bring her to the surface, was eating me alive.

●

To pass some time at Tilly's bedside, I tackled my email inbox, which was heaving with messages of sympathy, interspersed with death threats, media inquiries and marketing spam. Next, I turned to my voicemail, which had been clogged for over a week. There were thirty new messages. The most recent one had been left on Easter Monday by the mother of one of Tilly's friends when news of the poisoning had first broken. She didn't believe that the reports could be true. I deleted it before the end, and listened to the next message in the queue – this one left just moments before the first by another friend, also frantic with worry about what she'd heard on the news. I soon found a rhythm, stabbing the button to erase each message within the caller's first breathless syllables. The backlog was steadily dwindling, back from Monday to Easter Sunday. It was a perverse sort of time travel, forcing me to relive those horrible hours after my life snapped in half.

A nurse popped her head around the curtain to say that Ana had returned and was waiting for me in the caregivers' room. On my way down the corridor, I passed a large Greek family who had dominated the common spaces since I'd arrived in the PICU. They were supporting a ten-year-old girl who'd suffered burns in a housefire. Today, she was being discharged, and the atmosphere was almost festival-like as they chattered and laughed, and presented the staff with gifts of baklava and orange cake. I was relieved for them and for the little girl, but I couldn't help resenting their blatant joy. What if our turn didn't come?

At least Ana and I had the caregivers' room to ourselves now. She handed me two bags – one of clothes, and another of fresh fruit and sandwiches. 'This should keep you going until I come back tonight. Now, how is Tilly? What's the latest?'

'There's no real update. They stopped the sedatives two days ago, so she should start regaining consciousness any time.' I didn't add the doctor's rider – that, by now, they would have expected at least involuntary responses, like pupil dilation and automatic reflexes.

Ana squeezed my hands. 'She'll come back to us. I know she will.'

My phone rang. It was Duncan. The sight of his name curdled my stomach, and I looked to Ana. She nodded at me to accept the call.

'I take it you know I've been arrested.' His tone was strained.

'Where are you?'

'I'm at home. I've been bailed here under twenty-four-hour surveillance.' There was a deep exhale down the line. 'Look, I really need to see you. To explain things, so you don't get the wrong idea.'

I knew he wanted a chance to stop me from cooperating with the police. I didn't owe Duncan anything, but he sure as hell owed me. And most importantly, he owed Tilly. This might be the last opportunity for us to speak candidly before lawyers or corrections officers mediated every conversation. After all the lies, I wanted to hear the truth from him.

'I'll come,' I told him. 'But I can't stay long.'

Ana promised to wait with Tilly.

•

The entrance to Thornfield was cordoned off to contain the waiting media and rubber-necking neighbours. I ignored the lenses trained on me through the windscreen. One of the police officers approached and radioed someone inside. The front gates swung open.

There was another officer guarding the front door. Mr Turner was waiting for me in the library, he said.

The hallway was rank with the odour of dead flowers. Everything drained of its life force. When I passed the open door to the old ballroom, I had a flashback to our first-ever visit to the house after we'd taken possession. The vendors had left us their grand piano, and it was the only piece of furniture in the vast room. Duncan played me a Chopin étude by heart, and I was awed by the soaring melody glancing off the vaulted ceilings and bare walls. Afterwards, we'd made love on the bare oak floors. It had been so magical, and I'd felt like I was on top of the world. We'd fallen so far.

The officer at the library door told me to alert him if I felt unsafe at any time. I said I would, then pushed through.

Bo yelped in delight and rushed towards me, his tail wagging manically. I kneeled to hug him.

Duncan was sitting on the sofa, his face burdened, his hands clasped tightly together. How quickly we'd gone from soulmates to strangers, from allies to warring states. I was surprised at the cataract of emotions that swept through me at the sight of him – fury, sorrow, despair, hatred and, as much as I loathed admitting it, even something approaching love.

He rose, his arms outstretched, and I recoiled. 'Don't touch me.'

Duncan bowed his head. 'I'm so sorry.' He slumped back on the sofa, and it was a motion of such defeat that I fought the urge to comfort him – the ghost of a feeling from before. 'I've handled things so badly. I was just trying to protect you.'

'Stop it. Don't pretend any of this was for me.' I drew a deep breath and sat on the sofa opposite him. Bo sprang up beside me. 'I need you to tell me the truth.'

He nodded.

'Did you poison Tilly and Nina?'

'God, no. *No.* I'd never do anything to hurt anyone, but especially not our daughter. Please, Skye, promise you believe me.'

'I don't know what to believe.'

'I didn't have anything to do with it,' he insisted.

'Then who?'

'I can only guess that it was one of my brothers. Maybe both of them.'

I stood up and crossed to the windows. I couldn't look at him. Outside, the pool water had turned murky, and the sky was a dark slate grey. 'You've been working with Hawk Eye?'

He paused. 'Dad worked with them for years. We needed them to run interference.'

I turned back to face him. He was standing now.

'And you had me followed?'

'For your own protection.'

'Protection from what?'

'The media. Jamie. Hugo. Everyone.'

'Who asked Viktor Utkin to plant that evidence in Tamara's apartment? Was it you?'

A pause. 'Yes. Jamie and me.'

'Why would you do that if you weren't responsible for the poisoning?' I had to work hard to control the emotion in my voice.

He moved towards me. 'It was Jamie's idea. I didn't want to do it. I felt sick about it. But we had to buy time.'

'For what?'

'If the police had a reason to search us, we knew they'd find other things, and that it would get very bad. We needed time to get things in order.'

'You mean, you needed time to destroy evidence.'

'Look, I never condoned what my father did. I tried to get out years ago. But Dad – well, you know he could be controlling, but you have no idea what was going on behind the scenes. He made it impossible for me to leave.'

A serrating pain nicked my temples. Part of me was desperate to believe him, but I couldn't let him fool me again. 'You're acting like you're innocent. But I saw the photos you kept in that file, Duncan. What you made those poor girls do for your gratification. You disgust me. You're as guilty as the rest of them.'

'Those aren't my photographs!' He shook his head. 'I can't believe you'd think I'd be involved in that. They belong to my brothers and my father. Not me. Never me.'

'How stupid do you think I am? If they're not yours, why do you have them hidden away? And why's your handwriting all over them?'

'I'd pieced together where they must have been taken from flight logs. I only kept them for leverage. That's what I need to explain.'

'What are you talking about? Leverage for what?'

'I was going to tell Jamie and Hugo that I was out. At Yallambee, before Tilly got sick.' He was standing right in front of me now. 'We were supposed to meet on the Saturday morning to discuss the estate. Remember? With Dad gone, I finally had a chance to cut free.'

I tried to push past him, but he grabbed my shoulder.

'Skye, listen. I had all the banking codes, pay-offs made over the years to conceal the sexual abuse claims brought against my brothers. Those records and the photographs in that file were the ammunition I needed to negotiate an exit. But Jamie and Hugo must have worked out what I was planning.' His eyes were shining. 'I think they poisoned Tilly as a warning shot. Maybe Nina knew too much.' He wiped away his tears with the back of his hand. 'I wish I'd told you all of this before, but I didn't want to put you at risk. I thought the less you knew, the better. Everything I've done was to keep you safe. To protect you. You have to realise, I'm a victim in all of this too.'

That doublethink was his birthright, and I wanted to tear him apart. 'You think *you're* a victim?' There was no point in trying to calm my voice. 'Because of you, Tamara was charged with murder. She could have gone to jail. You gaslit me into thinking I was going mad. You had me locked up in a psych ward. You've kept me from my daughter when she needed me most.' My tears were thick and angry. 'And what about all the lives you've destroyed because of your family's greed?

All the suffering? You're a monster, Duncan. Not a victim. Do you understand that?'

Duncan slammed his fist against the wall. 'Give me a break. I've never heard you complain about the money.' He brought his face close to mine. 'I picked you up from the gutter and treated you like a queen. You've loved every moment. You've loved the lifestyle.'

I pulled away, but he wrenched me back.

'If I'm guilty of anything,' he continued, 'then it's of trying too hard to protect you and Tilly. We have to stick together. I still have people out there who will help us. We'll be okay.'

'Do you think Tilly's okay?' I screamed. 'Look what your family has done to her!' I was weeping now, sobs that broke from the deepest part of me. 'Don't you care?'

'Of course I care! I'd have made Jamie and Hugo pay. But you had to go running to the police, didn't you? You cratered my plan. Now we're all exposed.'

'Not me.'

He shook his head. 'You don't get it, do you? You're a Turner now. You don't have anyone else. And that frightens you shitless.' He offered me his hand. 'I know it'll take some time for you to trust me again. But you, me, Tilly and Cody – we're a family.'

'A family?' I gave a bitter laugh. 'We're not a family.'

I crossed the room and opened the door. Bo followed me. When I looked back at Duncan, he was fierce, defiant. I saw Campbell in him. 'You might as well know – neither Cody nor Tilly are even your children.'

'What are you talking about?'

'I suggest you ask Jamie.'

His face disfigured with fury, and he stumbled towards me. 'You fucking whore!' he yelled. The mask had slipped.

With Bo at my heels, I stepped into the corridor, slamming the door behind me.

THIRTY

MEI

THURSDAY

All night, the horrors inflicted by the Turners gnawed at my brain, and I barely slept. I was devastated about Laifu and then sickened when Rebecca White phoned to report her abuse at Jamie's hands. At the outset of this investigation, I could never have imagined the extent of the Turners' depravity.

On Thursday morning, when I rolled over bleary-eyed and turned on my phone, there was a message waiting from Abe Cohen. *Hi Mei. Here's a link to our article. Thanks for your help.* He and Bonnie had broken their story overnight, and now the rest of the world's media was scrambling to catch up on the scandal.

Horrific crimes alleged against family of late mogul and philanthropist, Sir Campbell Turner, and his global luxury empire

After an extensive investigation spanning a decade, The New York Times *is finally able to publish revelations concerning the late Sir Campbell Turner, the renowned Australian-born business tycoon and founder of multinational luxury goods business Turner Corp, and his three sons, Jamie, Duncan and Hugo Turner.*

Shocking revelations about the family's connection to organised crime and sex trafficking have come to light as Australian federal investigators pieced together the circumstances surrounding the recent fatal poisoning of Nina Turner – the wife of Jamie Turner – and the poisoning of Sir Campbell's six-year-old granddaughter, Tilly Turner, who remains in a critical condition. The Australian Federal Police are working with the Federal Bureau of Investigation and their international counterparts to investigate the extent of the family's criminal activities across the globe.

Following their arrests, Jamie, Duncan and Hugo Turner are facing charges in Australian federal and state courts relating to money laundering, sex trafficking and sexual abuse of minors. They have all entered not guilty pleas, and have issued statements through their attorneys vehemently denying the accusations against them as 'categorically untrue'.

Once I'd briefed Heather on the information from Martin Fairhurst and Rebecca White, she sent me away to do more digging. We were closing in on Jamie Turner, but we still didn't have nearly enough evidence for a conviction for Nina's murder and Tilly's poisoning.

There was still plenty to follow up – the terms of Sir Campbell's will, the lab analysis of the materials found at Yallambee, and testimony of employees at Turner Corp and the family's household staff. But the starting point was Nina's autopsy report, which was well overdue. If arsenic poisoning was not the confirmed cause of death, then we'd been heading down the wrong path from day one.

I put a call through to Barbara, the coroner.

'Didn't DCS Wilson update you?' she asked.

I explained that the investigation had been taken over by Heather Dixon's team at the AFP.

'Well, the Turners have done their very best to frustrate the process.'

'What do you mean by that?'

'First of all, Jamie Turner objected to the autopsy for personal reasons in his capacity as the deceased's next of kin, which set us back forty-eight hours, and then his lawyers challenged the release of Nina's medical records on privacy grounds. Although their arguments were baseless, it caused a further delay to the forensic pathologist's access.'

I couldn't believe the extent of Jamie Turner's subterfuge. What more could he possibly have to hide?

THIRTY-ONE

SKYE

THURSDAY

I met Mei in the hospital courtyard. Sonia had promised to wait with Tilly and to phone me immediately if there was any change in her condition. The detective and I perched side by side on the concrete rim of a flowerbed, clutching takeaway coffees while the wind snatched at our hair and clothes. I burrowed my fingernails into the styrofoam cup to quell my anxiety about what was coming. Over the phone, Mei had said she had something important to tell me.

'Nina's autopsy report came through this afternoon,' she said. 'As we expected, acute arsenic poisoning is confirmed as the cause of death. But the pathologist found something else too.' She scanned my face. 'You didn't suspect anything?'

I had no idea where this was heading, but there was a skipping sensation in my stomach. A hint of dread. 'I'm not sure what you mean.'

Mei's face tightened. Something bad was coming. Had Nina been pregnant? Or battling a secret illness? I wanted her to spit it out.

'On Easter Saturday,' Mei continued, 'when Nina was admitted to hospital, she presented with numerous injuries – heavy bruising on her abdomen, scars, burns, internal bleeding.'

My mind whirred. I couldn't recall any mention of Nina having been in an accident.

Mei continued: 'The pathologist had to exclude injuries caused by the arsenic and resuscitation attempts, and pre-existing conditions, before he could confirm his findings.'

'I don't understand,' I said. 'What caused them – the injuries?'

'According to the pathologist, they were consistent with a sustained pattern of physical abuse inflicted over many years.'

I clamped my hand to my mouth. I thought I was going to vomit.

'Did you ever suspect that Jamie was physically abusing Nina?' Mei continued.

I shook my head. I couldn't find any words.

'You never noticed any bruising or other injuries?'

I cringed at my stupidity. For years, I'd laughed with Duncan about Nina's prudish clothing. She'd rarely bared her skin – it was usually concealed beneath long sleeves, full skirts or trousers, and high necklines and scarves, even in the sweltering summer heat. This explained her reticence to swim, even on a burning hot summer's day. Her reluctance to spend time with me in situations where I might have worked out what was going on. The fractured wrist she'd explained away as a skiing accident. The burn on her hand she'd blamed on the hair iron. I clawed back through my memories, and now it seemed so obvious. She'd been suffering in plain sight. I thought of Good Friday at Yallambee, when I'd seen her and Jamie in the spare room and had assumed they were making love. But now the image in my head was so clearly one of abuse.

Mei put her hand on my arm. 'It's easy to miss the signs. She wanted to leave Jamie, you know. She spoke to a lawyer a year ago about moving the children to England. She never mentioned any marital problems to you?'

'We weren't close,' I conceded. I didn't say that I'd assumed she looked down on me; that I'd assumed she thought I wasn't good enough for the Turners.

'Did Nina have any close friends she might have confided in about what Jamie was doing to her?' Mei asked.

Nina and Jamie had been at the glamorous pinnacle of Sydney's social scene, and she had hundreds of friends and acquaintances, but when I thought about it, her closest circle consisted of the wives of Jamie's friends and her colleagues on the boards of the Turners' charities. All of them were connected to her husband. Many of those bonds were superficial. Perhaps she'd confided in some of those women what was going on in her marriage, but if so, why hadn't any of them helped her leave Jamie? And why had none of them come forward since her death?

For all of Nina's privilege and social standing, I saw now that Jamie had isolated her. He'd coaxed her away from her family and friends in England, then insisted she leave her legal career when the twins were born. Over time, he'd surrounded her with his people. Did she feel she had no escape? And for all of those years, I'd been right there, in a position to help her, if only I hadn't been blinded by my own insecurities.

When I explained this to Mei, she wasn't surprised. 'That's the pattern,' she said. 'It usually starts with isolation and control, and then the abuse escalates.'

'Why wouldn't she have gone to the police?' I asked, but I already knew the answer. Jamie had the money and the power. He would have found a way to turn it around on her. He would have painted her as crazy. He would have hired the best lawyers and deprived her of access to her children. As unbearable as it must have been for her to stay, there had been no viable option for her to leave either.

And I was in no position to judge. Like Nina, I'd allowed Duncan to lure me away from my friends and into his world. He'd increasingly dictated who I spent time with. Had my past, my rootlessness, my lack of family ties been what had drawn him to me? Had I been an easy target, and misconstrued his control for fierce love and protection?

'So, you think Jamie was responsible for the poisoning?' I asked.

Mei nodded. 'We don't have any direct proof. But circumstantially, all paths lead to him. We believe Nina was threatening to expose him and his family. Jamie tried to make Nina's death look like an accident. He organised the weekend away at Yallambee with no staff, which was highly unusual. The location was sufficiently remote that there would be delayed access to medical treatment. It was all carefully premeditated.'

'Why Tilly too?' I asked, barely able to breathe.

'Honestly, I don't know,' Mei said. 'It could simply have been a mistake. Or maybe Tilly overheard something she shouldn't have and that made her a target. Maybe she was intended to be a diversion to take the focus off Jamie and Nina. We may never know why.' She clasped my hand. 'I'm really sorry.'

•

My head was throbbing by the time I returned to Tilly's bedside. I nuzzled her hair. It smelled of antiseptic. I traced my fingers up and down the flesh of her inner arm, and around her delicate wrist. I kissed her forehead. I sensed her in there. She was reachable. She had to be.

I'd muted my phone to avoid the calls rolling in from friends and acquaintances now that the news media was blazing with stories about Duncan's family, but I couldn't hide from them forever. I resumed clearing messages. My voicemail box had clogged again. Eventually, I'd whittled down the backlog to four. They dated all the way back to Easter Saturday.

I pressed play. There was a furious one from Duncan, trying to locate me and Tilly at the hospital after we'd arrived by ambulance from Taree. It was only ten days ago but it felt like a different lifetime. I deleted that and the next two messages, which were also from him.

I was down to the last one. '*You have one new message,*' came the computer voice in its automated staccato rhythm. '*Left at two twenty-one pm on Saturday the sixth of April.*' I must have missed this call when I was travelling with Tilly in the ambulance from Taree to Sydney.

'Skye, it's Nina.'

My mobile turned slippery and plunged to the floor. It was chilling to hear her voice, rasping and strained, from beyond the grave. By then, she was battling the effects of the poison. Within hours of her leaving this message she would be dead. Did she suspect what Jamie had done? Had she phoned me with a desperate plea for help? I was furious with myself for having missed her call, and for not having listened to her message sooner. It could have saved so much anguish. It could have saved her life.

With my heart in my throat, I replayed her message.

'Skye, it's Nina. I've just heard about Tilly.' Her voice cracked, and she broke off into sobs. 'I'm so sorry. I've made a terrible mistake.'

There was a rushing in my head.

'If you tell the doctors it's arsenic right away, they'll know what to do to save her.'

What? No. This wasn't happening.

'Please – don't tell my children,' Nina continued. 'I'm begging you. They're my world.' Her terrible confession arrived in ragged gasps. 'I had to make it look like food poisoning. It had to seem like my death was an accident. For the children's sake. So they wouldn't think I'd chosen to leave them.' I thought back to the awful hangover I'd woken with on Easter Saturday. The stomach cramps. Duncan and I had both felt ill. She'd poisoned us too.

'I've tried so hard to stay, but I can't do it anymore. I was so careful to protect the children. That's why I served them a different meal. It was only in the rice.' Her voice twisted into a harrowing scream. 'Why did she eat the rice?'

And then the flashback came. Tilly's wiggly teeth. She couldn't eat her burger. I'd taken her into the kitchen at Yallambee that night. I'd dished her up a bowl of food. I saw it as clear as day. A bowl of vegetables and rice.

Something tore inside me then. I crumpled to the ground, blood rushing in my ears. The horror of it was too much to bear.

I was the one who gave the arsenic to Tilly. It was me.

SKYE

It was a clear spring morning, and the white froth on the cherry trees flashed through the taxi window as we wound our way into the city. I'd arranged to meet the others outside the Hyde Park Barracks.

The driver delivered me right to the entrance of the fore-court, which was humming with tourists and school groups queuing for the museum. There was an electric charge in the air.

I spotted Mei first. She was standing straight-backed outside the cafe, her dark hair sleek and shiny. When the crowd parted, I saw she was deep in conversation with Rebecca and Tamara. All three of them looked strong, battle-ready. Rebecca raised her hand when she saw me.

Together, we crossed Queens Square into the fray of the waiting media. We had arrived for the opening day of the Turner brothers' trial in the New South Wales Supreme Court.

A picture of the four of us ascending the courthouse steps was beamed out across the world and headlined every major global news bulletin. That picture would forever symbolise the fall of the Turner dynasty.

•

The trial dragged on, of course, but eventually my part in it was done, and I could make my long-anticipated departure from Sydney. The heat lingered long after the suburban scatter had dwindled to low sky and open pasture. By the time I spotted the hand-painted sign at the turn-off, dusk had fallen. I steered off the main road and onto the dirt driveway that traced the rise of the hill.

When we arrived, I opened the car door to an opera of cicadas and birdsong. Bo shot out into the undergrowth after a rabbit. The cottage was smaller than it had appeared in the photographs, but there was a shed for my kiln and the garden was astonishing – ancient and wild. And beyond the clifftop, the ocean stretched to a clear horizon.

Tilly had fallen asleep in her car seat, but she woke when I unclipped the buckle. I bent forward so she could clasp her hands around my neck. I lifted her out and set her down on the path beside me. Every day she was stronger, but the road ahead was long. We would travel it together.

Here, in this place brimming with life, we would make a fresh start.

Here, no net ensnared us.

We were free.

ACKNOWLEDGEMENTS

See How They Fall was born in Dr Paula Morris's classroom when she accepted me into her Master of Creative Writing programme at the University of Auckland. Paula, I'm so grateful for your astute feedback and guidance.

A huge thanks to my MCW cohort – Andrea Pollard, Aniwa Codyre, Anna Woods, Candice Tutauha, Craig Clark, Eamonn Tee, Hannah Norton, Katie Newton, Sarah Shortt and Yvette Thomas – for the laughs and for keeping me (semi) sane on the rollercoaster that is writing a novel.

I'm also grateful to authors Angelique Kasmara, Caroline Barron, Rose Carlyle and Tom Moody for their early positive feedback which gave me the confidence to persevere.

To Kate Stephenson of Hachette Aotearoa – thank you for championing this novel when it was a half-written Word manuscript, and to Rebecca Saunders of Hachette Australia for joining forces with Kate to publish the book.

A huge and heartfelt thanks to my brilliant editors: the aforementioned Kate Stephenson and Rebecca Saunders of

Hachette, my US editor Luisa Cruz Smith of Penzler Publishers, and my hawk-eyed copyeditor Ali Lavau and proofreader Theresa Crewdson. Any mistakes that remain are mine alone. My thanks to Alex Ross for the stunning cover design. Huge thanks also to Sarah Brooks and Emma Dorph of Hachette Australia for their deal-making and to Amelia Mysko of Stampede Ventures for believing in the novel's potential for a screen adaptation from the get-go.

Thanks to the many others who supported *See How They Fall*: Dom Visini, Mel Winder, Sacha Beguely, Tania Mackenzie-Cooke, Suzy Maddox, Nic Faisandier and Sharon Galey at Hachette Aotearoa; Kirstin Corcoran and Alexa Roberts at Hachette Australia, and the many others working behind the scenes at Hachette across Aotearoa and Australia; Julia O'Connell and Charles Perry at Penzler; Aimee Glucina, Becky Zhang, Kelly Hills, the Mighty Moas and my wonderful beta readers: Cecilia Davis, Victoria Marquez, Emma Small and Alan and Monique Sutcliffe.

I also want to acknowledge the legendary Harlan Coben for sharing his thriller tips.

I'm so lucky to have the most amazing friends, old and new, near and far, who've been such cheerleaders throughout this process. Thanks to Ryan Mudie for giving me the push I needed to start writing, and to my old school and uni friends, my London girls, the Omaha crew, my old workmates, the school mums, and especially to Mon, Rissy, Caro, and Michelle.

I have to pay special tribute to my crazy whānau: Liz, Jock, Will, Vicky, Biddi, Ben, Nett & Baz, and my nieces and nephews. Mum and Dad, thanks for fostering my love of reading by ensuring my childhood home was packed with books, for telling the best bedtime stories, and for the regular library trips. Vicky, my beautiful sister, in law and in life, thanks for your love and advice. And my little blister Bridge, thanks for your next-level support and for always inspiring me.

Writing this book was the best job in the world because I got to do it in the company of my three furriest loves – Arthur, Coco and Max.

And finally, to Jason, my incredible husband who suffered through a gazillion drafts without complaint, and our three beautiful children, Sam, Will and Eliza. You're my everything. Thanks for bringing me such happiness every day.

PS: Sorry to all the lovely Vanessas.

Rachel Paris won the Phoenix Prize for the best manu-script in her Masters degree at Auckland University. She came to writing after a highly successful 20-year law career, specialising in fintech. She gained her Master of Laws at Harvard University. *See How They Fall* is her debut novel.